... His tongue touched her lips in a feathery motion, drinking in sweetness so pure he wanted to fall to his knees. He pulled her slight body into his.

A sharp pain hit his leg. He grunted and broke the kiss, making the break as painful as the pain in his leg. He glanced down. She'd dropped everything she'd been holding, her hands clutching the front of his shirt. Her cheeks were flushed. With hunger? Need?

She seemed at a loss as to what to do next. He stifled an urge to smile, irritation dissolving for the moment.

He grasped her hands gently, surprised by the rising desire to safeguard her. Resisting the appeal to reclaim her mouth, he tugged them from his shirt. Kneeling down, he gathered the spilled belongings. Just as he suspected, he'd been besieged with books.

copyright © 2012 by Kathy L Wheeler
All Rights Reserved

http://kathylwheeler.com

This story is a work of fiction. Names, characters, places, and incidents are either products of the author's imagination or used fictitiously. Any resemblance to actual events, locales, or persons, living or dead, is entirely coincidental.

All rights reserved.
No part of this publication can be reproduced or transmitted in any form or by any means, electronic or mechanical, without permission in writing from Kathy L Wheeler.

Cover Art © Novak Illustrations

Quotable

Kathy L Wheeler

Bloomington Town Square

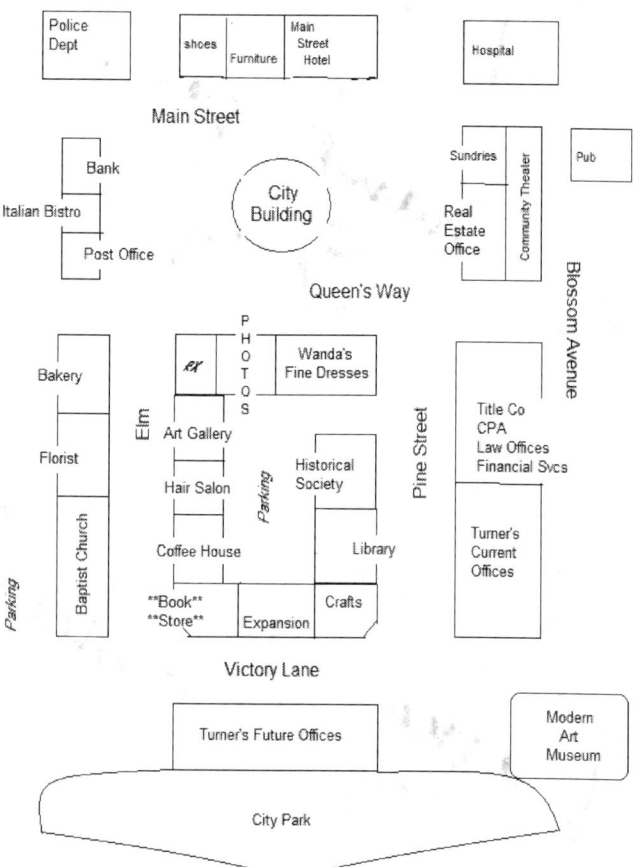

Cast of Characters

Genna Lyndsey ~~ co-owner of Renewed Interest Used Books
Rick Johnson ~~ Insurance Fraud Claims Investigator
Lorianne Gentry ~~ co-owner of Renewed Interest Used Books
Ashton Turner III ~~ Rick's best friend
Joanna Bakely ~~ Bookstore customer
Damon Wharton ~~ Genna's old boyfriend from college
Lewis Peale ~~ Head Contractor
Toddy Wilson ~~ Comic book nerd
Ida Finch ~~ owner of Bloomin' Arts & Crafts
Reverend Colvert ~~ Baptist minister
Josephine Phillips ~~ Curator - Historical Society
Wanda Buford ~~ owner of Wanda's Fine Dresses
Plank ~~ owner of Plank's Coffee House
Lester Van Horn ~~ Realtor
Selma Stotts ~~ Beautician
Sarah Pendergrass ~~ owner of Blooms & Florist and Bloomies Bakery Goods
Josh ~~ Bartender at Pat's Bloomin' Pub
Lillian ~~ Rick's assistant

CHAPTER 1

"*HE WHO SEES THE inaction that is in action, and the action that is an inaction, is wise indeed,*'" Genna Lyndsey quoted. She eyed the shelf where she needed to consign *Tribes of the Amazon* to its proper place. Definitely out of reach, she'd need the stepladder. Rain pounded the roof outside of her and Lorianne Gentry's little store, Renewed Interest Used Books.

Lorianne's rapid tut-tut-tutting of her pen on the counter had Genna casting a quick glance over her shoulder, slightly annoyed. The constant thump kept precise time with the unending downpour. She sighed, choosing to ignore the irritation, and turned back to the task at hand.

"Inaction that is in action? Really? That makes no sense at all, Genna."

"Of course it does," she said.

Genna pushed her black-framed glasses up on her nose. Matter-of-fact resolve was the best way to help Lorianne. "It's a quote from the *Bhagavad Gita*, you know...it's a San—"

"Genna!" She kept her back to Lorianne, wisely hiding the twitch of her lips at her best friend's exasperation. It would only aggravate her further.

Genna ignored the interruption. "...Sanskrit text from the

Bhishma Parva of the *Mahabharata.* It's an epic of sorts."

"The what epic?" The even tapping of Lorianne's pen faltered.

"The *Mahabharata* epic. Sort of a long narrative poem."

The steady rapping of the pen resumed along with Lorianne's frustrated sigh and the steady downpour on the roof. It reminded Genna of the call for a ceremonial Indian Rain Dance. It was working.

"What does that have to do with Gordon losing his job?" Lorianne demanded. Genna hoped the ceiling held. They'd had enough problems with the lights going out at whim. Last year's flooded basement and their current construction sent their costs soaring through the roof. *Sagging roof.*

Maybe the internet café idea was too much too soon. She chewed her bottom lip before letting out a soft sigh to address Lorianne's question. "Well," she said carefully. "Gordon kept calling in sick when he really wasn't, right?" She lifted her shoulder in a shrug. "That's an action, 'calling in' when he wasn't really. While sitting at home, 'not sick' that's the *inaction*…playing video games instead. In essence, I might add, that by your own observations of 'Gordon calling in sick when he wasn't really to sit home and play video games instead,' shows how wise you are, by seeing how his action for inaction in keeping his job really came into play. That's all." A crack of thunder rattled the old building.

"Now you're quoting *me*?" Lorianne's frustrated gasp had Genna biting back a grin.

Genna chanced another glance over her shoulder to see Lorianne shaking her head in amazement. It was more prudent to keep to the task at hand. She turned back and picked up the next new, used book to store in its designated place.

"Honestly, Genna, we need to find you a hobby," Lorianne huffed.

Genna moved one row over and bent two shelves down to place the book, *My Travels in India* between *My Travels in Indonesia* and *My Travels in Jamaica* before facing her friend, hands on her hips. "Well, the good news is that you won't marry him now, Lorianne. He doesn't have a job and you've discovered how wise you are by your admission of seeing his actions of inaction."

Genna spun around again and picked up the next book on the stack. *Walk in the Woods: Rediscovering America on the Appalachian Trail*. Hmm, this looked interesting.

"It's not like he'd taken any *action* to ask me anyway," Lorianne muttered.

The pen clattered on the counter. Genna snuck another peek. Lorianne had snatched up the mop and bucket and headed toward the office where a puddle of water was fast forming—obviously spurred into the *action* of cleaning it up.

DARTING INTO THE RUSTIC shop from the pouring rain, Rick Johnson spotted two other customers in the small, nondescript bookstore where he now found himself. He frowned at the sight of a nerdy guy hovering over a short, too-skinny waif with wild crazy hair wearing black sturdy framed glasses. Guy-nerd held a comic book and sported his own disorderly haircut and wire-framed glasses held together with...he strained forward for a closer look...yes, that was tape wrapped about the bridge. Girl-nerd was pushing her black glasses up on her nose, trying to step back. A sense of predatory defensiveness touched him.

He stopped so Guy-nerd could see him. When said subject caught Rick's eye, he backed off. Rick shook his head and hurried through a maze of what he was sure was someone's sense of organized bookcases. He was astonished at the amount of paperbacks anyone was creative enough to cram onto the massive shelves. These were all used books? He tried to tread carefully, to limit splattering water all over the place. There was no help for it.

There was no one else to blame; he was furious with himself. He'd procrastinated, waiting until the last moment to find the books Ramona had mentioned over two months ago that she'd wanted for her birthday. Now he was down to fifteen minutes before meeting her at the restaurant for a surprise dinner with some of her academic cronies from the university. He hadn't even thought of the surprise dinner. Such details usually didn't fail him. Although in his defense, due to all the recent rain, the investigative fraudulent claims business had skyrocketed.

Rick tripped down the aisles, checking labels someone had generously provided—sciences, in particular. The labels protruded from the wood shelves like little flags where each subject and category shifted from one topic to the next. If he had any hope for a night of Ramona's long legs wrapped about his waist and her sultry exotic charm inundating him, he needed those books. And who wouldn't? The senses of any normal warm-blooded male lived for getting lost in such dark, almost black eyes that tilted up on the ends, begging for seduction.

Not to mention brains and full pouty lips—the woman was a wizard in mathematics and civil engineering. If one was in the market for a package of an abundance of aptitude and sex appeal, Ramona fit the bill. Her professorship of environmental sciences and engineering at Bloomington College had her vying for aspirations of Department Head in the nearby future. Rick found her interest in old books a bit eccentric, but otherwise found her always willing. He wasn't about to turn all that sensuality away. Yep, he was a sucker for full lips on a brainy woman.

Rick turned his attention to the overflowing bookcases. The vast amount of books was staggering. He pushed a hand through his hair which sent water droplets flying.

Sorted by subject, practically two full bookcases, eight or ten shelves high, were dedicated to historical romance. Not just historical, mind, but Regency historical, medieval historical, American western historical, Tudor. He knew, because of the helpful little flags telling him so. Otherwise, he would have had no idea what the hell a historical was, medieval or otherwise.

Other shelves displayed contemporary thrillers—psychological and horror. Poetry. Reference. Cookbooks. Travel. Self-help, and... ah, hell!

Sexual therapy. Sexual dysfunctions. Sex enhancements. And one surprising title that caught his eye, *How to Overcome Premature Ejaculation*. Now he'd seen everything.

Curiosity got the better of him, and he flashed a quick glance around to make sure no one would surprise him by leering over his shoulder. Coast clear, he tugged the offending book from the shelf and flipped through the pages. Sexual sensory awareness. Okay, not so bad. Inadequate ejaculatory control, rapid ejaculations, plateau stage...

"But we would have a great time." The raised whiney tone startled Rick and he thrust the book back in its place, irritated at the heat on his face. At least it was placed out of the reach of small children and little old ladies, up high at the rear of the store.

"Forget it," she snapped. Their voices dropped to a murmur, and Rick heard a little bell signaling their departure. Guy-nerd's, anyway. Apparently, Nerd-girl-wild-haired-waif stormed toward the back of the store, setting him in mind of a miniature hurricane, muttering furiously under her breath. Her fury was quiet but apparent. "'*Is this a dagger which I see before me*?' Ha! I only wish."

Stifling a grin at this odd remark, he averted his gaze and continued a quick perusal of the shelves, moving off to an entirely different subject matter, of course.

Rick could hardly afford the 'few more minutes' when he finally spun in a circle at a loss. How the hell was he supposed to find some out-of-print books on Inductive Sciences in this mess?

Putting off his search until the last possible moment had been a foolish oversight. He looked at his watch and winced. Twelve minutes.

Seeing no one around to help, he strode to the end of the towering bookcases and paused in the center of a wide aisle. An unsightly sofa covered in faded floral print looked perfect in the setting. Just then he caught sight of Girl-nerd-waif inside a doorway at the back of the store, down on her hands and knees, slinging water about with an already soaked towel.

"Excuse me," he said. "If it's not too much trouble, I need help finding something?"

Startled out of obvious concentration, she glanced up at him from her position on the floor. Brows drawn, she didn't bother to conceal her exasperation behind the black nerdy glasses. He fought a sudden grin at the picture she made, somewhat adorable, in fact. But he was in a hurry. He cleared his throat. "I'm, uh, looking for *History of the Inductive Sciences, From the Earliest to the Present Times*, in three volumes, by William Whewell," he said. He kept his tone polite and gave her a gentle smile. She wore worn jeans and a rumpled tee. Poor thing, minimum wage was tough.

"*History of the Inductive Sciences?*" she repeated, cocking her head to one side. She stood and wiped her hands over her dusty jeans.

"Yes. And I'm in a bit of a hurry." He kept the smile in place, an effort as he glanced at his watch for effect. Definitely running out of time. Ten minutes to be exact.

He frowned at her gaping look. She needed to shut her mouth. The full lips were too distracting. Only why should he care, he couldn't guess. He should be thinking of Ramona's...

"Yes. *History of the Inductive Sciences, From the Earliest to the Present Times*, in three volumes by William Whewell," he said again, a bit more slowly this time. He was starting to doubt her intelligence. It was a long title, after all. "Is there someone here able to help me find them?" Looking past her into what he'd originally thought was a stockroom but was in fact, a small office. Those black, sturdy-nerdy glasses, he and his friends from high school had called them, failed to hide brilliant dark blue eyes. The glasses slid down a small upturned nose.

She pushed them up with a delicate finger, drawing attention to, he wasn't sure, but it looked like a streak of dirt crossing her left cheek.

"You mean Reverend William Whewell's *History of the Inductive Sciences*, the mathematician born in 1794, known for coining the phrase 'scientist'? The one who wrote *Astronomy and General Physics: Considered with Reference to Natural Theology*?" Her brow was still furrowed. Her obvious bemusement was in direct contrast to her reference of the author in question. It occurred to him that she might be having fun at his expense.

His eyes narrowed on her, considering the possibility. She didn't appear to be laughing at him. Breathing in willed patience, he let out a slow stream of air. Did she have the books or not? She was still talking, however.

"...co-founder and President of the British Association for the Advancement of Science." She didn't even pause. "You know, he also wrote on mechanics, architecture, and moral philosophy. Have you tried the internet?"

Did she ever take a breath? He followed her to the checkout counter, his gaze on the sway of her hips, subtle but alluring. He palmed a hand over his face. He really had no time for thoughts like these. "Look, miss, all I wanted was a used book. This is a *used bookstore*, right?"

"Well, yes, but—"

"But what?" Rick's exasperation started to give way. Unable

to stifle a sense of panic, his voice rose a degree. He knew he sounded unreasonable, but he really was out of time. He was going to look like a fool at dinner.

How had he let the time get by? He wasn't normally so disorganized. There was a new case sitting on his desk, a file he had yet to open. His mother had the audacity to start dropping the guilt bomb, deciding it was past time he married. Hell, he was only thirty-four. It felt like a betrayal of sorts. That was irritating in and of itself. He jerked his attention back to the matter at hand. How hard could it be to find a couple or three used books? And the clerk was *still* talking.

"*...and there was hardly a hole in it anywhere.*"

"Excuse me?"

"I said—" And she reiterated, enunciating as if to a very young child, "'*His ignorance covered the whole earth like a blanket, and there was hardly a hole—*'"

Rick let out a sharp laugh. "Never mind, I get it. You're calling me ignorant." Another quick glance at his watch. Eight minutes.

"It's a quote from *Mark Twain in Eruption*," she stated. "And I hardly ever use 'i' words." Frustration marred her brow. *Her adorable brow.* "Surely, you came prepared for the information you needed when you walked into a small used bookstore housing mostly paperbacks of the novel variety." She actually huffed. "Obviously not," she muttered.

For a split second Rick wished he wasn't in such a hurry after all. Such pragmatic, unembellished tones did not match the full lips or dark blue gaze. There was more to Girl-nerd-waif than met the eye.

Out of time, or not, he couldn't resist jerking her chain. "That's not what I saw on that shelf over there." He indicated with a jerk of his thumb and turned his most wolfish smile on her. Her now pink face was somewhat satisfying. She knew precisely to what, and where, he was referring.

She opened her mouth to say something. Stopped. Opened it a second time. Ah, hell...not that again. *Ramona. Ramona. Ramona.*

An inner resolve seemed to settle over her, and she drew herself up to her full height. He almost laughed. It couldn't have reached more than the top of his chin.

"Is there anything else I can help you find?" Polite indifference colored her tone.

"I just wanted a used book," he scowled, any urge to smile disappearing. Conscious again of the passing time, he refused to give in to the urge to check for the fifth—or was it the sixth—time?

"Oh. Well." her expression brightened, relief palpable. She spread her arms indicating the obvious. "As you can see, I have plenty of used books."

Her smile caught him by surprise, stirring something he realized was missing with Ramona. Full lips across small even teeth stirred his senses.

A sudden whiff of honeysuckle tickled his nostrils, reminding him of lazy summer days gone by when his parents and siblings took vacations to their small farm in the country, a scent that had drifted through steamy heated air. Rick shook his head. Oh, for God's sake! All he'd wanted was a used book. Granted, a specific book, but...hell, what did it matter?

Those eyes, shining like dark blue sapphires behind the black nerdy glasses, struck him again by their brilliance. "Is something wrong?" She asked, brows drawn, inquiring.

He pinched the bridge of his nose, horrified by the train of his thought. "No...yes...well, I was particularly interested in the *History of the Inductive Sciences*." His voice came out rough.

The delicate frown touching her full mouth was quite engaging. *Ramona*, damn.

"Oh." She stopped with a thoughtful pause and a delicate shrug of thin shoulders. "Unfortunately, that item is considered rare and collectible. It's much too valuable for our little establishment." She smiled again. And, again, he found himself dazzled. The animation in her expression as some idea occurred, punched him deep within his lungs. "Oh wait, I have something that might help you. One second." She darted from behind the counter. The wind from her movement disturbed the contents of the counter. A lone piece of paper floated across the floor along with the scent of honeysuckle. Rick stooped to snatch it, midair, as much to breathe in the fresh scent.

His attention was drawn to strange lettering. Someone had gone to a lot of trouble, cutting words from a magazine. They were pasted on the page, similar to that of a collage. He had just enough time to scan the words 'You need to make better choices' before Girl-nerd-waif rushed back in, waving yet another piece of paper. He dropped the page he held next to a stamped envelope with similar markings. The whole scene reminded him of a corny police drama from the seventies.

"Here you are. I'm certain this will help." She smiled and the strange note fled his mind.

Rick snatched the paper from her outstretched hand, irritated that such a tiny person could crawl under his skin, and perused the note. "Antiquarian and Rare Books?" he read. "Delaware?"

"It's a place to start."

The serious, excited expression crossing her features made him grin until he stole another glance at his watch. "At this point, I doubt it will really matter." It occurred to him he might find himself back, looking for...something else. *A book*, of course.

Another quick look at Girl-nerd-waif with her wild dark curls gone awry had him smothering an unexpected urge to wipe the smudge of dirt from her face; that creamy smooth complexion was irresistible. Why he let himself get distracted with any kind of *nerd-waif* was contemplation for another time. *This* time was up. It was obvious his luck had run out in locating *History of the Inductive Sciences, From the Earliest to the Present Times*, in three volumes, on this night. The hand at his side clenched into a fist.

Thanking Girl-nerd-waif abruptly, he darted out into the pouring rain. Perfect.

GENNA GAZED AFTER THE closed door, slightly bemused after that bizarre encounter. Goodness, the man was a walking disaster. What on earth would he be doing looking for such a treasure in a little used bookstore known more for romance and contemporary thriller paperbacks? Her mouth watered at the thought of such a collectible in her possession.

She chuckled softly. He must not read much. Although, he'd zeroed in on the adult material quick enough, she thought, lips turning down.

Genna would have never seen the need for the erotic book section if Lorianne hadn't insisted on it. But her arguments that sex, a natural part of life, was so popular, had convinced Genna to at least give the category a try. Obviously proving the argument true, as she'd just witnessed.

Strolling to the back of the store, hands planted on her hips, she surveyed the office. The gray metal bucket Lorianne had placed under the leaking ceiling was already over half full. Lorianne had been so irritable, Genna insisted she could handle the shop on her own, should any late customers venture in, and sent her bad-tempered friend home. At the very least, it should have given Genna some much-appreciated quiet time. That's what she'd been hoping for anyway. But, now, seeing the brown water stain on the ceiling, worry filled her. Slightly bulging, it still managed to hold...so far, anyway. She pushed a wayward curl from her forehead. The insurance company was surely starting to tire of her.

Spinning on one foot, Genna let out a soft breath. This, her vision of Renewed Interest Used Bookstore. Its small house-like structure was situated on the south end of Bloomington's downtown area. The property had been in Genna's family for three generations. Of course, it hadn't always been a business. In the early days, the house provided her great-grandparents, then grandparents, a warm home. Even her parents had called it home until a brother she'd never known died of SIDS years before she'd come along. A sense of loss she hadn't felt in ages settled over her. It was only after his death that they'd decided to move from town and bought the house she now resided in. Five minutes from the store made things ideal as far as she was concerned.

It was in Genna's atypical friendship in Lorianne where the two had found the perfect niche and partnership, finally bringing Genna's dream of owning her own business to fruition. A bookstore where she could read and dream to her life's content. Most times, Lorianne dealt with the customers. Lorianne had an insatiable need for personal contact, whereas Genna was more than happy to handle the accounting, stocking, and general mundane office upkeep.

She let out a sigh of contentment. Little had changed the building over the years. They'd squared off a section near a door that led to the stairs of an unfinished basement that held storage for extra stock intended for their new expansion. And if they were able to keep the basement from flooding again, Genna eventually envisioned a large enclosed space designed for children's activities. The possibility of relocating their small office would free up valuable space on the main floor.

Large windows faced the street on two sides of the building. They allowed a plentitude of natural light during daylight hours. Her little store boasted character with uneven hardwood floors and bookcases from floor to ceiling, not placed in any symmetrical sense. She and Lorianne had found overstuffed chairs and tables in a variety of shapes at yard sales and used furniture stores.

She drifted to the only sofa, a faded floral print in a comfy warm yellow any college student would love, and plopped down. With Lorianne's natural sense of flair, they'd scattered sitting areas sparsely throughout. It had the overall effect of coziness and intimacy.

Reveling in the quiet, Genna looked at the elaborate entrance she'd spent a good-sized portion of her inheritance on. The oversized, double dark red mahogany doors added warmth, even if it stole the entire southeast corner. Large center bevel curves, tinged with light pink, tinted the glass in various pieces. The door was a masterpiece, creating one of the most unique entrances in town.

Unfortunately, humidity caused the basement door to stick. The railing needed repair. And now, another new roof. But the property was her legacy, and she loved every crack in the plaster and etched groove in the wood floors.

It was the perfect location in Bloomington's antiquated historic district. The area was filled with a contrast of restored and dilapidated structures, half a block from the town's main square. She sighed, looking back up at the sagging ceiling. Her bottomless peace and satisfaction was about to cave in. The rain was definitely playing havoc with her nerves.

Construction had already begun in the vacant building next door. The ceiling would require additional expense. No doubt she'd have to rework the budget.

All the chain bookstores were adding coffee bars, and her research assured success, doubly encouraged by the presence of Bloomington's private university.

Genna sighed again. It didn't look to be an early night, no matter how badly she wanted to settle down to read her quick date for the evening, *A Guide for the Perplexed*, by E.F. Schumacher. Mr. Schumacher's view of how man's learning related to the four fields of knowledge had caught her attention from a customer bringing in his trades. At only a hundred and forty-two pages she would have made quick work of it, too. Her gaze settled on the metal bucket, then moved up toward the ceiling. Well, maybe later.

The lights flickered once overhead then petered out. Finding her way to the counter she groped for the flashlight below. *"'What light through yonder window breaks?'* Thank you, William Shakespeare," she mumbled, stomping *carefully* down the basement stairs for the junction box.

CHAPTER 2

THE NEXT MORNING RICK laid on his back, arms folded behind his head, reflecting over dinner with Ramona and her friends from the university. Her reaction to his not having found the books she'd asked for some two months earlier was curious. She hadn't even seemed particularly surprised he hadn't found them. In fact, it was almost as if the whole ordeal was a test of some sort and he'd passed. Only by passing, he'd failed. It was certainly not a mess worth puzzling over. The fact of the matter was he liked sophisticated women. He liked beautiful women. He really *liked* Ramona.

She drifted to him as natural as a bee to honey...like honey...suckle. It was enough to make him think of...of the clerk at the bookstore? Who was *not* his type! She was not sophisticated. She was not beautiful. Okay, she *might* be brainier that he'd first believed.

Worldly? No.

Cultivated? No.

Ambitious? *No*. Still...despite all efforts to the contrary, the annoying little bookworm kept invading his morning. That was an excellent name for her. Bookworm. He pushed thoughts of the annoying bookworm away.

Easier said than done when the memory of sweet honeysuckle pestered him into unwilling more thoughts. How his impression of a 'close to below average' on the IQ chart struck, knocking him in the head when less than a moment later he'd learned just how deceiving looks could be. Questioning the specific author of the inductive sciences nonsense, reciting cryptic passages, even offering to help research where he might find the blasted thing. That was the surprise. *She* was a surprise.

He rolled over and groaned. Said Bookworm was *not* sexy. He was just horny. Which was why the thought of her open mouth and how it might feel on parts of his anatomy, straining for attention was...well, making it strain more. Rick buried his head in the pillow, desperate to clear her from his mind. Think of Ramona, think of Ramona, think of Ramona. Think of Bookworm...no! Ramona.

An inept little clerk with blank unseeing eyes that shifted so quickly into an intellect—it caught him off guard, that's all. He huffed out a disgusted breath. So what if she'd turned into an unexpected scholar right before him? He preferred women who were not complicated—women who were independent. When he looked at Ramona, he saw confidence, capability, *experience*. She was wise to men like him. He was no one's hero. Just like he preferred.

The idea that a bookworm could invade his orderly world was ridiculous. That petite thing couldn't weigh more than a hundred and ten pounds. And that hair. He couldn't imagine what she had to do to contain that dark curly—he swallowed—soft hair. The tips of his fingers tingled at the thought of helping her out.

Lady Bookworm certainly lacked the sophistication he normally found himself attracted to. Though, admittedly, someone could get lost in those brilliant dark blue eyes, *if* one wasn't too careful. Not him, of course. Jesus. The thought was ludicrous.

He doubted she even smiled all that often. Brows drawn together looking like some thesis had popped into that genius little head. Trying to find a way to convey it to the less literate population—a smiled tugged at his lips.

He pushed away his thoughts of the mousy little clerk, *again*. No, he would not be going back to that bookstore, he decided. Certain distractions he could do without. Any rare books he needed in the future would entail taking her suggestion by way of the internet, or a store—somewhere in Delaware—or at the very least, the next county.

Jewelry. Jewelry was always a good fallback option. Jewelry unleashed options for sex. Experienced sex. Capable sex. *Worldly* sex. He rolled once more onto his back and lifted the covers. One glance at his lower regions decided it. Ramona loved jewelry.

CHAPTER 3

"IDEAS COME WHEN WE do not expect them, and not when we are brooding and searching at our desks. Yet ideas would certainly not come to mind had we not brooded at our desks and searched for answers with passionate devotion.'"

"Where is that from, Genna?" Mrs. Bakely asked.

Genna rested her gaze on the elderly woman perusing the shelves of the over-abundant historical romance section. Regency. Her graying hair was pulled to the nape of her neck in an old-fashioned coiffure, blue-eyes twinkling with laughter.

"Max Weber's *Science as a Vocation*," she said, returning to her task of logging more books to be shelved.

"You are just a wealth of information, dear."

"Thank you, Mrs. Bakely. Sometimes these things just pop into my head." Genna smiled, picking up the next book.

"Do you have anything new from Suzanne Enoch or Cathy Maxwell, dear?"

"Not since you asked a few days ago. But if anything comes in, I'll be sure to hold it for you." Genna lifted her pen to her bottom lip and contemplated Mrs. Bakely's question. "You might try something from Karen Hawkins. I believe she and Suzanne Enoch are friends. In real life, that is. She has a terrific sense of subtle humor." Genna scribbled Mrs. Blakely's preference on her notepad.

"I'll keep that in mind. How is that dear Lorianne doing? Have she and Gordon Flypaper set a wedding date yet?"

"His name is Stiper, and, no. No wedding date, as of yet." Genna glanced at the elderly woman, hesitating. Then lowering her voice, confided, "I have a feeling there won't be a wedding date."

"Oh?"

She straightened and set her eyes on the computer screen. "*'Marriage is neither heaven nor hell, it is simply purgatory,'*" Genna told her.

"Well, I suppose that is one way to look at it." Mrs. Bakely smiled. "Although, my Victor and I had a wonderful marriage."

Genna stole a glance at the front door, and lowered her voice more. "I think she and Gordon may be finished."

"Oh, my. Really?" Mrs. Bakely turned from the shelves and pierced Genna with a sharp gaze.

"Yes. He sort of...well..." The bell to the shop tinkled. Genna started with guilt.

Lorianne breezed in. "Hello, Mrs. Bakely."

Genna took in Lorianne's pale, blotched face her makeup didn't quite hide. Dark lashes framed cornflower blue eyes, suspiciously puffy. Her wheat-colored hair almost as crazy as Genna's. Which was *not* normal. She frowned. Lorianne always looked perfect.

"How are things this morning?" Lorianne asked.

"Fine." Genna's response was automated. Then, before she could stop herself, blurted out, "Though, we did have an interesting visitor last evening." She lowered her voice, embarrassed.

"That's nice." Lorianne's distraction stopped Genna.

"Are you okay, Lorianne?"

"Of course!" she said with appalling brightness. The falseness in her tone hit Genna like a discordant note in an otherwise perfect sonata played by Mozart himself. Lorianne buried her face in both hands. "Oh, you were right about Gordon. He is such a loser. Why do I keep picking losers?" The tears in Lorianne's muffled voice broke Genna's heart. "You were right! Gordon's *inaction* is a huge problem, as well as his action of calling in sick to work." She raised her head and gave a shaky laugh. "Lord. Now I'm quoting you. At the very least, making sense of what you say."

"Oh, Lorianne. It will be okay." Impossible to take offense, Genna ran around the counter and embraced her friend in a fierce hug.

"I know." Anger tinged her voice. "My hero is out there. Somewhere."

"Elizabeth Barrett Browning wrote, '*All actual heroes are essential, and all men possible heroes.*'"

"You are the best friend ever!" Lorianne hugged her back just as fiercely. Her tears flowed freely, saturating Genna's rumpled gray t-shirt. "What would I do without you?"

"WHY ON EARTH WAS he looking for the 'History of the Pervert' —what was the name of it?" Lorianne wrinkled her nose.

"*History of the Inductive Sciences, From the Earliest to the Present Times.*"

"We didn't have it?" Lorianne asked with a straight face. She felt much better having had a good cry the night before and the hug from Genna. Gordon was now old news.

"No, it's a collectible. And rare." Genna munched on her salad, eyes focused on something unseen. "He seemed fairly agitated. Like, since it was an old book it should be in a used paperback bookstore. And he looked at his watch. *A lot.*"

They both giggled. Then Genna said, "He was very

attractive."

Lorianne gaped at her friend in surprise. Genna never noticed how anyone looked. Attractive or otherwise. Her friend was all about academics.

"So, uh, what do you mean attractive?" Lorianne disguised nonchalance was weak at best, but Genna didn't seem to notice.

"Oh, well, he, umm, he was kind of tall. Yes, tall. And, umm, uh, agitated."

"You've already said agitated." Lorianne sipped her soup to hide a smile, observing Genna from beneath concealed lashes. Genna pushed lettuce around her plate with her fork.

"Oh, yes, well. He had dark eyes. Brown, I believe."

Genna's cheeks turned an engaging pink, scrunching her nose as if wondering why she would notice his eyes. Lorianne fought the urge to laugh. "Maybe you should go out with him," she suggested.

"What! He's a customer," Genna said in horror.

"Did he buy anything?"

Genna's glare and lack of response did not put Lorianne off.

"You know," Lorianne started. She kept her tone light, knowing she treaded on thin ice. She debated the wisdom of bringing up the past, but decided she just couldn't help herself. The past was not a subject Genna was usually willing to discuss, but it needed discussing. "You haven't gone out with anyone since that imbecile in college. Damon, was that his name? It was only after he took advantage of your doing all his homework that you started with this…" She waved her hand in the air. "…unrelenting recitation of odd quotes you throw out at random."

Sure enough, Genna thrust her chin out in defense, eyes glittering. "You know how I feel about 'i'—"

Lorianne cut her off. "—Oh, don't glare at me like that. He took advantage of you and you know it," she said gently. Then, added with bitterness on Genna's behalf, "I just wonder how he passed his tests in order to graduate."

The look on her Genna's face was one of absolute panic. "There was...was that guy last year, I-I forget his name now," she stumbled.

"Barrett?"

"Yes, that's right. Barrett," she said in relief.

"Nice try, Genna." Lorianne smirked. "Barrett worked at the coffee shop next door and we walked over there for lunch almost every day until he moved out of town. I wouldn't say you *actually* went out with him. And he was weird."

"'*The more I see of men, the more I admire dogs.*'"

Lorianne waited, and as expected, Genna cited her source. "Just a general comment from Jeanne-Marie Roland."

Lorianne lifted a spoonful of soup, then stopped with it paused before her lips. "There you go again, resorting to the most ridiculous quotes," Lorianne told her. "You don't even *have* a dog." She put the spoon in her mouth.

Genna looked at her with wide unblinking eyes where a suspicious sheen gleamed, her black glasses magnifying the pool.

But Lorianne continued, with little caution. "I may keep picking the wrong man, but you don't even give yourself a chance." She lowered her spoon and meeting her friend's direct gaze. "You just hide yourself in the most obscure text you can find." Lorianne lifted her spoon again and sipped. Swallowing, she chuckled. "Though, where you come up with some of the stuff that pops out of your mouth amazes me."

TEARS CLOGGED GENNA'S THROAT. She knew Lorianne's intentions were not malicious. True, she buried herself in books and facts. At least books didn't use you and make you feel like you were only good enough for your brains. So what if she'd helped Damon with his homework? He'd had to work, hadn't he?

But the lump in her throat was hard.

Air fled her body like a leaking balloon. He'd been attractive, ready with a quick smile, and she'd fallen—hook, line and sinker. It's wasn't as if the guys were lining up to date a short, skinny, brainy *she-devil*.

She sat taller and sniffed back the tears in a defensive effort. Like she hadn't benefitted from helping him through his degree program of public relations! Ha! She'd applied several of the methodologies she'd learned. While it hadn't seemed so at the time, the subjects were just as fascinating as she found most subjects. Could she help being a veritable sponge?

Slumping again, she rested her chin on her fist. If only she were a little taller; a tiny bit more of an elegant sponge that maybe didn't soak up quite so much.

And her hair? Short of shaving it clean off, there wasn't much else she could. And that just seemed a little too drastic. She picked up her fork and shoved the lettuce around her plate with a viciousness that surprised her, landing some of it on the floor.

"What are you mumbling?" Lorianne demanded, jolting her back.

Genna refused to look up, attacking another piece of lettuce with hostile fervor. "I was just saying '*the ability to discriminate between that which is true and that which is false is one of the last attainments of the human mind*,' that's all."

"I hate when you say 'that's all,'" Lorianne grumbled.

"James Fenimore Cooper."

"I suspected as much," Lorianne said sweetly, lips curled with sarcasm.

Genna jutted her chin out, hurt by Lorianne's insensitivity. No one knew about Damon, except Lorianne. And why was she bringing him up all of a sudden? She hadn't seen him since the day he'd graduated almost five years ago.

Lorianne let out an exasperated huff. "Look, I have tickets

for Bloomington's Art Museum fundraiser for Friday night. Now that I'm not seeing Gordon any longer, why don't you go with me? It will be fun. We'll dress up and make a girls' night of it."

Genna groaned. "How did you get tickets to the art museum's fundraiser? They don't have country dancing, do they?"

"Very funny," Lorianne retorted. "They were from a client of Gordon's. I don't see how he'll have any use for them."

"I don't know. I'm just not comfortable in that sort of setting," Genna objected, pained with the turn of the conversation. She put a hand up to her wild hair. She hated dressing up. Makeup was a nightmare. And shoes? Forget it. She would fight her. She would.

But Lorianne drew her greatest weapon—a sweetly disguised beg. "Genna, you are the smartest and prettiest girl I know. It's the perfect place for you."

Genna squeezed her eyes tight. Knowing Lorianne's decision was resolved, she was sunk.

"I won't take no for an answer. It will be like before you met that idiot—" she held out a palm to Genna's protest. "I know you don't like 'i' words, but he was an idiot. Admit it!"

"Okay, I'll admit it," she said darkly.

"Good." Lorianne's face lit up. "We'll go shopping tonight. Wanda will love helping us out."

"Tonight?" she squeaked.

"It will be great."

CHAPTER 4

GENNA WANDERED ABOUT THE large atrium in the Bloomington Modern Art Museum alone, wine glass in hand, taking periodic sips. Sometimes unable to stifle her bewilderment when confronted by some "interesting" piece of abstract art of marble, canvas, even video, thinking of the strange film she'd watched for an amazing twenty minutes on some kind of booby trap series of events.

The minute they'd stepped through the door some blond-haired, silver-eyed Adonis zeroed in on Lorianne. She wasn't jealous. Lorianne couldn't help that her long blond hair fell down her back in perfect waves, or that the unusual shade of her cornflower blue eyes framed by dark long lashes made even the most staid of men trip over his own feet to reach her.

Genna stopped before an odd, yet fascinating statue of a bronze, elongated figure smooth in detail. She studied it for a moment trying to decide whether it represented a sleeping woman or an exotic plant. After a moment, she decided on the woman and moved on. The low hum of chatter settled over her as she meandered from exhibit to exhibit.

She wondered idly if Selma Stotts, the beautician who worked the miracle on her hair, could actually sculpt art. The ability to tame her overrun curls, and bring out her eyes with just a few strokes of make-up brushes, had been an amazing sight to behold once Genna had finally been allowed to look. True artistry.

Both Selma and Lorianne had convinced her to leave her glasses home, donning her contact lenses for once. She'd hardly recognized herself in the mirror. Though she could feel little wisps of hair escaping confinement, a few softened the effect, they'd assured her.

Genna perused the art, stopping at something drummed up in sort of a glass and mirror concoction. She really should study more modern art form and theory. Art was much more fascinating than men. She smiled.

She set her empty wine glass on a passing tray and found an alcove where she could comfortably observe other patrons who'd donated, what Lorianne insisted was, an outrageous amount to attend. The museum's clientele included an interesting mix of dressed to the nines wealth to artsy folks with long free-flowing hair, men and women. She and Lorianne had opted for little black cocktail dresses. Wanda Buford, of Wanda's Fine Dresses on the town square, had been thrilled to help them, just as Lorianne had predicted.

Sounds resembling a babbling brook trickled from the large fountain centered under a domed ceiling. Caught up in her surroundings, Genna started when a warm, deep resonating and *familiar* voice, interrupted her musings.

"Interesting group, isn't it?"

She froze. From the corner of her eye, dread gripped her when she recognized the maniacal customer who knew nothing about rare and collectible books. Well, perhaps not maniacal, but impatient, to be sure. She excused the fact that not many people did know about rare and collectibles. But really, in a nondescript, mostly used, paperbacks bookstore?

He was just as attractive as she'd remembered. Only then he'd been dripping wet, hair plastered to his head. She masked a wince. His height of over six feet was intimidating.

The black Armani suit emphasized broad shoulders. She wasn't sure it was an Armani, that would be Lorianne's department, but it was the only men's designer name that came to mind. Something else she should study. His black silk shirt made an odd combination, finished off with a stunning silver tie. It was an illusion so overpowering, it made her long for the sudden safety of home, with her newest conquest, Living Biographies of Great Philosophers. She'd had a tough time finding that volume too as it was currently out of print. Making it a rare collectible!

She frowned, taking an unconscious step back from his smothering presence.

Genna's cheeks heated under his scrutiny, the pulse throbbed in her ears. She prayed it didn't show on her face. Protective shields surged, she blurted barely above a whisper, "Paul Gauguin said, '*I shut my eyes to see.*' I...I think he envisioned this crowd."

He laughed softly. "Agreed."

RICK SEARCHED HIS MEMORY for the sound of her hushed voice, running an appraising glance over her small frame—with discretion of course, slim legs beneath a simple black cocktail dress, very enticing. Bared, graceful, sexy shoulders and dark hair struggling to escape a sophisticated twist at the nape of her neck did something to his insides. Eyes hidden by thick lowered lashes beguiled. Warmth, bordering on hot, swarmed over him. Surely, he would have remembered meeting her. His gaze focused on full, glazed lips, tinged to soft peach. God, to taste something so delectable.

"Would you care for wine?" he asked, snagging two glasses from a passing waiter. He handed one to his dainty, plainly shy, companion without waiting for an answer.

"*'Good wine is a good familiar creature if well used.'*" He smiled at her flushed face when she realized she'd spoken the thought aloud. She took a quick gulp.

"From William Shakespeare's Othello, isn't it?" he murmured.

Rick leaned in. A drop of wine on her bottom lip absorbed his attention. His fingers itched to brush it away, or—he swallowed—released a raging obsession to daub it with his tongue. Instinct and decorum warned him otherwise. That's when the faint aroma of wild honeysuckle drifted up to him. *Very* familiar.

When she lifted her lashes and looked him square in the face with dark blue eyes, it hit him with a force as strong as a kick in the gut. Son of a bitch. Girl-nerd-waif from the bookstore! He groaned, managing somehow to keep it inside.

Straight from the kick in the gut was the immediate heat. It swelled through his lower regions. It was those damned books on that back shelf making him feel so hot. He pressed his lips together. It was the only explanation.

His smile seemed to freeze on his face. He couldn't remember the last time he'd been at a loss for words. Well, yes he could. It was their last encounter, when she started spouting facts on that ridiculous rare book he'd been hunting for.

"Genna Lyndsey, small used bookstore entrepreneur," she said holding out her right hand.

"Ah, *better choices*," he breathed. "I remember now." He could still see the note he'd witnessed then dropped on the counter. Words cut out to spell out an odd message. He wanted to ask about it, but thought it unwise to do so. He took her outstretched hand, captivated by its cool elegance and fragile form, in his warm larger one. He angled his head to one side, at her questioning expression.

"Your name?" Intelligent eyes bored into him like midnight pools of radiated brilliance, elevating the level of his pulse. He seemed to have trouble reconciling this well put together creature with the scraggily tiny thing from the other night. Shocking, the difference.

"Rick Johnson." He let her hand slide from his. "You *own* the bookstore?"

"My friend and I own it together." Her gaze drifted from his to the surrounding atrium giving him a moment to acclimate the two.

"Have you owned it long?"

"Three years," she answered absently.

"I didn't recognize you with your hair pulled back," he accused with a mildness he did not feel.

She trained those compelling eyes on him, placing a self-conscious hand up to smooth back a few rebellious wisps. She dropped her eyes to the wine glass she held and said, "'*Long on hair, short on brains.*'"

"Although that is a lovely French proverb, I doubt *you* are short on brains." His tone came out more sharp than he'd intended. He took a measured breath. It was time to get control of the conversation. "I find it interesting that you own a used, paperback bookstore."

"I like to read."

GENNA CAST A DESPERATE glance around for Lorianne. She spotted her quickly enough—the blonde hair. She stood across the room, facing a monstrosity of a canvas with painted stripes in neon colors more appropriate for psychedelic birthday wrapping paper. Even soft strategic lighting, placed throughout the atrium, failed in toning down its loudness. Twenty feet by twenty feet of outrageous, splattered paint was difficult to subdue. It would have been fun to see the price on the two-inch by two-inch card next to it.

On the verge of what she would consider an abnormal sense of panic, Genna willed Lorianne to turn around. But she could tell by the slant of Lorianne's head and slight thrust of her pert and perfect breasts, she was knee deep into flirtation with the same attractive male who had snatched her attention the moment they'd walked through the door. If he were standing any closer he would have been in her dress instead of leering down the front of its cleavage-popping dip. Good grief, they'd be here all night!

She was *not* bitter, she insisted silently. It was just time to go. That's all.

Genna could site hundreds of idioms on controlling the mind. Unfortunately, her E.S.P. was nonexistent in the "real life" sense. Past experience reminded her she was well forgotten. Despite the odds against her, Genna bore her eyes into the back of Lorianne's head, willing her to turn around.

It didn't work on Lorianne, but Genna felt another uncanny sense of someone doing the same to her. She looked quickly around. There, toward a display of wooden sculptures in a bizarre presentation of the Universe, she gasped in shock. Damon? It couldn't be. Yet, he lifted his glass in a silent salute, giving her a dazzling smile. "'*False in one thing, false in everything.*'" The words slipped out under her breath.

"Excuse me?"

Genna sent a startled glance to her new acquaintance, having completely forgotten him. He was staring at her, his expression baffled.

Panic seized her. In no way was she willing or...or able, to talk to Damon. She felt ill. Hair still dark and curly, eyes sharp and piercing, remained trained on her. His smile...she didn't want to think of his smile, it irritated the...the *heck* out of her. She wanted no part of his game.

What was he doing in Bloomington? And why suddenly

appear after all this time? She didn't care. Desperation seized her. She had to get out of there. Willing her accelerated heart to slow, she steadied her breath and pulled up. She needed to think.

Smile, she needed to smile. She pasted on a bright smile. It was false but she couldn't help that. She turned with gritted calm to her companion, "Well, it was very nice meeting you…uh—" His name. *She'd forgotten his name* and she never forgot names. Mortification swamped her.

"Rick?"

"Yes. Yes, Rick," she said relieved. "If you'll excuse me, I…I see my friend."

"A pleasure meeting you as well, Ms. Lyndsey," he acknowledged, inclining his head in a polite gesture.

Genna slipped quickly through the crowd. She avoided eye contact with everyone before making it to the ladies' room. She bent over the sink, breathless. Why *was* Damon here? And why was he staring at her, like he wanted to eat her up? Like a hawk swooping in on a small defenseless rabbit? Getting tangled in his lies again was not a pleasant option.

And what was it with the 'I-couldn't-tell-a-collectible-from-a-best-seller guy, Rick…Rick…she forgot his last name. Frustration filled her. How was it he could make her feel as if her knees wouldn't support her own weight? One glance in the mirror showed cheeks flushed and eyes wide. This was not what she wanted to feel about anyone, ever again. Maybe she should get a dog.

RICK WATCHED LITTLE MISS Bookworm rush from the atrium, black swirling skirt gracing a small, shapely derriere. She kept her eyes glued to the floor, dashing down a darkened hallway instead of going to a supposed friend. Presumably, destined for the ladies' room.

She was a regular Cinderella running from the ball, he

laughed to himself. He shook his head, shocked to find she was the same person he'd met earlier in the week with the wild hair, dusty jeans, nerdy glasses, and dirt streaking her face. His pulse kicked up a notch. He frowned. He should have invited Ramona. Nah, he'd take his chances on the hottie bookworm when she came back for her *friend*.

Scrutinizing the room, he caught sight of Ash talking to a busty blonde. Then he caught sight of a man gauging Ms. Lyndsey's departure with great interest. He'd heard her sharp intake of breath. It could have been excitement. Or panic? He wasn't sure. But one thing was for certain...she'd flown out of there like she'd seen a ghost.

The sharp-dressed man made a move in her direction, but as luck would have it found himself blocked by a group of twenty-somethings, angling for a look-see of the tin cans and barbed wire exhibit.

Ramona forgotten, he snatched another glass of wine for people-watching. A smile curled his lips—bookworm-watching, in particular.

CHAPTER 5

THE NEXT MORNING GENNA sat on a tall stool behind the register going through a stack of recently acquired Regency Historicals. Mrs. Bakely drifted to the counter. Genna leaned down and gathered the small stack she'd set aside for her favorite customer.

"Can you believe this rain, Mrs. Bakely?" Genna asked. "Here you are. One new Karen Hawkins came in and two Cathy Maxwell's. Unfortunately, no new Suzanne Enoch's this time. You'll enjoy the Karen Hawkins. I promise." Genna beamed at the sixty-plus year old woman. "That will be $11.40."

Mrs. Bakely grinned. Her silver hair in its usual coif was secured neatly at her nape, blue-gray eyes peering as sharp as ever. The unusual color struck Genna as familiar.

"Thank you, dear. I trust your judgment implicitly. Where is that charming Lorianne this fine Saturday morning?" Genna accepted a twenty-dollar note.

"We had a bit of a late night. We attended a fundraiser the museum was hosting." She made a special effort striving for a bland tone, and handed her change and the receipt. Genna stepped around the counter to hand over her purchase. "Thank you for coming in, Mrs. Bakely."

Moments after Mrs. Bakely's departure, where the shop bell had tinkled with a dainty chime, it now revolted in protest with its new entrant.

Startled, Genna's gaze darted up. Lorianne rushed through the door holding two large lattes, sporting the same black dress from the evening before, her glorious hair no worse for wear despite the rain. Genna's lips tightened. She turned back to logging more used paperbacks on the computer. Contemporary thrillers. Murder.

"I'm so glad you made it home okay, Genna. I had a wonderful time last night," Lorianne gushed. She stepped forward and set the cups on the counter.

"'*The tongue like a sharp knife...kills without drawing blood*,'" she responded coolly, not meeting her eyes.

"Oh, no. You're mad at me, aren't you?"

"Buddha," she said. Genna picked up the stack of books she'd just logged, determined to keep her hands occupied. She walked over to the homicide section, tossing a glance over her shoulder. "Nice outfit." She choked back the guilt.

Lorianne lowered her eyes. "I'm sorry, Genna. But I met the greatest guy. He's the one, I know it!" The door tinkled, interrupting Lorianne's glowing commentary.

An attractive woman Genna didn't recognize strolled in and began perusing the bookshelves. Heavy, long black hair swung in opposition of her gait. Genna scowled. She couldn't detect one single flyaway or frizz.

Genna turned back to Lorianne, lowering her voice, but refusing to relent. "Well, thanks for inviting me last night, then deserting me." She was surprised at her own bitterness. In a quick swoosh the air left her body. What did it matter anyway? It only gave her more time to read.

"We just got separated," Lorianne whispered. "Besides I saw you talking to a pretty hot guy," she accused.

"Yes, well." Genna was at a loss for words, irritated at feeling a blush warm her cheeks. "Well...'*Lost time is never found again*,'" she sputtered, slamming the books on a nearby shelf, hiding behind fury.

Lorianne's eyes narrowed on Genna. Genna's fingers shook. Surely Lorianne was sick and tired of hearing a walking Quote Book when said Quote Book happened to be a little put out. But Genna couldn't seem to help herself. Her feelings were hurt.

"'*Every path hath a puddle*,'" Lorianne retorted, surprising her.

Genna's mouth dropped open. "Y...you." Her voice raised a fraction. "'*It is generally unwise...to raise an issue when one is not prepared to accept the likely response.*'"

Lorianne rolled her eyes. "'*As the wind blows you must set your sail.*'"

"'*Better to remain silent and be thought a fool than to speak out and remove all doubt.*'" Genna punctuated the sentence with a tilted chin and crossed her arms.

"Humph." Lorianne's eyes flashed. "'*What is not started today is never finished tomorrow.*'"

"How are you doing that?" Genna demanded, keeping her voice low.

"I've known you a long time," Lorianne hissed back. "Do you think I can't read? Or that I *don't* read?"

The perfect-haired customer sauntered to the counter, appearing oblivious to the surrounding tension. Genna hurried to the register while Lorianne moved toward the back of the store as the customer set her selections down. She opened her purse and reached for her wallet.

Genna flashed Lorianne a telling glare. This wasn't over by any stretch of the imagination. Genna was ringing up the purchase when the subject matter of the books finally trumped her temper.

Sextacy, by Caroline Aldred, and *Mathematics and Sex*, by Dr. Clio Cresswell.

Stealing a glance from lowered lashes, Genna realized the woman was quite striking. Well, no matter. Lorianne had an instinct about people and the subjects they might be interested in. It was none of Genna's business what customers chose to read.

"That will be $18.38," she told her. She avoided eye contact, placing the contents in a clear plastic sack. A brown paper bag would have served better. With a demure thanks for her business, Genna handed over the purchase.

The door jingled her departure.

Genna met Lorianne's gaze for a long moment. "'*After sorrow comes joy*,'" she murmured, anger fleeing as quickly as it had risen.

"'*After darkness comes light*.'" Lorianne smiled and rushed forward.

Genna surrendered. "'*The best is yet to come*?'"

"For sure!" Lorianne finished with a hug.

RICK HADN'T INTENDED TO get into the car and drive for coffee. He had an excellent coffee maker on his nice, shiny granite countertops in his over-the-top, state-of-the-art, all stainless kitchen. But when he woke that morning, he felt a restlessness he couldn't pinpoint.

He woke, a throbbing hard-on tenting the covers. Disturbing thoughts of Bookworm, though 'bookworm' didn't quite seem to fit after the erotic dreams he'd suffered through all night. It was that damned black dress she'd had on. Pissed or frustrated, he couldn't decide which, when she hadn't returned to the atrium to locate her friend. He should know—he'd watched for her for over an hour.

When he'd finally made his way down the hallway where

she'd disappeared, strictly to make sure she hadn't ended up in some kind of perilous situation, he found a door leading out of the building. Cabs lined the curbs, waiting for inebriated clientele. Apparently, she'd ditched her friend...if she'd even had a friend.

Rick paused at the door of Plank's Coffee Shop, and held the door for a beautiful blonde, save for the smudged makeup, carrying two larges coffees. Well, at least someone had gotten lucky. It appeared she hadn't quite made it home from her Friday night party. Hmm, busty, too. Surely, she wasn't...no, of course not.

GENNA TOOK A SIP of the coffee Lorianne generously put forth as a peace offering. Eyes drawn by research that had facilitated her exploration for the brown-eyed Rick lay on the counter in front of her. The previous week she'd located copies of the *History of the Inductive Sciences, From the Earliest to the Present Times*. She hadn't been able to resist. She tugged on the piece of paper and stared at it.

An unfamiliar, altogether unwelcome, surge of desire took hold. She'd already given him a head start with the company in Delaware. With an abrupt turn, she wadded the strip of paper and tossed it in the wastebasket. Her attention was snagged by an envelope with odd lettering.

Reaching down she pulled out the envelope and a letter. Someone had gone to the trouble of cutting out words from a magazine and glued them to a white sheet of paper. Blatantly immature, it must be someone's idea of a joke. "You need to make better choices." What in the world?

A crash from the office startled Genna from the paper in her hand and she dropped it, racing to the back of the store. Her shoulders sagged at the sight. Portions of the ceiling littered the floor where the rain had, finally, had its way.

CHAPTER 6

"DID YOU GET A hold of the insurance company?" Lorianne asked.

It was Monday morning, and for once, Lorianne was situated in front of the computer logging paperbacks, this time of the Young Adult variety.

"Yes, they're sending out an adjuster this afternoon," Genna sighed. "It sure seems like we're having a lot of problems all of a sudden. The power going off at whim, now the roof caving in. Not to mention the flooded basement last year."

"Well, we've had an awful lot of rain," Lorianne said, not looking up.

"I guess so." Genna turned a melancholy gaze out the windows. "Lorianne? Did you see a note with words from some magazine glued to a piece of paper?"

"Yeah, I'm sure someone's just goofing off."

"Who would play a joke like that? It gave me the creeps. Well, if I had time to feel anything."

"Uh, Gordon?" Lorianne's tone dripped sarcasm.

"Oh." Genna stopped and glanced over at her friend. "Yes, I suppose he would. That makes sense."

"What's with that Mrs. Bakely, Genna?" Lorianne asked,

changing the subject. "Does she strike you as a bit odd? I mean, she must come in here at least three times a week, and buys no less than three books at a time. She can't be reading nine books a week!"

"*Separate not yourself from the community.*" She turned back to Lorianne.

"Good Lord, Genna."

"A little obscure?"

Lorianne raised an eyebrow in answer.

"Yeah, I think it's from the 16th century. Something like 'Hillel.' I can't really recall."

"There's a shock," Lorianne mumbled.

HARRISON MERRICK JOHNSON ANSWERED to Rick, though his mother still referred to him as Merrick in times of aggravation. He shoved blunt fingers through his hair, ready to pull it out by the roots. Delving into the paperwork covering his desk, he tried to absorb details the insurance company had provided him. Apparently, pushing erotic thoughts of bookworm-waif from normally, structured thoughts, was impossible.

It didn't help that he'd just hung up on his mother after surviving the endless intrusive questions on when he planned on bringing his latest date to Sunday brunch. He pleaded work.

He had a feeling this new case was about to change his life. He hated premonitions of that sort. They unbearably proved irritatingly accurate.

His assistant, Lillian, an astute, matronly woman, maneuvered her way into a chair in front of his desk. "The building was constructed in the late twenties with the same gothic structure Bloomington boasted with its unusual downtown façade," he read aloud.

"What's so unusual about that?" She drummed her fingers on his desk.

"It's not so unusual," he retorted. "And nothing over the course of the last eighty years has yielded anything all that remarkable in its history. Hmm, part of Bloomington's original downtown."

"That makes it a registered Historic Landmark, doesn't it? Is it on the National Register?"

"We'll need to check, but I suspect it is. Here's the problem. The past two years more than five claims have been filed. Unusually high." Insurance companies frowned over that many claims in such a short span of time. He scanned through several more pages. "Ah. The roof was replaced almost three years ago. The most recent claim is the ceiling caving in damaging the office furniture." Oh, he had a really bad feeling about his future.

"Okay, so the roof has been replaced and the ceiling has caved in. In less than three years. What else? Have you seen all the rain we've had?"

"Sarcasm does not become you," he told her. Shaking his head, he went on. "Last year the basement flooded with plumbing problems. Looks like it ruined a lot of the store's inventory."

"What kind of inventory?"

Rick thumbed through a few more pages and groaned. He didn't even bother to smother it. "Books." He refused to look up, anticipating her questions. "Faulty wiring reported six months prior to that."

"None of those seem all that unusual," Lillian stated. "It's an old building. Well, except for the roof leak."

It was true about the rain. One look out the window from the third floor of his office on Main Street at the unrelenting rain, he decided it probably *was* a natural disaster. Would it never end? "The only thing lacking in the report is fire." His voice had a cynical twist. "The property appears to be in the unique position of being desired by a development company for parking, and the owner holding onto it for sentimental value. And its historic distinction, if you read between the lines."

"Who's the development company? That could certainly change the semantics," she said, "and a developer would have the knowledge and resources to manipulate what the naked eye might assume."

He shot her a look, a sharp pain in his lower gut spearing him.

For the first time in the ten years since Rick had established his consulting firm, Fraud Management Specialists, Inc., he felt a frisson of unease trickle up his spine. He'd designed the system so a potential customer could send their request to the Abstract Department. They stripped all personal information from the documents: names, addresses, locations and the like, so Rick and the other analysts could render an objective first overview.

Rick frowned, not vocalizing his thoughts. It didn't take a college degree to ascertain that the development company in question belonged to his good friend Ashton Turner. Ashton was in the middle of a large construction project just south of the downtown area of Bloomington, conveniently located across the street from where the historic landmarks began. Rick pulled his lips to a grimace. If Ash was the developer—and how could he not be—ethically, Rick should pass the case to someone else, to avoid any possible conflict of interest.

But the prick of apprehension on the back of his neck served as warning. "Lillian, we need to get the other details for this case." He could feel Lillian's eyes boring into him, but he kept his gaze firmly on the paperwork in front of him.

Lillian retreated from the room without a word. Her sharp green eyes would nail him. She talked in hushed tones from her desk, and five minutes later walked back in. He glanced up. She held another, thicker, file in her hands.

Lillian handed the stack over and planted herself back in the same chair. "What's the problem?"

"I don't know." Alarm bells sounded off in his head. "I just need to see the whole thing." His tone dismissed her, but she stubbornly remained.

Slowly, methodically, laboriously, he made his way through the documents. The insurance company had been quite comprehensive in their findings. The property was 215 East Elm. He located the map documenting the location. Though he needn't have bothered. It was the bookstore. Memories assaulted him of the girl-nerd-waif-bookworm with the wild hair, slim legs, black dress, and dusty jeans. He really should turn the case over to a colleague.

Instead, he studied the content of each photo before handing them over to Lillian, one by one. The flood damaged basement. Stacks of boxes and plastic bags of books. One pictured a pipe under the sink in what he assumed was a small bathroom.

"Look at this, Lillian." He laid the print down and came around the desk next to her while she examined the photo. "Are there gouges on the pipe? Of course, even if there are, it doesn't prove anything. That could have been done trying to fix other problems."

"Are you trying to convince me or yourself?" She peered up at him.

"The building *is* old." But his instincts were screaming.

She ignored him, and moved to the wiring photos. Several of the wires had been crossed. It was certainly not up to code but… His dread grew, pulse racing.

She was smart, anyone could see that. How hard would it have been? Wires weren't heavy. Would she destroy her livelihood for insurance money? And what of her friend? He wasn't even sure who she was.

Then there was the mysterious man he observed watching her. An accomplice? A threat? A *partner*? That thought didn't sit well at all. What of the paper with the cut-out words? '*You need to make better choices.'* Was Genna Lyndsey sending it to someone? Or had someone sent it to her?

"Rick," Lillian demanded. "Are you going to level with me? What is it about this case that has you so antsy? You look like you are about to self-combust."

Rick sucked in a deep breath and let it out slowly. There was no choice now—he'd have to make a stop at the bookstore.

He rounded the desk, sank into the chair, and sifted through the papers again.

"Rick?"

"The insurance company's original report should indicate what the business would gain through total loss," he said.

"If I'm to assist you, you'll have to tell me what's going on," she bit out. "I won't be kept in the dark."

He met her piercing green eyes. She was right. If he trusted anyone, it was Lillian.

"All right," he agreed. "Turner Development has a large project across the street from this property." He pointed at the address. Unnecessary as it was, the information seared his brain.

"Has he made an offer on the property?"

"If he hasn't, it's a sure bet he will in the near future." He grimaced.

Her eyes, sharp and assessing, made him shift uncomfortably. "He's a friend of yours. From way back, if I recall."

Yes, he was a friend. When they were sixteen, he and Ash defied old Asshole Turner, Ash's father, by sneaking out of the house to hang out at the lake. Unfortunately, a fight had broken out and some of the kids ended up in trouble with the law. Ash hadn't wanted to tell his father about it, but Rick talked him into doing the *mature* thing. Then when Ash hadn't shown up at school the next couple of days, rumors surfaced that Ash was in the hospital. Rick had ditched his afternoon classes, determined to find out the truth.

Hospital lights glaring, sick to his stomach, Rick found the room and hesitated at the door. When he peered in, he was shocked to find he barely recognized his friend. Nose and arm broken, head concussed, and sporting a gash running from close to the corner of his eye down to mid-cheek. His stitches would have given Frankenstein competition.

Though Ash never admitted what happened, Rick knew deep down Old Turner had beaten his own son to a pulp. It made Rick ill to realize it would never have happened if he'd just trusted that Ash knew his own father.

After "the incident," Rick sat with Ash every day after school. He'd been in the hospital for over a week. Assuaging guilt to a small degree spurred Rick's assistance in getting Ash to Rick's grandmother's. Yeah, they went way back.

Could Rick be an independent judge on this case if his friend turned out to be involved? *Could* his friend be involved?

Instincts were critical, and his were sounding off like a tornado siren seconds before the storm hit. "Yes, he's a friend."

"There's something else, isn't there?" Lillian said, jolting him back to the present.

And how the hell was he supposed to explain Genna Lyndsey, bookworm connoisseur? He didn't answer.

She stood abruptly. "Don't forget your dinner date tonight," she told him and strode from the room.

"Ah, hell," he said irritably. He needed sleep, and it had been as elusive as sunshine.

CHAPTER 7

Rick ordered a bottle of 2001 J. Lohr Estates Hilltop Cabernet, his patience waning as the waiter popped the cork to pour a small measure for his approval. He couldn't understand why he was so fidgety. He accepted his glass from the waiter and swirled the contents, then gauged the color. He breathed in the rotund flavor, relaxing a bit from the aroma. He met Ramona's smoky eyes, emanating heated desire, over the rim of his glass. As usual, she was stunning. Beauty seeped from her smooth olive skin, her white designer dress clinging to every curve.

Her eyes sparkled with excitement over the late birthday present he'd bestowed moments earlier. Funny, how the enticement he'd felt a week ago seemed so much less intense.

Her delicate wrist now sported a beautiful freshwater cultured pearl bracelet secured with an eighteen-karat gold safety clasp. A sense of observing outside of his own body stole over him. He placed a hand over hers when she reached for the glass the waiter had just poured.

He closed his eyes, bringing her wrist to his lips. His senses brought to mind a drop of red wine lingering on full, shiny, peach-tinted lips...and...that damned whiff of honeysuckle. His eyes snapped open at the intrusion.

"What is it?" Ramona asked him. Her voice was husky, inviting.

"I must have overworked myself today. I have a new case. The paperwork from the insurance company is analytical and tedious."

Yeah, and had Genna Lyndsey stampeding his thoughts more than once, the suspicions, up and down, driving him crazy. He plucked his hand from Ramona's and snatched up his wine.

"What's the case?" She brought the glass to her lips. His eyes followed her movements.

Rick thought about what he'd learned. To his relief, she hadn't been lying about a friend. They, indeed, owned the bookstore together, just as she'd said, and for three years. Though there he'd found one interesting twist.

"Just some claim investigation." Just pools of brilliant blue eyes boring through his every thought. *Nothing exciting*.

The building belonged to Genna Lyndsey, and had been in her family for over three generations. It was only the business that belonged to the two of them. He wondered how often that scenario played out in other businesses.

Rick tried to make sense of what either one would have to gain by sabotaging their livelihood. The payoff from the insurance company, he'd found, was not substantial enough to warrant the actions. The only other suspect that came to mind was Ash...at least on the surface. Nothing like a little mystery and dilemma to liven one's life.

Rick must have sounded convincing, because Ramona let the remark go and said, or rather purred, "This has been a wonderful birthday." Yes, she was purring. It had never irritated him before.

Her voice dripped with seduction, tearing him away from visions of sturdy-nerdy glasses perched on a pert nose, hosting other secrets.

"First, *The History of the Inductive Sciences, From the Earliest to the Present Times* – all three volumes – 1847 Edition. An ex-library copy," she informed him, excitement leaving her breathless. "A-all the way from L-london," before she stuttered, blushing.

He watched her, puzzled.

"Can you imagine? The hinges are cracked, but still incredibly intact. It even has the library numbers and foot spine. But it's a very clean copy..." Her voice faded. Shooting a quick glance at her wrist, "and this lovely bracelet, of course."

He smiled at her, but those premonitions attacked with a vengeance.

GENNA STEPPED THROUGH THE door gasping at the brisk, cool, damp air. The afternoon had turned quite lively at the bookstore with an unusual number of regular customers bringing in their used books to exchange.

She glanced at her watch; it was late. If she could have shooed Toddy Wilson out sooner, she'd already be home and curled up with *Darwin's Ghost* by Steve Jones. It was an updated version of Darwin's theories. But Toddy had stubbornly refused to leave, hugging another comic to his chest, as if it stabbed him through the heart to give it up.

Wrinkling her nose, she wished he'd bothered with a shower. Why didn't he just buy the silly comics? She pushed a lock of hair off her forehead, but it just sprang back. Regardless, she was happy at Renewed Interest's growth. Things would only get better once the transformation of the vacated space next door was completed. She'd leased it to renters for years.

But now, she could hardly contain her excitement. Enlarging the business was the next step. Soon, she and Lorianne would be able to include music, a children's area, and, of course, the internet cafe. Construction had already started, making her downright giddy.

She clicked off the list aloud, "Bookshelves on order, painters starting soon. Stock sorted, logged, and stored in the basement, ready for the additional categories."

She grinned. Exciting times were ahead. "Still need the inspection for the wiring and plumbing for the new café." But the structural aspects of the space were finished and things were finally falling into place.

Lorianne had secured suppliers for newly released paper and hardbacks. Things were so busy and hectic, it was a wonder she could keep up the real chore—the paperwork.

For once, all those ideas that had filled her head over the years were starting to pay off. There were always other items they could incorporate.

"We'll add reading lights, bookmarks, greeting cards." The list was endless.

Interesting how the inventory of the *slight* erotica section seemed to be expanding. As embarrassing as it was, Genna was certain they would have to dedicate an entire area to it eventually, perhaps its own room. The basement. "Lorianne's natural instincts at work." She giggled.

It was too bad Gordon had turned out to be such a loser. He'd been a great help setting up the database for their inventory and record keeping. But, she sighed, "His actions in keeping his career from moving forward were something out of their control."

Genna was so lost in thought when she slid the key in to bolt the door, she started at the deep, but familiar voice, "Whose actions are out of control?" She should be used to it by now. She wished he'd quit sneaking up on her though.

IRRITATION FILLED RICK, NOTING the dark storefront and the hour Genna Lyndsey heedlessly took for granted. It seemed an unnecessary risk, loaded down with her purse and another bag, her back to the street. Probably filled with books, he surmised. Hell, there was a building under construction just across the damn street. Rain fell in a gentle mist.

"Where is your partner?" he snapped.

"She went home hours ago," she said cheerfully.

His jaw clenched with an unnatural exasperation.

"Is something wrong? I'm no expert, but you seem a little out of sorts."

"I just drove up to get some coffee next door and I see you locking up your store with no regard to personal safety." He encroached her personal space to make his point—certainly not for the sweet fragrance of wild honeysuckle. He breathed deep.

"Oh." He saw her steel herself against the surge of emotions assaulting her when she turned and met his angry gaze. The stiffening of her spine, the deep pools of her eyes, color indiscernible under the night sky. Her gaze measured him intently through the black sturdy glasses. "'*I cannot think well enough to be intelligible*,'" she whispered. Her delicious mouth parted slightly. It was all the invitation he needed. He blamed the wild honeysuckle.

Without a second thought, he moved his mouth over hers slowly, deliberately, allowing her ample time to step back should she have wished. It didn't matter that the door was to her back and she had nowhere to step back to.

Definitely, the wild honeysuckle. It drove him wild with desire. Just the feeling of her timorous nature kept him from devouring her outright, tempting as it was. His tongue touched her lips in a feathery motion, drinking in sweetness so pure he wanted to fall to his knees. He pulled her slight body into his.

A sharp pain hit his leg. He grunted and broke the kiss, making the break as painful as the pain in his leg. He glanced down. She'd dropped everything she'd been holding, her hands clutching the front of his shirt. Her cheeks were flushed. With hunger? Need?

She seemed at a loss as to what to do next. He stifled an urge to smile, irritation dissolving for the moment.

He grasped her hands gently, surprised by the rising desire to safeguard her. Resisting the appeal to reclaim her mouth, he tugged them from his shirt. Kneeling down, he gathered the spilled belongings. Just as he suspected, he'd been besieged with books.

Frustrated with himself...no, *her*, he stood and handed over her purse and the overfull bag. "Where is your car?" he demanded, reaching for anger.

Her flinch told him how harsh he sounded, but damn it, it was dark, it was raining, and it was late. She was on the outside edge of downtown, for God's sake. Crimes happened in small towns. Maybe not as frequent as large cities, but they happened, all the same.

"In the church parking lot." She pointed across the street. Her voice was husky, barely above a whisper.

"I don't see any cars," he said tersely, with a glance to the west. He shouldn't have kissed her. The blood rushing through his body angered him.

"In the lot behind the church."

"That's just great."

With a determined gait, and a firm grasp on her elbow, he marched her across the street, down the side of the church to the parking lot behind. With each step, his anger grew. No lights! There were no lights, whatsoever. Well, the traffic light, but that didn't count. Not to mention the construction property. She was a disaster waiting to happen. He would be angry to see anyone so careless. His mother, his sisters, his dog...only he didn't have a dog.

He figured the little Toyota Camry was hers, as the only other car he spotted was a new Cadillac. She didn't seem the

Cadillac type. He snatched the keys from her hand and hit the lock release activating the lights. He jerked open the door and planted her bodily inside. The bag with the books fell to the ground. He snatched them up as well and thrust them at her before slamming the door closed.

"Lock the door," he glowered at her.

Hands on hips, he stood there while she lowered the window. Her eyes glittered with a rage he wouldn't have thought possible. "'*Passion and Reason, Self-division cause.*'"

"Yeah, yeah, I know. From the 'Choras of Priests,' Mustofa 1609," he told her. He leaned in the window, and to his satisfaction, she reared away from him. "You want *passion*? You already have it. You want *reason*? Anything could happen, small town or not," he spat. He cupped his hand on the back of her neck, and dragged her forward. He would have felt her breath had she dared to breathe. "*Self-division*? Definitely." His voice softened. He couldn't help it; he touched his lips to hers. Their moist promise furthered his frustration. "Go home," he growled. He released her and stepped back.

Rick waited until she drove off, taillights winking at him. It was only then he remembered he hadn't asked her about the note he'd seen on the counter. He really was losing his mind.

Guilt swarmed him. Intimidating shy bookworms was not his usual style. Of course, he'd not associated with shy bookworms before now. He'd always heard the smart ones had no common sense. He started his stride around the church, along the street. Catching a slight movement from the corner of his eye, he flattened himself against the building. His pulse throbbed, muscles tensed.

This was exactly what he'd been trying to get her to understand.

CHAPTER 8

ASHTON TURNER SWIVELED HIS chair and peered out large corner windows from atop the fifth floor of his office. He didn't see the beautiful sunrise. Didn't register a morning clean and fresh from rain for the first time in a week.

He was irked to no end that he was still thinking about a blonde haired, blue-eyed beauty who was as clingy as she was enchanting. He'd read her insecurities like a neon sign on a dark bleak highway. He wanted to call her, but every male instinct he'd ever possessed told him to steer clear and wide.

She was typical of the women he went after. Willing and able. He'd scoped out the patrons at the fundraiser, spotted her the moment she'd walked in with her friend. A friend who could not touch her in sensuality and beauty. No, his beauty had been decked out in a black cocktail dress that molded her form like honey on a stick. Her figure lush and inviting. Ash ran his fingers over the scarred indention on his face out of habit.

He still hadn't figured out why she had been at the fundraiser. She hadn't been there to contribute her own money, that much was certain. He could tell that from her lifestyle. Once he'd pegged her, it was a sure bet she'd be going home with him. Of course, they'd had to look for her friend, but once satisfied they weren't leaving her friend behind, it was a piece of...cake.

The two nights following continued into sheer ecstasy when they'd meandered back to her house where the interruptions there suited him much better.

She lived in a small two-bedroom house on the outskirts of town. Granted, it looked as if the house had charm, and clutter. And it did. Clutter of clothes that covered every piece of furniture she owned. Not to mention shoes that overran every square inch of floor space. Pumps, boots, mules, clogs, sandals. He grimaced at the thought that he knew that much about women's shoes. Her bathroom counters sported every conceivable kind of moisturizer and cosmetic known to womankind, and him, apparently. He winced, couldn't believe it, but he'd found it *charming*.

Which must be why he'd spent three consecutive nights with her. Not his regular mode of operation, usually his only indulgence being one night stands. She'd needed to eat, hadn't she? He frowned. To his surprise, she hadn't said much about herself. Thinking back, she hadn't really said anything about herself. Not where she'd come from, who her parents were. If they were living or dead. Where she went to school, where she worked. In fact, when he took the time to consider what conversations there were, and to *his* credit, there hadn't been many. And to her credit, she'd distracted him by doing rather creative things to his willing body. It was, in retrospect, what stirred his senses about her, appealing to his own enthusiasm for adventure.

She was quick with her laugh and spontaneous in her nature. Specifically, her sexuality. It was genuine, he was sure of it. At least, he was almost sure of it. There was a certain amount of innocence in her he hadn't expected. Oh, not the sex. He had neither the desire nor inclination for virtuous women. No, there was something in the hunger of her kisses, the spark of excitement lighting her eyes. A practiced woman could not fake such passion. She made love with the lights on without a shy bone in her beautiful body.

Unexpected desire clenched his insides, thinking of her long blonde hair brushing his neck. And before he'd realized it, she was tracing his scar with her hot moist mouth. The hurt he remembered, tingling at her touch. No one ever touched him there. No one...save her. She'd never asked him about it. If she had, he would have walked out right then. Just like he always did when they dared to bring it up. She seemed to know instinctively he would shut down. But through her actions she'd slipped past the reserve it had taken years to obtain.

Sure, she'd slept with him the first night, but he'd turned on the charm. He couldn't blame her for that. He'd known she was an easy conquest, and he hadn't hesitated to take advantage of the opportunity. He knew his appeal to women. Well over six feet, with dark blond hair and gray eyes. What was not to be enjoyed? Everyone knew that a man who was not an easy capture could have any woman he wanted. He was not above admitting the creativity had been an easy incentive for three nights *in a row*. But he *was* above admitting he could just as easily be someone else's conquest.

Ash rubbed the jagged scar on the side of his face, the one last gift from his father at the age of sixteen. He'd never realized until that moment in the library of his father's house how much his own father despised him. Only Rick knew what had happened, or thought he did.

Ash pushed those thoughts from of his mind, and the humiliation that night entailed.

Ash would give it a few days before he called her back. There was a certain protocol when it came to controlling women. He knew nothing if not women.

Tuesday morning was cool, fresh and clear. A nice change,

Lorianne thought, letting herself into the bookstore. She flipped the lock into place on the door, smiling. Genna would think the heavens were falling in as Lorianne had never come in this early before. But no, looking out the windows, the sun was definitely shining.

Usually, Genna was knee deep into logging books and had half of them shelved long before Lorianne had even woken up. Not to mention the daily bookkeeping and sweeping of the floors.

Lorianne, swamped with guilt, had had trouble sleeping. Hence, the early morning onset. Her weekend had been full and sweet despite the rain. Inklings of trepidation were determined to undermine her good luck, but she shoved them away and smiled. Just because Ashton hadn't stayed over the evening before after staying two nights in a row didn't mean they had to move in together—and just because he'd left sometime around three that morning, mumbling something about a meeting didn't mean he wasn't going to call her.

A dreamy anticipation filled her. Ashton was everything Gordon wasn't, plus some. Ashton. She loved his old fashioned name, and sighed with what could only be considered a historical novel throwback. It made her feel like a damsel in distress, a weak-kneed heroine, whom he was sure to fall all over.

A small giggle escaped. She could hope, couldn't she? She loved how his height complimented hers, how his dark blond hair set off deep olive skin and corded muscles. Masculine in every sense of the word. Athletic, too, if stamina was any indication. She laughed again, feeling a little giddy.

The long ragged scar on his face showed he'd battled the world. She'd reveled in the feel of it against her tongue. But instinct whispered his reluctance to talk about it. And if there was one thing she had in abundance, it was instinct. Growing up on the streets honed instincts like nothing else ever could. Her breath choked on memories, threatening to surface. She shoved them away.

He was her Prince. Communicating with her mouth, leaving the words behind was an excellent way to show him how she felt. Butterflies tickled her insides.

Lorianne took a turn around the store, absorbing the quiet. Her feet echoed on the worn wood floors. It was nice. No wonder Genna welcomed these early mornings.

Where was Genna anyway? It seemed unusual that she hadn't made it in by this time. She'd probably walk in and spout something from Robert Browning like *'The year's at the spring / and day's at the morn / Morning's at seven / The hill-sides due-pearled.'* Lorianne chuckled, unable to hold back from giving Genna competition on quoting the outrageous, if she thought so herself. She flipped the switch on the computer and let it boot up. She might as well shock Genna completely, and readied the counter to log more new, used books.

The latch of the lock clicked and the bell on the door alerted Lorianne to Genna's arrival. She glanced up from the computer to tease her friend about the lateness of the hour. But the sight that greeted left her speechless.

Genna's wild curly hair, if possible, was even wilder. She must have pulled her jeans and t-shirt right out of the laundry basket. Even though Genna never minded the scraggly-and-wrinkled look, it wasn't usually quite so distinctive. Her expression was the biggest disturbance. Brows drawn together, lips pressed into a tight grimace, her face pale except for two bright red spots on her cheeks. A paper sadly crumpled due to her unnatural grip, crinkled in her hand.

"Genna, what is it?" Lorianne darted around the counter.

Genna handed her the rumpled paper, and dropped her head into her palms, fingers threading through her hair. Genuine concern spilled through Lorianne. She read the note. Then read it a second time—because she wasn't quite sure she understood it.

Hell, Genna was the one with the PhD.

"I don't understand. Why do they want to buy the building? And this offer—it seems, well...a little high."

"I'm not sure. And it's really high." Genna tossed her head, rebellion making a rare appearance. "This is the only legacy I have of my mother, grandmother and great-grandmother. I *won't* sell."

"Don't worry, we're not selling," Lorianne shrugged. "It's our business and our livelihood." She scanned the note again. "It doesn't even say who the buyer is. We'll just tell them no." That settled, she handed the crumpled paper back. Matter solved. "The sun is shining. It's going to be a beautiful day."

"Yes." Genna's gaze was still riveted on the paper.

"You don't think this is the end of it, do you?"

"No."

Genna pursed her lips into a thin line, a dark look seizing her usual gentle features. It was that fierce look that made Lorianne very glad they were on the same team. "'*Difficulties exist to be surmounted*,'" Genna murmured.

"Well, that's encouraging," Lorianne smiled. Nothing could bring her down today.

Rick sat behind his desk, head resting in his hands, and groaned. He couldn't seem to dispel the image of that astonishing, yet spine-tingling meeting the night before. He wasn't usually caught so off-guard.

It was certainly unexpected. Unexpected in how Genna Lyndsey, with one tiny kiss and full lips, had managed to entice and thrill him like he'd never kissed before. Sleeping had been out of the question. He exhaled slowly, sounding more like a hiss.

He'd been assaulted with an intimacy that left him lightheaded with desire. Heavy-hearted guilt banged him over the head. That trek to her car—his overbearing arrogance, even for him it was a bit much. He found himself lucky she hadn't run him over.

At least the books she'd dropped had knocked some sense into him before he'd done something stupid, like ravishing her on the sidewalk. His shin sported a bruise as proof. Thank God. Not that he hadn't wanted to. But God, that sweet, luscious mouth, so sweet, had hounded him all night.

Not an hour before, he'd been having a perfectly lovely dinner with an exotic beauty. He smiled thinking of her blue...Black! Black eyes. Sultry and exotic. Wild curly no, no, no. Heavy, straight black hair. He was sure he and Ramona would have been celebrating her birthday in a fervent frenzy when visions of a girl-nerd-wild haired waif stole every private thought of a lust-filled, passionate evening.

Oh, the picture his mind conjured of that petite body beneath him, no barriers, cloth or otherwise. He pulled at his suddenly too-tight collar. Genna Lyndsey needed a protector not a lover. *Lover?*

He would call Ramona. Yes, that's what he would do. Call Ramona. Later. He shook his head to put his brain back in working order.

The door in the outer office sounded, shaking away his reverie. It was time to buckle down to business. He had a fraud business to concentrate on.

Ash might be knee-deep into shit. Genna, too?

CHAPTER 9

THE WEEK PROVED BUSY for Renewed Interest. With business growing by leaps and bounds, Genna should be euphoric...and she was. Really. She never minded staying late—in the end it would all be worth it. After the flooded basement incident that had damaged most of their inventory the year before, she and Lorianne were lucky. It had already more than doubled with return business. Bloomington was moving into the early days of summer, and soon the tourist business would be overflowing. Well, as overflowing as Bloomington ever got.

Genna's gaze strayed to the windows. If the weather cooperated, things would be perfect. But no, rain. Again. It pelted the streets. The roof. Her head. Mood just as morose. The lights were out again and Lorianne was down in the basement wiggling the faulty wiring. Genna admired her for it- she was terrified of the dark- but Lorianne was determined to face her fears.

Genna frowned. Their most recent letter from the insurance company had denied the claim on the leak in the ceiling. Something about 'failure to maintain the maintenance,' whatever that meant. Frustrated, Genna flung her pen on the counter. They'd replaced the roof not so long after they'd started the business. Three lousy years ago. The joys of entrepreneurship, she huffed. She would fight the insurance company. She jerked the pen back up with a sweep of her hand and a scowl.

She glanced at her watch, letting out a tired sigh. There were still things to take care of before closing time. She placed logged-in books into a box ready to store in the office until she and Lorianne could shelve what they could the next day, saving the rest for the basement. She hefted the box up when the bell tinkled its customer welcome. She turned to the door—the box tumbled through her hands.

"Hi, Genna." That coo sounded exactly the same as it had the last time she'd seen him. Damon Wharton.

"That *was* you at the fundraiser." She'd almost forgotten about him. Goosebumps prickled her skin. Her mind seemed to separate from her body in an odd detachment. Had he actually cooed? Yes. Too bad she hadn't recognized how fake it was in college. It was strange to think of someone cooing.

This must be how the outer body feelings felt, floating somewhere above—observing, viewing. She wished she could get her telepathic powers to work as well. Her gaze slid to the spilled books. She pushed her glasses up further on her nose. She found herself comparing his lesser height to the taller Rick. Damon's weaker chin to the angled planes of the stronger-jawed Rick. Damon's darting eyes to the wide-spaced, clear gazed, dark-eyed Rick. Damon's thin lips to Rick's firm, velvet, fuller ones.

"'*Knowledge is power*,'" she whispered.

"Excuse me?" He looked confused.

Good, her outer body informed her. She reached for the books, annoyed to find her hands trembling. She took her time, careful to keep the books between them. She didn't want him near her.

"Of course it was me. You ducked out before I could say hello." Such mock severity. She almost laughed outright, but for the irritating familiarity.

She ignored his teasing tone and snapped at him. "I was in a hurry." She frowned. "I'd only intended to be there for a short time." She pushed her crazy hair off of her face and stood. "Why are you here?"

"I wanted to talk to you." He put his palms out in a gesture of surrender. His tone indicated a nonchalant water-under-the-bridge, let-bygones-be-bygones.

Ha! Over her dead body, *inner or outer*, said.

"We're old friends."

She pressed her lips together. He was trying to cajole her. Genna struggled to maintain an even, conciliatory tone. "No. Not friends," she corrected, marveling at her coolness. This outer body thing was really something. "They announced your name at graduation and you walked by me. *Right by me!* Kissed another girl. In front of everyone." A thought struck her. "No one knew about me, did they? *I* was the other woman!"

"I'm really sorry." He sounded contrite.

She narrowed her eyes on him. Like she would fall for that. What an idio—loser. "Why are you in Bloomington?" She did notice, *from above*, how her hands clenched into tight fists. She must have dropped the books again and not even realized. She scooped them up, dropped them in the box.

"I'm here to broker a deal with one of the artists represented at the fundraiser." Her inner body shivered with disgust. The outer body appeared calm, however. That was a relief.

"You could never, ever make up for what you did to me." She glared at him. He had gall bringing back pain she'd thought long gone. Unfamiliar fury raged through her.

"I really am sorry," he said. "I've had time to think about you. You've grown up." He made a move toward her. She jumped back.

"What happened to *her*?" It irked to ask the question.

"It...it just didn't work out." He cast an appreciative glance around. "This is a really nice place you have here."

"Yes, it is." The comment angered her, her nails cut into her palm.

Damon turned soulful eyes on her. "Do you think we could start over?"

It took her a moment to fully realize what he'd said. Thank goodness her outer body had more sense, jarring a response. "'*Experience is simply the name we give our mistakes.*' Oscar Wilde said that."

The confused expression on his face had her choking back a laugh...the outer body's anyway.

"What?"

"I call *you* 'experience,' Damon."

"But..."

Lorianne clomped up the basement stairs. "Genna, where are the...? Oh." She stopped, eyes narrowed.

Genna seeped back into her body again, the outer body slipping away. She turned to Lorianne, unable to keep the desperation from her tone, and said, "Lorianne, this is Damon Wharton. From college? You remember?" Clearing her face of any expression, Genna swung around to confront Damon. "Lorianne should be able to help you find whatever it is you think you need. Thanks for coming by." She spun and walked. Deliberate and certain, straight to the office where she collapsed inside against the closed door.

Genna inhaled deeply. Once she was certain her knees wouldn't fold, she made her way behind the desk and dropped into the chair. The small room was the perfect refuge that for years served as a kitchen for her great grandparents. The usual comfort she took in the enclosed space had deserted her. She still was still shaking. The bell on the front door jingled, signifying his departure. *Final* departure she dared to believe. Lorianne popped in the door.

"He's gone," she told her. "What was *he* doing here? I thought he lived in Tucson or Timbuktu. Doesn't he?"

"How would I know? It's been years. I find it odd that he shows up out of the blue."

"Are you okay?"

Genna nodded slowly. "Yes. Yes, I am." Relieved to find she really was. "Another loser whose actions did not serve him well."

Lorianne grinned at her. "I knew you would be. No telling quote to mark the occasion?"

Genna gave her wan smile, but blood inflamed. "*'For violent fires soon burn out themselves; Small showers last long, but sudden storms are short.'*"

"Perfect. I doubt he'll be back," Lorianne predicted. The bell on the door jangled again. She wrinkled her nose. "Let's hope." Lorianne pulled the door closed when she stepped back, leaving Genna to sag in the chair.

"Hi, Toddy," she heard Lorianne say.

CHAPTER 10

LOOK AT THIS." GENNA held out another letter. "It sounds...I don't know...threatening, somehow. The last one was over a week ago."

Lorianne read aloud.

Dear Ms. Lyndsey:

My client is willing to increase his current offer on 215 East Elm and 220 East Elm, by an additional ten percent. I would strongly urge you to consider this offer carefully.

Due to the aforementioned building's old, outdated, dilapidated, and dangerous structure, my client is willing to keep this offer firm for fifteen days from the date of this letter.

The building in its present condition warrants much less, and you should consider yourself fortunate by his generosity. I urge you not to ignore this letter as it is sent in good faith.

Regards,

Lester Van Horn

Van Horn Real Estate

"I don't understand the sudden interest." Puzzled, Lorianne

handed it back.

"Neither do I. And I'm not sure how to find out." The lights flickered once then darkness, again. "Oh, this infernal rain!" Genna stormed.

"Lester Van Horn." Lorianne's tone filled with disgust. "He is such a weasel. He once tried to feel me up when I happened to be sitting next to him, and his date at the movie theatre one night." She shuddered.

"Well," Genna paused, then, sighed, "sometimes it's tempting, I have to admit. Hand me that flash..." But Lorianne was already holding it out. "Back in a minute," she said, and went to the basement stairs.

Genna had to push a little harder on the door to get it open. The wood swelled in the humidity. She hated going to the basement in the dark almost as much as Lorianne. The stairs, though solid, always felt less so in the gloom. She grimaced, not to mention the reminder of the unsecured railing. The thought always hit when it was dark.

She heard the bell on the door and hurried down to the fuse box. A slight jiggle to the wires usually did the trick. Genna reached the fuse box, and reached out to tap the loose wire, but the lights came back on before she touched them. She hesitated a moment then decided it would be okay. She would get an electrician, soon, she promised herself. Another item in the 'To Do' column.

The basement was so creepy, it felt like a haunted house. The only natural light came from one small window up high, at street level. She looked around. Most of the space remained unfinished where her father had started covering batts of insulation, but at some point ended up distracted with some other project in the interim. In the dim light, the shadows made her think of spiders, ghosts, and other silly things. Her sense of relief was so palpable, she was breathing hard when she reached the top of stairs.

"...goofy Lester Van Horn sent the letter. So we don't know who his client could possibly be," Lorianne was telling Mrs. Bakely. Annoyed, Genna rolled her eyes, listening to Lorianne spill their private business to one of their best customers.

"*'Things without remedy should be without regard; what is done, is done.'*"

Lorianne and Mrs. Bakely turned simultaneous glares toward her, each raising a brow indicating their impatience. So similar, Genna choked back an outright laugh. "What! It's William Shakespeare," she defended.

Disregarding her, Mrs. Bakely said, "The Town Council meets Tuesday nights." A short pause ensued. "I'm on the Council, you know," she said.

Genna nodded, not sure of the point she was trying to make.

"That's nice, Mrs. Bakely," Lorianne smiled. Obviously, Lorianne hadn't either. Genna's thought was a little ungracious.

"The Town Council?" Genna encouraged.

"Um hum," Mrs. Bakely reiterated. Her bobbing head, threatened the bun on the nape of her neck. "There's new business that has to do with the construction across the street."

Genna's gaze sharpened on Mrs. Bakely, then moved on the windows to the south. She'd been hoping that monstrosity would be finished soon, so it wouldn't be such an eyesore. "And you think they may," she tilted her head in the direction to the 'eyesore,' have some interest in our business?"

"Not the business, necessarily." Mrs. Bakely perused the paperbacks on display next to the register. "More likely, the property itself."

Genna gasped with sudden understanding.

"Why would they want the property, but not the business?" Lorianne asked. Frustration filled Genna with Lorianne's apparent dimness, but just as quickly assailed with guilt. It wasn't like her to be so impetuous. Thankfully, Lorianne's head was down and she appeared none the wiser, still logging books into the system. New Adult.

Mrs. Bakely set her customary three books on the counter. Lorianne lifted her head and rang up the purchase. She smiled brilliantly at their best customer, and Genna thought tears shimmered in the elderly woman's eyes.

"Here you are, Mrs. Bakely. Your regular amount of $11.40, please." Lorianne bagged the books and handed it to her.

Genna turned her gaze back out the window. "Why would they want to get rid of the building? For what possible reason?" Genna's question was directed more to herself than Lorianne or Mrs. Bakely. She studied the mass of unfinished concrete across the street and the sign in front of the building. Turner Development. She gasped, then turned to Mrs. Bakely, clamping her lips together. She shoved her glasses up on her nose. "Turner needs parking, doesn't he?" She hissed.

"Turner?" Lorianne stopped. "Turner. Development?" Lorianne stumbled to the sofa and sunk down, as if her legs couldn't support her. "Ashton's name is Turner."

"What!" Genna rushed to her side.

"Do you think he could be Turner Development?" She asked.

"Of course not."

"I think he has a lot of money."

"That doesn't mean he's them, Lorianne." A terrible sense of dread swept Genna. "When was the last time you spoke to him?"

"Several days. I tried to call a couple of times. But he hasn't called back," her voice broke.

"Oh, Lorianne. I'm so sorry." Genna clasped her hand.

"You were right, as usual."

"If it's any comfort, I hate being right."

"What's this about Ashton Turner?" Mrs. Bakely demanded.

Genna glanced up at Mrs. Bakely, surprised to see her still standing there. Her oddly familiar blue eyes flashed.

"Oh, n...nothing," Lorianne stammered.

Genna felt breathless with a rage she rarely experienced. "Well, he can't have it." Genna stood. Resentment worked its way from the pit of her stomach to the tips of her trembling fingers she clenched into a tight fist. "I own the building. He can't *force* me to sell. Besides, this building is on the National Register for Historic Preservation. Even if they could get me to sell they couldn't tear it down." It wasn't possible for anyone to take her property. It had been in her family for three generations, right? She tightened her lips. He'd have to kill her first.

"I haven't heard anything official," Mrs. Bakely said.

"When did you say the meeting was?" Genna asked, pacing.

"Tuesday night, six o'clock."

Genna looked over at Lorianne. Devastation covered her features.

"We should go to the meeting, Lorianne. It won't hurt to see what, if anything, is being said."

CHAPTER 11

JOANNA BAKELY WALKED OUT of Renewed Interest a determined woman. She had many regrets in her sixty-seven years of life. Having lived through the loss of both parents, a sister, a brother, a husband, and a son could do that to a woman.

Joanna's most remorseful memory in all those years was the mistreatment of her son's wife after his tragic and unexpected death at the age of twenty-one. Tears could still overpower her after all these years. Sadness swept through her, suffocating her. Parents should never outlive their children. Particularly, an only child.

She was so proud. Peter had grown into a vibrant young man. He was everything and more than she'd planned. Now in his third year of college he'd made it home for Christmas.

"Hello, Mother." He grinned at her, his eyes glittering with a mischievousness she hadn't seen since he was a child.

"Darling." She threw her arms around his neck. It seemed he was even inches taller. But then he'd dropped his bomb.

"I have a wonderful Christmas surprise." Peter moved to one side. Next to him stood a thin young girl of twenty or thereabouts. She had long, untamable red hair, freckles, and large blue eyes. Joanna's insides plunged toward the ground.

Her only son had brought home his own unexpected Christmas present—a new wife.

All Joanna saw was red. Rage.

Joanna pasted on a smile. "Hello, my dear. And you're in school as well?" So the conversation went. She was a beauty, of course. But, a waitress? Sierra. Peter, so like his father in that regard. Hadn't Joanna herself been such a beauty?

Joanna loved her son, enough to carefully keep her disdain and disappointment out of sight. She never attempted hiding it from Sierra, however. It was petty, hateful, spiteful, and vengeful. All hopes for Peter dashed in an instant.

Before the end of the holiday season—before he even returned to school, he'd collapsed. Suddenly Joanna's world was turned upside down. Devastated by her loss, her hurt became destructive. Toxic. Yet, how was she to seek refuge in another's loss? Peter was her son.

Unfortunately, Joanna lost sight of how Peter's death devastated others. His friends. His wife.

The memories made Joanna ill. When she finally rose out of her self-absorbed grief, she looked in the mirror and faced the truth. She'd been jealous. Joanna condemned herself and Sierra to a future she could not have foreseen.

Joanna clung to her anguish with arrogance, thought nothing about bullying her son's young, impressionable wife. He'd suffered through heart failure, the result of an undiagnosed enlarged heart.

Guilt attacked her anew. The pain as sharp as a pointed blade. She took a deep breath to still her racing pulse. The memories haunted her, assaulted her- and she deserved them.

Sierra, inexperienced and proud, had run away, never to return. The girl was only nineteen. Joanna was not so sure she wouldn't have done the same in her place. Left alone to deal with an angry, bruised mother-in-law who flaunted callous indifference to the younger woman's own torment, grief, *fear*.

Yes, Joanna loathed admitting how much responsibility rested on her shoulder. But truth was truth, and she lived with the anguish every day. Only years later did she finally see and acknowledge the part of her son she'd missed out on, cheated Peter, Sierra, *herself*.

Joanna inhaled a deep breath to steady her chastising thought. Her mistakes were horrendous. Things she could never retrieve with the passage of time. Shunning Sierra for her own resentment was shameful behavior. She might as well have sentenced the poor girl to her death.

But Joanna tried to make amends. If she could have found her, she'd have made up for her awful treatment. But no luck. After she had years of searching, she'd all but given up hope when the private investigator she'd long since dismissed ran across an obscure article in the St. Louis Post.

A drug bust that had ended badly for one young woman. A woman...by the name of Sierra Gentry. Said woman had a child. *A child*. A seventeen-year-old child set to graduate from high school. The memory still had the ability to choke her.

She swallowed hard. A little more digging, a little more money, was all it had taken to answer long ago questions. Joanna had been ready to storm the school, had in fact contacted the school counselor, a Miss Castor.

Miss Castor, thank the Lord, had taken an interest in the child. But she said the child was a loose cannon- Unpredictable and wary. To Joanna's reluctance, she followed Miss Caster's advice, allowing Miss Castor to see Lorianne through high school and somehow, into college. It was a miracle, as miracles go.

Joanna kept very close tabs on her newfound grandchild, though from a distance, difficult as it was. Terrified she'd make the same mistakes with Lorianne she'd made with the child's mother.

Yes, Joanna had borne her share of torment. But Joanna was ready to make up for a lifetime of self-condemnation. She pressed into her meeting with Calvin Herald of Herald and Koombs Law with a new sense of purpose.

"Joanna, are you sure about this?" Calvin ran fingers through thick silver hair. "This seems a bit impulsive. I've known you a very long time, and one thing you are not is impulsive."

Joanna tapped the pen she held impatiently on the desk, tut-tut-tut. "You must trust me, Calvin. This decision is a long time in coming. I know *exactly* what I'm doing."

"Okay, my dear," he said, resigned. "Stop that infernal tapping and sign on the dotted line." He slid the estate documents across the desk.

Determined to do it right this time, she sighed with flourish. Lorianne would know the truth.

Experience was an excellent teacher.

CHAPTER 12

Friday morning, Lorianne unlocked the door early for the third day in a row. Her sleep was totally screwed up. The rain was not helping. Not once had she heard from Ashton Turner since he'd gone home early Monday morning after waking her slowly, skillfully, completely. Three nights they'd spent together, then, nothing. The all-American guy. Wham-bam, no thank you, ma'am.

Okay, so he *wasn't* the one. It still hurt. She wouldn't have minded a couple of more days. Resentment shredded her. Angry tears stung her eyes. She shoved them away with the heel of her hand.

She dreaded the moment Genna remembered to ask about him. Why? He wasn't a Gordon. Hell, maybe he was. All men were creeps. He was probably no better than Lester Van Horn, well, at least not much better. Okay, maybe a lot better. But only in looks. Well, and touching. Gees, she might as well add kissing...above and below the belt. Okay, damn it. He was the hottest guy she'd ever been with. A real life 'step out of the Regency' good looking, dark, brooding hero. She'd wanted to swoon. Oh, Lord. She was reading a *lot* more than she was telling Genna about.

The lights flickered then winked out. Lorianne grabbed the flashlight and stomped to the basement, hesitating at the door. She hated the basement. Musty, stale air had followed her, her whole life.

Hell, coming home from school every day would have made an HBO Special for 'how *not* to raise your kid.' Bracing herself before the door, she steeled herself for the trek down. She started down, careful of the rickety railing. She hated the dark. That's why she slept with the lights on.

She couldn't count the times she and her mother had slept in cars or homeless shelters. Once in an alley covered with a cardboard box after Clark had deserted them.

Clark. The one man who should have been her father, whose expectations she couldn't live up to. *Never enough.* She hated thinking of him, too. She *hated* him. The bleak thoughts truly were in the dregs. Damn historical novels, again. "What kind of word was 'dregs' anyhow? It's a stupid word," she said, out loud and cross.

She'd reached the bottom step when the bell on the front door jingled. She frowned. She must have forgotten to lock the door. She tapped the suspected wire, but the single light bulb decided not to play nice and remain stubbornly off. The door at the top of the stairs slammed shut.

Lorianne froze, breath caught in her throat. The flashlight slipped to the floor with a clank. Shaken from her frozen state, she dropped to the floor trying to find it, but it must have rolled out of reach. Familiar panic spread up from the base of her spine, to her nape to her fingertips.

"Damn, where are you," she screeched. At the same instant her fingers grazed the cool metal. She snatched it up, and like a wild savage, hurried to the top of the stairs tripping, on the top step. She shoved on the door.

Stuck. Hysteria ripped through her. "Open the door," she

cried. "Please, open the door." Tears streamed down her face, sobs racking her body. "Please, please open the door." Terror stripped her of all reason. She pounded until her fist was bruised. She sunk to the floor begging for someone to *just open the door*. "Pleeeeeassee," her voice came out in a whisper. Darkness closed in, the musty, stale air, choking her.

GENNA WAS FURIOUS. WHAT was it with those stupid insurance people? The letter she received in her mailbox last night practically accused her of sabotaging her own building. They assigned an examiner to investigate the legitimacy of her claims from the last two years. That, with the unrelenting rain, was enough to send her flying over the edge. Would it never stop?

She put her key in the door but the lack of a click brought her out of her reverie. The lights were out and Lorianne was nowhere to be seen. It was so quiet, the hair on Genna's neck stood out. Every telepathic notion she ever knew or didn't know she possessed, screamed.

She thrust away the silly ideals. More importantly, she'd been informed, the examiner would be contacting her sometime that day. She hit the light switch on the wall but found it already in the 'on' position. The lights were out again, adding to her aggravation. At least they'd given her notice regarding the examiner's visit. She could have just been left in the dark. Oh, that was rich, she smirked. She really needed to call an electrician.

Today. She would call today.

Dropping her purse on the counter, Genna slipped off her sweater and tossed it to the side, then bent down for the flashlight. Gone. It was always under the counter. Genna straightened. Honestly, Lorianne needed to put things back where they belonged for these kinds of emergencies. Maybe it was in the office. Natural light streamed in from the windows to the south, framing the construction across the street. Scowling at the mound of concrete, Genna made her way to the office and pushed back the door.

Something wasn't right. She sucked in sharp breath, stunned. Hand across her mouth, she muffled a scream. Her chest felt as if it would burst. Complete disarray. The office was a war zone. Desk drawers were emptied on the floor. The chair tilted on its side. Files from the cabinet strewn about the room. The trash bucket dumped upside down. A cold knot formed in her stomach. She backed out of the office. The shop doorbell tinkled, the dainty sound, eerily out of place now. She spun in fear.

"Ms. Lyndsey? Genna? What's wrong with the lights?" Rick Johnson strode through the door, trying the light switch. Hands on her ears, eyes squeezed tight, unable to hold back any longer, the scream wrenched from her.

SOBS SOUNDED FROM A closed door. Alarmed at the sight of a chair wedged under the knob, Rick scrambled to pull it away. It was impossible to open from inside. "Move back from the door," he said.

The door was blocked. "Lorianne, move back. We can't open the door," Genna yelled.

He ignored her shock and resentment when he lifted her bodily and set her aside. He eased the door ajar, careful of its obstruction. The obstruction was one very distressed young woman. Genna squeezed past him to her friend. "Lorianne. Lorianne, it's okay. It will be okay." She dropped down on her knees and embraced her friend. Her voice cooed softly and as if soothing a child.

"Is there a flashlight?" he demanded. He knew he sounded was harsh, but he was having trouble containing his fury.

Genna fumbled around her friend, then handed it up. He flipped it on, but the bulb was flickering. What was it with the lights in this place? "Are there any batteries?" He grated.

"The office," Genna told him. He darted to the room he'd thought was a storage room the other night. Astonishment surged through him. Now he understood the panic. How dire did Ash want this property? Was he really willing to risk his own business this badly? Rick found the batteries under the desk beneath an overturned drawer. He righted the trash container and pitched the old ones and tested the switch.

When he returned, Genna had her friend situated on the ugly sofa with fading flowers. He had to admire the level head she exhibited. Grimly, he cast the beam through the basement door. The stairs were hazardous. He jiggled the railing, and a portion fell to the bottom, disappearing in the gloom. The place should be condemned, historic landmark or not.

He trekked down carefully. Once he reached stable ground, he flashed the light around, dust motes dancing in the beam. Close to a third of the area had been finished with sheetrock though remained unpainted. It looked as if someone had started and intended to finish, but somehow got interrupted and never got back to it.

An old sink was off to the right in a far corner with a small toolbox on the floor nearby, partially opened. Rick guided the beam around where boxes appeared organized and stacked uniformly. Large plastic garbage bags held books. Excess inventory—made sense. The wall to the left and the wall he was facing showed batts of insulation between two by fours, giving the space an eerie Halloween feeling. A single bulb hung from the ceiling in the center of the room. He channeled the shaft of light along the corners searching for a breaker or fuse box. A building this old had him doubting it had breakers. He located the fuse box in the corner above the old sink. He shined the light in the box, careful not to touch anything.

Finger marks looked to have brushed dust away. But that

could be someone's efforts to replace a fuse. Sweeping the light surrounding the area, he saw a box of fuses in the sink, obviously unused for running water. He shined the light into the box again. Upon closer examination, he noticed a lead wire not tightened down. It was a wonder the place hadn't caught fire. He pulled a pair of pliers from the toolbox and tightened the cap. Miraculously or not, depending on who you were, the lights came back on. His hike back up the stairs, slightly less hazardous. There was still the issue of the rickety railing.

"Thanks," Genna said.

"There was a loose connection."

"We know. We usually have to jiggle it to get the lights to come back on."

"There is something funky with that wiring. You should have it checked out." He studied her reaction carefully. The narrowed eyes. Definitely suspicious.

"Are you okay?" He directed his question to Lorianne. Her fingers shook as she reached up to push long blonde, tangled hair from her face. She was striking. Unfortunately, not in a bookish sort of way.

"Who are you?" she mumbled. Rick turned an annoyed gaze on Genna. She hadn't even mentioned him? How flattering. He felt a smirk of satisfaction at her blush, though her eyes shot daggers. He had no doubt *if looks could kill...*

"I'm Rick Johnson. Genna didn't tell you about me?" He quirked a brow, and almost laughed outright at Lorianne's questioning look toward Genna—and Genna's murderous one. She was still pissed off about that kiss-madness the other night.

"Nooooo." The word was drawn out, almost a question but not quite. If anything, it drew Lorianne's attention away from her frightful experience, if only for the moment. Her long hair was naturally curly, eyes blue. Black mascara tracks trailed her cheeks.

"Call the cops," he instructed Genna. "Did you see anyone?" he asked Lorianne. From the corner of his eye he watched Genna dig through her purse.

"N...no," Lorianne shuddered.

"What happened?" he demanded. The grim picture that was forming in his mind both terrified and infuriated him.

Her voice trembled. "The lights went out, so I grabbed the flashlight and went to the basement to check the fuse box. They go out a lot when it rains."

"Take a deep breath." He forced his tone to remain gentle. Rick made himself do the same so as not to traumatize her more.

Drawing in a shaky breath, she said, "I heard the bell on the door, but I thought I had locked it behind me." Lorianne wrinkled her nose as if that would help her remember. "I...I guess I didn't."

"Can you think of anyone who would lock you in the basement?"

"Lock me in?" She whispered. She paled at the implication. "No. I begged them to open the door. I could hear them moving around. Were we robbed?" Another shuddering breath shook her. Her face was white and strained. He put his hand over hers. It was clammy.

"Are you claustrophobic?" He wouldn't be surprised.

"I...I don't like the dark." A violent shake rippled her shoulders.

"They were looking for something. The office is turned upside- down."

Her dazed expression and surprise relieved him. "But, why?" Her confusion was apparent. He got up and walked over to study the door jam. He came back and positioned himself on the arm of the old sofa.

"The door doesn't appear to be jacked with." He was talking to himself now. He focused his attention back on Lorianne. "Where was Ms. Lyndsey?"

"I must have left it unlocked," Lorianne confessed. "I'm not usually the early one. "I...I haven't been s...sleeping v...very well, so I've come in early all week." Reaction started setting in. She was shivering with nerves.

"What do you mean, you aren't usually the early one? And why haven't you been sleeping well?" He moved again, this time lifting a sweater from the counter to drop across her shoulders.

"I...I'm not sure," she said. But she cast her glance down, away from his.

"Could it be a boyfriend?" Her glance was quick and sharp, then down again. If he hadn't been watching her he would have missed it.

He had to strain to hear her response. He frowned. So she wasn't going to implicate Ash. Her appeal to Ash was clearly defined. A beauty, with long blonde hair cascading down her back, the typical fragile-lean-on-your-man-type. The kind Ash ate up for breakfast, then a quick so-long.

"And, Genna?" He hadn't meant to ask that.

"Genna?" Her laugh was more a bark. "No. I mean, well," she hesitated.

An uneasy chokehold stole over him.

"Her old boyfriend from college did pop up this week. Just out of the blue." The anger that flashed in her eyes surprised him.

He waited.

"I was in the basement checking the fuse box earlier in the week. The lights had gone out that day, too." He followed her gaze to Genna. She stood at the counter, punching numbers into her cell phone. She lowered her voice—Rick had to lean in to hear her. "When I came back up the stairs, he was here."

"Was she glad to see him?" He winced at the turn he directed the questions. It was none of his concern. But what if he was the one who'd ransacked the office? He was looking out for her interests, right?

Genna dropped her cell on the counter and moved to her friend. "The police are on their way." She sat down next to Lorianne and tugged the sweater tighter around her friend. As different as night and day. Their closeness touched him. "Are you okay?"

"Yes," Lorianne said. Her glance never wavered from him.

Rick opened his mouth to tell them the actual reason he'd stopped by, but something stopped him, the words lodged in his throat.

"'*Cease, warring thoughts, and let his brain / No more discord entertain / But be smooth and calm again,*' James Shirley." Genna said softly. She pulled Lorianne's head to her shoulder in a protective gesture.

His gaze followed hers to the windows where Ash's new office building under construction loomed. The whole situation smelled like rotting fish. He didn't like it. Not one little bit.

"Yes," Lorianne whispered, eyes closed.

Could Genna be sabotaging her own business? At the risk of feeling relieved, there was at least another suspect. Unfortunately, it was his most trusted friend.

The police timed it perfectly. Rick never got his answer.

CHAPTER 13

ENSCONCED IN GENNA'S SMALL Victorian home, Lorianne found she had questions for her friend. "What did that Rick guy mean, you hadn't mentioned him?" Lorianne asked.

Genna came through the bedroom door carrying a tray with tea and crackers. Lorianne loved Genna's little gray house with white trim. It was Genna's pride and joy—another legacy from her family. Every worn stick of furniture and faded pillow treasured.

Genna had stuffed Lorianne in an old Queen Anne style bed in her spare bedroom, overrun with fluffy pillows in greens and yellows. Large arched windows overlooked the street, letting in natural light. The sort of refuge she'd needed. Lorianne struggled to a sitting position.

"Huh?"

"Nice try." Lorianne pulled the sheet up to cover a grin. "What did he mean?"

"Oh, nothing, I'm sure." But tell-tale stains of scarlet appeared high on Genna's cheeks. Whitened knuckles gripped the tray she held.

"That's not how it sounded to me," she muffled through the covers.

"Oh, all right," Genna huffed.

"What?" Lorianne dropped the sheet from her mouth and snatched the tray from Genna's hands before she dropped it. "Sit down," she ordered. Lorianne was not about to let her out of any details. "Spill it."

"He's the customer who wanted the William Whewell volumes."

"Oooohh," she said, and picked up her cup. Lorianne blew across the rising steam. Genna's berating glance had her biting the inside of her cheek to hide a grin. "Go on."

"What else is there?"

"Plenty, I'm sure."

"'*Nothing is more useful than silence,*'" she scowled.

"That sounds familiar," Lorianne took a careful sip. She could be as patient as anyone.

"Meander of Athens. You probably heard it in your English Lit or Humanities—"

"Anyway?"

With a sigh, Genna continued. "I ran into him at the fundraiser."

"Ah, he was the hot guy I saw you with. Uh huh, go on."

Genna's scowl deepened. "He came by the shop when I was closing up one night, too."

Oh, this was getting better and better. She just knew it. Lorianne waited, pleased at the heat surfacing in Genna's face.

"He sort of kissed me."

"*Kissed you*!" Tea splashed over the edge of the cup. "And you didn't tell me?"

Genna rolled her eyes. "Why didn't you tell me about Ashton?" Genna retorted.

Lorianne dropped her eyes to her cup, unable to stop her fingers from trembling.

"Because I haven't heard from the son of a bitch since he

left after fucking me three nights in a row." As quick as that, Lorianne was struggling to hang on to a control that was as fragile as the cup she held, resenting the pity in Genna's eyes.

"I'm sorry," Genna whispered, her regret sincere.

LORIANNE SHRUGGED. OBVIOUSLY, AN effort to convey it didn't matter one whit. But Genna knew better. Lorianne's situation in life had started out unfair. She didn't talk about it much, and most of what Genna pieced together was sketchy.

She knew Lorianne had grown up in a single-parent household. Known they'd moved around, known she'd never met her biological father.

Really, in retrospect, the only time Lorianne even came close to opening up about her mother was after a few drinks. She'd told Genna that her father had died within a year of her parents' marriage. After which, her mother had remarried almost immediately. Details were sparse after that. Lorianne never learned his actual name, said she never knew what to believe from her mother.

"What a pair we are." Lorianne gave a shaky laugh.

Genna took Lorianne's cup and placed it on the tray and set the tray on the bedside table. She reached over and clasped Lorianne's hand. "You know, you *are* going to find your prince. I'm willing to bet he is just around the corner."

"Don't be ridiculous. You're just spinning fairy tales and you know it."

Genna shrugged. "So? I think it's true." Maybe her telepathic powers were finally kicking in. Lorianne was special. It was odd, in a way. Lorianne was beautiful, quick, fun, and confident. But her insecurities were deeply rooted. And Genna loved her in spite of them. One only had to look in her eyes to see the frightened little girl.

Lorianne hadn't grown up with the loving support of parents

like Genna had. "'*Fairy tales do not tell children the dragons exist. Children already know that dragons exist. Fairy tales tell children the dragons can be killed.*' That was G.K. Chesterson."

"I don't like the words 'fairy' and 'tale,' remember? Especially, in a sentence where 'tale' follows 'fairy'." Lorianne tossed her head.

"They aren't all like Clark, you know. Besides, don't you think Clark really did love you? He wasn't a dragon."

"The *dragon*!" she spat. "Of course he didn't love me. If he had he would never have walked out."

"Maybe he didn't have a choice. I think you are still looking at it through the eyes of a six-year-old. A six-year-old victim."

"You're being ridiculous again." All of Lorianne's hurt and insecurities sounded in that one statement. Genna could hear and see it, like a movie trailer in the theatre, with Dolby Surround Sound, complete with a mega picture.

"Am I?" Sarcasm did not mask her fear.

"Yes."

Lorianne snatched her hand away and slid deeper in the bed, planting the covers over her head almost knocking Genna to the floor.

"I mean it, Lorianne. You were really young. *Really* young," she emphasized. "Who wouldn't crave the attention? And he gave it, too. You said he took you for ice cream, amusement parks, the zoo. Things lots of dads do with their kids."

"Stop it," her muffled voice shot from under the covers.

It was time to play hardball, Genna had coddled her long enough. "You should hear yourself talk about him after you've had a few drinks! '*I* wouldn't have minded having Clark for a daddy. *I* dreamed about it. Then *I* would have a dad like other kids. Then no one would have made fun of *me*.'"

"Stop it! Why are you doing this?" Lorianne threw the covers off her head, tears spilling down her cheeks.

Guilt swarmed Genna, but she plowed forward. "Because you think you aren't good enough! That's why," Genna jumped up and paced the floor. Her voice rose with every word. "You *are* good enough—*better* than good enough—and to let men use you just because you are scared? Like that little girl—always afraid they'll walk away. So you give them everything you've got, no holds barred, up front." Genna dropped to her knees next to the bed and took Lorianne's hands. "And when they do walk away, it breaks my heart, because you blame yourself. And it's not you. It's them!"

Lorianne tried to snatch her hands away, but Genna tightened her grip.

"It wasn't your fault he left. It wasn't your fault your mother died of a drug overdose when you were seventeen. You were just a kid. You did what you had to, to survive. But so did she. Don't you see?"

"Clark didn't leave because of you. He left because he couldn't stand to see what your mother was doing to herself, or to you. And you weren't his kid. If he'd taken you, you probably would have ended up in the foster care system. I think he loved *both* of you very much.

"When your mom said you were too bossy and head strong, she was probably just teasing you. She probably never guessed how much it hurt you. Moms love their kids, and I refuse to believe yours was an exception."

"But he left," Lorianne whispered, "and I don't know why."

"You may never know why. But I can *promise* you, he did not leave because of you." Genna plopped back down on the bed and hugged Lorianne.

Lorianne's body shook with silent sobs. "I just wanted him to love me."

"He did love you. I'm certain of it. You are the most lovable person I've ever known."

CHAPTER 14

SATURDAY MORNING RICK POURED coffee in his cup, debating his approach to Ash. It just didn't seem possible that he would deliberately destroy someone's property. But Ash had grown up with one helluva teacher in Old Asshole Turner. The phone rang, jerking his hand. Hot coffee splattered. "Damn." He snatched up the receiver.

"I've been trying to reach you for a week," Ash said.

"Why?" Rick kept his tone mild. He refilled his cup and waited for Ash's reaction.

"Why?" Ash repeated.

"You're trying to buy the bookstore across the street." It was a statement, not a question.

"How did you know that? It's not supposed to be common knowledge. That Van Horn has the biggest mouth."

Rick would have laughed at his outrage, but there were more important issues to discern. "I didn't hear it from Van Horn." He grimaced. "Why keep it a secret?" Calm façade threatened to give way to impatience.

"I didn't say it was a secret. I said it wasn't common knowledge," Ash said.

"Are you seeing a girl by the name of Lorianne?" That

should stir things up.

"What is this?" Ash bristled. "And what do you know about *her*?"

"Are you?"

"We went out a couple of times, but it's done." Ash's sudden blandness raised the hair on Rick's neck.

He closed his eyes, dreading the next unavoidable question. "Did you come out of the Baptist church the other night, late?"

"What are you talking about?"

"Someone was prowling around the bookstore the other night, near the church. Was it you?" He was growling now, his impatience breaking through.

"What if I was? I have a construction project across the street." Definitely, defensive. But Rick set him up.

"You'd better have a good reason," Rick grated out. He slammed the phone down, furious he'd let his temper get the better of him.

Ash wanted that property. He had motive and opportunity. Who else could it be? He must have been using Lorianne to access information. He'd known Ash a long time. It sickened him to think his friend could use someone so ruthlessly. But facts were facts, and using women was one thing Ash did and did well.

Maybe Ash had finally become Ashton Turner, Jr. The influence couldn't be denied.

Fifteen minutes after he'd hung up the phone, he realized he'd never found out why Ash had been trying to reach him for a week. He dumped his cold coffee down the sink.

ASHTON SAT ON THE sleek, white sofa in his ultra-modern living room, and dropped the phone in the cradle. His home looked as cold as he felt, not an out-of-place shoe anywhere. He ran tired fingers through his hair. That was comforting, his oldest friend hanging up in his ear.

Life, just perfect. Wasn't it complicated enough with apparitions of a blonde-haired, blue-eyed she-devil plaguing him at every turn? He blew out a pursed breath. This insomnia would be the death of him. Even when he slept it was fitful and full of erotic dreams waking him just before his climatic conclusions.

Then when he'd fallen asleep, near dawn in his estimation, the sun streamed through the blinds, hitting him square in the face, jarring him from that much-needed slumber. And after all the rain, the sun had to finally show itself. Ash stormed to the kitchen and rinsed his cup. He refused to feel guilt over some insecure, clingy airhead. But, had she clung?

Succumbing to the inevitable, Ash showered, then armed with more coffee, made straight for the office. His playboy image would start to suffer soon if he kept showing up before his secretary. The thought brought a wry twist to his lips. He sat behind the desk and contemplated the mound of paperwork. Saturday, and he was at his office. What a sad life he led.

A sharp wrap on the door startled him. An elderly woman with her gray hair pulled back in an old-fashioned twist walked in. Shrewd blue, familiar eyes pierced him like lasers.

"Good morning, Ashton."

"To what do I owe the pleasure?" Never show weakness—that was his motto.

She sauntered about, taking in the plush demeanor. The heavy oak desk piled with files, the drafting table in the corner covered with the Bloomington Office Park project blueprints. She picked up a pen and tapped it against her fingers. She was nervous.

She took her time, but worked her way to one of the chairs facing his desk. Her dress was wispy. It floated around her in an elegant swirl of rainbow colors when she sat with a deliberate calmness, save for the moving pen. "I knew your father, you know," she started.

"Oh? So you knew how happy the son of a bitch was in real life, huh?" He refused to hide the bite of sarcasm from his tone.

She laughed softly. "We called him Junior."

Now that was an interesting piece of news. No one he'd known ever referred to him as anything but Asshole Turner. "You must have known him a long time ago."

"Yes. We were in school together. Elementary through high school."

"And who might you be?" he asked her.

"Joanna Bakely. My late husband was Victor Bakely."

"*The* Victor Bakely, The man Victor Town Park is named for?"

"The same," she concurred, inclining her head.

"What brings you by, Mrs. *Victor* Bakely?" Scorn echoed through the room. It didn't seem to faze her.

"Call me Joanna." Her smile reminded him of a mountain lioness sizing up its prey.

"Okay, Joanna." He leaned back in his chair and studied her, placing his fingers together in a contemplative gesture. The familiarity about her nagged him, set him on edge. The tilt of her head? The flash of her eyes? Something.

"I'm here to speak with you regarding your parking garage venture."

He stilled. "Is that so?" Ash tried working that angle three years ago to no avail.

"I realize the need to modernize Bloomington. But I wonder if you are going about it quite right." Her tone was conciliatory, but...

He waited, every instinct screaming to use the patience he'd spent years honing.

"There is an old building located just to the south of this property and east of your new development. Kitty-corner from Ida's craft store," she clarified. She rose and stepped to the window. He swiveled his chair to follow her movements, eyes riveted on her.

"I checked into that possibility some time ago," he said. He kept his tone bland, devoid of anything, as the hair on his nape raised. "The space is not nearly large enough." He swiped a hand over his eyes again and took a measured breath, trying to make sense of this unexpected visit.

"When you consider the location, it's actually perfect," she told him. "You could install a five story parking garage that could be utilized for holiday events—even for the city park."

"That's all well and good, but what of the owner?" His frustration was clear. "They adamantly refused to do business three and a half years ago."

"Maybe they are willing to do business now." He heard something catch in her voice that sounded suspiciously like regret.

"What could possibly have changed in the last three years?"

Rather than answer, she faced him. Her scrutiny made him feel like squirming in his chair like an eight-year old child in the principal's office. Or worse...waiting for his father to mete out punishment in his cigar-smoke-filled library. He clenched his jaw, annoyed. This was ridiculous. "What is your interest in this matter, *Joanna*?"

"Suffice to say, Bloomington is a historic town, *Ashton*. My interest is in the welfare of the town." He could read a good lie when it stared him in the face. After all, he was the consummate expert. Nothing like seeing yourself mirrored in someone else.

Then she clobbered him.

"Are you aware that someone is trying to damage the property you have your sights set on?"

This was going too far. "What the hell is that supposed to mean?" He ground out.

The pen in her hand stilled. All signs of nerves dissipated, her eyes trapping his. "Just what I said." The fury on her face sent a chill up his spine.

He shoved it away. "I believe you are going to need to be a little more specific." Again, he opted for the blandness that always served so well.

"My granddaughter is a business owner, and I'll not have you putting her in danger."

Stunned by her accusation, he demanded, "Maybe you should explain." This day was not getting any easier.

"I know that you want to buy Renewed Interest's property," she said.

Now he was pissed. That damned Van Horn. The man obviously couldn't keep a secret to save his life. Momentarily speechless, he watched Joanna Bakely saunter toward him like the prey he felt he was. Her gait was measured, calculated. He leaned back in his chair, portraying a relaxed position. It would take more than an old lady to fluster him. His disbelief grew in monumental proportions when she placed her hands either side of him on the arms of his chair and put her nose to his.

"Don't mess with her." Her voice was pure venom. "I'll hand you back to your daddy in a box." She moved back swift as a cat. Bringing her hand up under his chair, she tipped him backward. Before he could right himself, she was gone.

"Son of a bitch!" he yelled at the empty room. Hoisting himself to his feet, Ash reflected on her words. He moved to the windows where he could see Ida's Craft Store and the bookstore's expansion project.

Her granddaughter was Genna Lyndsey? Nothing made sense. He had no designs on Genna Lyndsey. He didn't even know Genna Lyndsey. He shook his head trying to gather his thoughts. And what did Joanna Bakely mean, 'putting her in danger'?

Fury clouded his brain. That's all he needed, another chick

to complicate his life when he couldn't seem to get haunted blue eyes out of his mind long enough to have a decent night's sleep.

Ash snatched up the phone. Time to find out what Van Horn had to gain by spilling Turner Construction business all over town.

CHAPTER 15

GENNA'S BATHROOM COUNTERTOP WAS not large enough for all the armor Lorianne saw fit to prepare her for the town council meeting. Not to mention two people crowding the mirror.

"You look great," Lorianne said, obviously pleased with her handiwork.

"Are you sure?" Genna wrinkled her nose at her reflection.

Lorianne insisted she dress in sophisticated heather gray wide legged pants topped with a double-breasted cropped jacket, straight from Lorianne's closet. The four-inch heels she'd purchased for the museum the other night made up for the extra-long length. The additional height boosted her confidence.

Genna turned, gauging her backside; it looked good. There wasn't much to do about her wild hair, so Lorianne secured it to the nape of her neck. It would have suffice.

"We'll just add a touch of mascara and blush after you put in your contacts."

Genna never understood how Lorianne had learned so much about clothes, makeup, and hair. She certainly had an aptitude for turning the mundane into extraordinary with minimal effort. And quickly, at that. The evidence was reflected in the mirror. She glanced over at Lorianne's simple pale pink jersey knit dress. The scooped neck showed way too much cleavage and the skirt hailed several inches above her knees. *Her* hair was wild on purpose—blonde, wavy, long, and full. It just wasn't fair.

Genna sighed. "Are you sure all of this is necessary?"

Lorianne ignored her. "I swear, those jeans you had on today should be burned, but it would probably be considered an ozone hazard and put the Environmental Protection Agency on our asses."

Genna squirmed under Lorianne's scrutiny when she stood back to observe her handiwork.

"You probably won't have to say anything at the meeting, but it never hurts to be prepared," Lorianne told her.

"Gray pants will prepare me?" Genna's brain was mush.

"We need to know who likes us and who wants our building torn down for parking, right? That's what you said to Mrs. Bakely."

"Yes, but I was just guessing. And remember, she said she hadn't heard anything official."

Lorianne's impatient gaze pierced her. "This will give you more confidence. Trust me."

Genna responded with a snort and turned back to the mirror to see if her image was just a mirage.

"Right. Any words of wisdom before we head out?" Lorianne asked, tucking a stray tendril behind Genna's ear.

"'*Resolve, and thou art free?*' Henry Wadsworth Longfellow.'"

"Is that the best you can come up with?"

THE TOWN COUNCIL MEETING was just being called to order when Genna and Lorianne slipped into the large, dingy paneled room full of folding metal chairs. They sat on the end of a wide aisle near the back. A podium outfitted with a microphone was centered in the aisle at the front, and faced a semi-circle dais. The town council members were already seated toward the public.

Genna spotted several familiar townspeople from the mediocre portion of the historic business district. A low hum filled the room. She smiled when she caught Mrs. Bakely's subtle wink. She felt, rather than heard, Lorianne's sharp intake of breath. Casting a quick glance in her direction, Genna witnessed Lorianne pursing her lips together—with fury or determination, unable to decipher which. Her gaze swept the room trying to spot the source of Lorianne's ire. She couldn't. No time.

When the meeting finally began, the council waded through several administrative items: approval of expenditures, traffic considerations, and outdoor warning device disposal plans—whatever that was—before finally reaching the historical preservation Conduct of Hearing. Genna couldn't decide if Lorianne would expire from extreme boredom or flat-out irritation, based on her restless bearing and the rapid tapping of an emery board she'd wrestled from her purse against her thigh. Thank goodness there wasn't a hard surface within reach.

Shifting audience members and the rustling of papers rose Genna's curiosity. Mr. Plank, from the coffee shop next door, sat next to Ida Finch of Bloomin' Crafts and Gifts. Reverend Colvert, from the First Baptist Church looked decidedly uncomfortable, knees almost touching his chest. He was very tall. Mrs. Wilson, Toddy's mother from Wilson's Photography, patted her hair. All waiting for the next session to begin, amid a few other members scattered throughout.

Mr. Plank, a man in his late fifties, wore a hard expression. His purchase of Plank's coffee shop in Bloomington several years before, had been a quiet transaction. No one knew much about him. He just appeared one day. But coffee was a staple in American culture, so he did very well. The coffee shop was always busy.

Ida Finch, on the other hand, was very protective of her age.

No one in town could or would venture a guess. At one time, it was considered social suicide. But if one kept their speculations out of her earshot, she was a very pleasant neighbor. Her small frame and frail hands hid a mighty ferociousness. Her smile might appear guileless and genial, her voice soft spoken, but Genna had once witnessed such an escapade when Wanda Buford made the mistake of comparing her to Wanda's great-grandmother. Ida still refused to speak to her.

Genna didn't own Mrs. Finch's building, just her own and the one between where Genna and Lorianne's new internet café would reside.

Reverend Horace Colvert was anything but genial and guileless. Years behind the pulpit had honed a resonance designed to wake the dead. She watched with envy as the reverend damned all new development, and raised issues of God's intentions for the sinning people in Bloomington. Such ability to stand up and speak to a crowd so effortlessly was mind-boggling. She flinched as his fist pounded the podium in fury. The sound, magnified by the microphone, left her surprised the wood hadn't split like a blow from a karate chop.

He turned unflinching eyes to her and Lorianne, catching Genna off guard. "I move that the bookstore be condemned as a hazard to the community. That store is a disgrace," he boomed.

Genna jerked in her seat. She could feel the blood drain from her face at the accusations. What could he have against a small used bookstore?

"What is this?" Lorianne whispered.

"I-I don't know," she squeaked. Genna pulled her composure into a shell, fragile as it was.

"Reverend Colvert, you'll direct your remarks to the Council, sir," Mayor Dan Thomas reprimanded. The mayor shuffled the papers before him, then shook his head. "Reverend Colvert, this property is not for sale, nor does it figure in any of the city's business at this time. You are out of order, as this item is nowhere on the agenda. Please be seated."

"She sells pornography," Reverend Colvert roared. His 'pulpit' resonance reverberated off the gray walls and cement tiled floor. Genna could feel the window panes rattle in their flimsy wood frames.

Blood rushed her ears. She heard nothing but her own heartbeat. Her stomach twisted into knots, bile formed in her throat. She'd never been attacked before, let alone in front of a whole town.

"Sit down, Reverend. This is not your lectern," the mayor reiterated, undaunted by his bluster. The reverend raised his head and started to stalk toward Genna and Lorianne. White spots danced before Genna's vision.

She thought she might faint. But to her relief, he stopped at a seat in the front row. Not without casting them a last look of disdain.

Unfortunately, Josephine Phillips, the Museum Curator, piped up. "He's right!" She had a mousy voice that matched her mousy hair, pointy nose, and bony arms. She shot a questioning look to the reverend. Why, the old biddy was his puppet.

It was true the erotic portion of their little business was growing, and for such a small town, Genna had to admit surprise. But it wasn't out of proportion with any other category in the store, say, the Historicals.

Lorianne's gasp sounded, and she drew up for attack. Genna squeezed her hand and whispered, *"The best answer to anger is silence."*

"Bullshit!" Her eyes flashed with outrage. "How do you think of those things in a time like this?"

Genna glanced around at the faces staring at her. Shock registered on Wanda's and Ida's expressions. Sympathy from Sarah Pendergrass, owner of the florist and bakery. Disbelief from Paris Jones, The Antique House. Righteous indignation on Selma Stotts, beauty shop entrepreneur. And condemnation from Mrs. Wilson.

Mr. Plank on the other hand was his usual quiet self, those hard black eyes taking in everything around him. Lester Van Horn, the real estate agent, looked smug. Genna truly felt she might pass out from the reverend's unexpected ambush.

"That's quite enough, Mrs. Phillips." Rancor colored Lorianne's scathing retort. "We have just as much right to our business as you do to yours."

"It's okay, Lorianne. Sit down." Genna could hardly manage a whisper.

"No," she said, with easy defiance. Lorianne was as impressive as anyone when she pulled herself up to her full height. "We work as hard as anyone. We're members of the Chamber and good citizens. What is this really about, Reverend?"

Mayor Thomas pounded his gavel. "This meeting is not over, people."

"Come on, Lorianne." Genna jumped up and dragged her to the door, frantic to escape.

ASHTON'S SURPRISE AT SEEING Lorianne at the meeting paled in comparison to the soft pink dress she wore. Her hair surrounded her head like an angel's halo. The minute she'd walked in he was on his cell phone to Rick. "Meet me at Pat's," he demanded, then clicked off. He didn't like the thought of her looking like an angel. An angel, his ass.

Ashton watched the unfolding scene with undisguised interest, as did the rest of the town members. His glance slid to the circular dais where the town council members sat. His gaze particularly resting on the enigma of Joanna Bakely. Her look was fierce, and he thought it must have been with great effort that she did not come out of her chair, over the desk, to flatten

Reverend Colvert with a personal vendetta. Her lips were pressed together, brows drawn. Oh, yes, she was fit to be tied. He bit back a smile.

He turned his attention back to Genna Lyndsey, Joanna's granddaughter. She couldn't have resembled her less. When Josephine started to agree with the Reverend, Ashton made a move to stand. But to his surprise, Lorianne launched herself out of her chair, ready to flay the onslaught. Something like...pride squeezed his ribs. It was obvious to him that Genna and Lorianne were great friends.

Genna whispered adamantly to Lorianne, who reacted strongly. A minute later Genna tugged her through the door.

In a flash they were gone.

"GOOD LORD, LORIANNE. HOW do you walk in these things?" Genna complained as they fled Town Hall. They'd stopped in the ladies' room, where Genna attempted to soothe Lorianne's temper. But Lorianne was not in a mood to be placated. Lorianne insisted they head east toward Bloomin' Sundries. Bloomin' Sundries was closed for the evening but that wasn't their destination anyway.

"We need a drink, Genna. You should have let me trounce them."

"I don't really drink. You know that."

"Well, *I* need a drink." Lorianne set the pace of an Olympic walker up for the Gold. "I'm so mad, I could spit. I'm so mad, I can't even think of another word for being mad."

"'*When angry, count four; when very angry, swear.*'" Genna couldn't contain a slight hysterical eruption of laughter.

"No shit," Lorianne spat.

Their destination was Pat's Bloomin' Pub, located directly behind the variety store off of Main Street. They made quick work of the short walk despite four-inch heels which made Genna stumble more than once. But Lorianne was experienced and caught her arm every time before she could fall. They crossed Pine and slipped passed the community theatre into Pat's.

Pat's offered the sanctuary of low lighting and wooden floors. Bar stools filled up quickly as other townspeople filed out from the council meeting. Apparently, they'd spent more time in the ladies room than she'd realized.

Genna cringed. She had no desire to see anyone from that council meeting fiasco. Ida Finch sat at a table near the door. "Do you suppose she walked here?" Lorianne whispered to Genna.

"Of course, I did, girl! I'm not dead, you know," Ida offered up a winsome smile, "With Mr. Plank's kind escort." *Kind?*

Mr. Plank said nothing, as usual. Genna felt the warmth on her cheeks, hoping the low lighting disguised it. For the life of her, every quote she ever knew flew out of her head. It wouldn't do for Lorianne to discover that. She'd never hear the end of it.

"Come on, Genna." Lorianne tugged her to a barstool, saving her from saying anything.

Lorianne raised a hand. "Hey, Josh. Give us a couple of White Russians."

"I don't think that's wise, Lorianne," Genna protested.

"It tastes like chocolate milk. You'll like it."

"Hi, Genna. You look terrific."

Genna turned where Toddy Wilson stood a little too close. She shifted away. His soft voice reminded her of her own lack of confidence. He was proprietor of the Picture Photo Studio next door to Wanda's Fine Dresses on the town square, or rather son of the proprietors; he was in his early thirties. He'd grown up in Bloomington, and helped his mother since his father's unusual demise several years before. He'd been spending a lot of time at the bookstore. His shy smile tugged at her. She did appreciate his support. "Thanks, Toddy."

Josh set two high-ball glasses filled with milk in front of

Lorianne and Genna. Genna reached for the glass and lifted it for a quick sniff. No way would she even consider tasting it if it smelled funky. Wrinkling her nose, she took a teeny sip. Wow, it did taste kind of like chocolate milk. She glanced at Toddy. "How is business?" she asked. Anything to take away the torture she'd just escaped.

"It's good. Graduation is just around the corner, you know."

"Yes, I suppose it would be then." She took a little larger sip. It really was good.

"How are things going for you?" He asked.

"Okay, if the lights would stay on for any length of time."

"What's wrong with the lights?" He trained intense dark eyes on her, her attention drifted to the taped hinge on his glasses. Goose bumps prickled her skin.

"I'm not sure. I'm going to have to call an electrician."

"I guess you were at the town council meeting?"

She nodded, taking another drink.

"It was pretty active then?"

Ignoring his question, she said, "Your mother was there. I thought she was going out of town." Amazing how they could make it taste like that. Lorianne was a genius. She smiled at her friend.

"She is, in a few days," he said.

Genna twirled her straw absently in her drink.

"What happened at the meeting? You seem agitated."

"Oh," she choked, obviously having swallowed wrong, "nothing, really." He needed to move back, his invasion of her personal space was a bit too intrusive.

Toddy leaned in closer. "Would you please go out with me? I keep asking, but—" she cringed. Oh, not that.

"N-no," Genna stuttered, "please quit asking, Toddy." His nerd stance resonated to a distinct Captain Kirk persona. In his own mind, she was sure, because she certainly didn't see him that way. This was not going to turn out well.

"I could fix your lights for you." His voice had lowered, and she struggled to hide a groan as he pushed his tape-clad glasses up further on his nose. A moment of déjà vu flashed before her. Is that how she appeared to people? Over-the-top shy, geeky-glasses that wouldn't stay up? Lord knows her hair was as wild as Toddy's, if not more so. She couldn't contain a whimper of despair.

She could have sworn Toddy's timid demeanor was more than he displayed currently. But he'd crowded her at the store, hadn't respected her personal space at all. She narrowed her gaze on him, glanced down to see what he was drinking. Moist, heated breath teased the hair behind her ear, creeping her out. She slurped the last of her drink. Whew, that was heady. "Toddy, I...I—" she started.

"I could pick you up tomorrow night after you close," he interrupted. "I could check out *your* wiring at the same time." Oh, no. Another slurp, but it was gone. She'd drunk it all. He wasn't talking about the wires in the fuse box. She sucked hard on the straw but all she got was air.

"Toddy, I-I can't go out with you." She struggled to offer a plausible excuse, other than 'you creep me out.' "I have too much to do." It was lame, but she couldn't bring herself to be out and out rude—hurt his feelings.

Josh set another drink in front of her. She took it, gratefully, and quickly inhaled another drink. A light-headed sensation swam over her. She blinked.

"Sure you can. It won't be like that Barrett guy you used to see who worked for Plank. It would be like a real date," he gushed.

This was too much, and on top of everything else. His attention was starting to be a nuisance. Irritated, she clenched her teeth. Enough was enough. "Toddy." She managed to keep her voice light. "'*Due to Lack of Interest, Tomorrow is Canceled.*'"

"What?" His gaze angled on her, vague with confusion.

"1969. It's a book by Irene Kampen." Genna dropped her feet to the floor and rushed for the ladies' room. Zig-zagging her way through the maze of tables, her face burned with embarrassment.

Was she too mean? She hated hurting people's feelings, but why wouldn't Toddy take no for answer? Her four-inch heels clicked like tap shoes over the wood floor, pounding her ears. Was it too much to hope no one else noticed? She made it without stumbling. Refusing to look around, she bolted through swinging doors that separated the restrooms from the bar. Behind the doors was a small lounging area, complete with a small sofa Pat's was famous for. She wasn't about to sit on that couch. She knew its reputation.

Genna jerked on the handle for the ladies' room. Locked. She focused her intent on the doorknob, practicing her telepathic powers.

Whose business was it whether she had dated Barrett or not, anyway? She pushed her nerdy glasses up on her nose before remembering she'd worn contacts, bringing to mind, once again—her own total nerd status.

ASHTON WAVED AT RICK when he stepped through the door from a booth along the windows. The blinds had been lowered earlier to keep out the afternoon sun. They were still down, though it was dark out. The crowd at Pat's Bloomin' Pub was picking up. Talk of the town council meeting buzzed. Reverend Colvert would be pleased his show for the town was making the gossip mill. News traveled fast in Bloomington. Pat's provided the perfect vehicle for the fodder.

"Did you make the council meeting?" Rick asked him, sliding into the booth.

"Oh, yeah. You missed it."

"What do you mean?" Ash watched Rick cast a glance around the bar, not giving him his full attention. Not yet, anyway.

"Reverend Colvert laid one out on Genna Lyndsey."

Rick's head snapped back. Ash would be surprised if he hadn't popped a tendon. He almost burst out in genuine amusement at the look on Rick's face.

Rick's narrowed eyes, compressed lips, and creased forehead was interesting, indeed. "What happened?"

"He accused her of selling pornography." Ash laughed outright. But then a picture of Lorianne rising to full height, preparing to wage war on her friend's behalf floated before him. It would have been worth millions to see her clobber the self-righteous bastard.

It was time to admit he wanted her. So what if she clung to him—licked him all over—kissed him in places he hadn't known were so sensitive, made love with the lights on, and made him feel like a knight in shining armor. He glanced at the bar where she was flirting shamelessly with Josh.

Rick interrupted his thoughts, drawing back his attention. "You mean that pitiable little section she has on the top shelf at the back of the store?"

Oh, yes, interesting, indeed, Ash smiled. When was the last time Rick cared enough about a woman to have such a knee-jerk reaction? Suddenly, he felt light-hearted. Not so alone.

The vision in pink ignored him, never looked once in his direction. Not for long, he vowed.

RICK'S FACE HEATED, REALIZING exactly what he'd revealed. But a prickle tingled along the nape of his neck. He swiveled in his seat, senses heightened. Striding through the door was the dark haired guy he'd noticed at the art museum.

"Who's that?" Ash asked.

"I don't know, but I have a feeling it's Bookwo—uh...Genna Lyndsey's old boyfriend from college."

"Now why would you have that feeling?" Ash's sardonic tone set him on edge.

"I just do," he bit out. Rick followed the man's movements as he weaved through the tables. He pulled out a nearby chair and seated himself in the far most corner near the pool table and leaned against the wall. His gaze drifted to Lorianne's form-fitting pink dress and the vacant chair next to her.

"Where's Genna?" Rick growled. Without waiting for an answer, he leaped to his feet and darted for the restrooms.

Genna stood against the wall, arms folded across her chest. Her attention focused on the doorknob to the ladies' room. Irritation ruptured through him. He rated less than a damn *doorknob*! After dismissing him with a quick glance, she said, "'*Silence is one great art of conversation.*'"

Frustrated with emotions, he could or would not identify, Rick pulled her startled body along his. "Sure," he said, unable to resist such a tempting morsel. "I'm all for silence."

His mouth descended onto hers, leaving her no chance for protest. Not that she had the opportunity to try. Shock left her mouth gaping open, and he took full advantage.

His tongue captured hers and he stroked it over with his-suckled, tasted, savored. Sweetness engulfed him. She clutched his shoulders. Surprise filled him when she angled closer. He'd expected a whack across the cheek. Surrender was the last thing he'd anticipated. Her mouth was hot, responsive. Her tongue tentative at first, but before long fire burned through her to him.

The effort to tear himself away was agonizing. It left his heart thundering in his chest. He pulled in a measured breath. "Nothing to say, Ms. Lyndsey?" Unable to hide the lower husky quality, he infused humor. Anything to conceal his heated reaction.

A long audible stream of air escaped. "*A cluttered mind is little better than an empty one.*"

He grinned, distinctly happy with the outcome. "I don't know about that," he whispered. He touched a soft, quick peck to her lips and stepped back. "I'll be waiting for you, waif." Now why had he said that?

Timing was everything. The ladies' room door opened and Selma Stotts strode out. She shot a speculative gaze over them. He quelled it with one of his own.

Battling an urge to tug Genna down on the infamous Pat's couch, he grasped her by the shoulders instead, and pushed her gently towards the open door. He didn't wait to hear it latch. It had taken all his strength to stop with one simple kiss. Simple—sure.

Masking a grin, Rick sauntered back into the bar and stood just beyond the swinging doors. It was as good a spot as any to observe the alleged college boyfriend. He was pretty, all right, with dark curling hair cut short. Features so perfect, so symmetrical, that any more delicacy would have made him too beautiful for a man. Rick grunted out a laugh. It would appear his only physical downfall was his height. Five seven or so. Rick scowled. Of course, Genna being so tiny would have made them an ideal couple.

He shot the alleged boyfriend a look so fierce it drew his startled gaze. Pretty Boy's look cleared and his eyes narrowed. Rick continued his stare-down. He didn't give a shit how anyone perceived it. Rick pulled his shoulders back and straightened. His scowl was so intent on his subject, he grunted, surprised when Genna rounded the corner right into his chest, stepping on his toe. "For such a little thing, you sure can hand out the bruises," he mumbled, steadying her. "What the hell are you wearing?" He felt like he'd just been knifed in the foot.

"Ooh." Wisps of hair escaped its hold.

Vulnerability stemmed from her. Something hard cracked within him. It was so pronounced; the effect was physical. The soft scent of wild honeysuckle threatened to drop him to his knees and press his lips to her belly. Blood rushed to the obvious appendages. Hopefully, no one would notice.

Pretty Boy would have to go through a rocky mountain to get to her. He almost grinned outright at her red face. Hell, he wanted to kiss her again. That moment set a resolve in him to claim her. Completely.

"What are you doing here?" She demanded, her voice lowering.

He was hard pressed to keep a straight face. "Isn't it obvious?" He shot back.

"'*Clumsy* pest-ing *is no joke!*'"

He couldn't help it. He grinned. Cognizant of trying to keep her attention from Pretty Boy, he baited her. "I believe the proper phrase is '*Clumsy* jesting *is no joke.*' You know, from Fables *The Ass and the Lapdog.* Aesop, 6th Century B.C." He took great pleasure in upping her.

"I know what it is; I modified it to suit me!" More tendrils slipped free when she tossed her head. Damn, if he didn't want to run his tongue along her mouth and feather her neck with his lips. Seeing that unruly hair trying to escape its confinement at the back of her neck teased him. Tempted him into setting it free. Set her free. She had no idea the extent of her allure. His lower regions did, however.

Over her shoulder, Rick could see they'd attracted the attention of the alleged college boyfriend, along with half the town. He battled to keep her attention, but she managed to glance around. It was enough. She stiffened when she caught sight of *him.*

GENNA THOUGHT HER HEAD would likely explode before she

could take refuge in her small bedroom and curl up. Toddy Wilson asking her out, if that wasn't enough, yuck. Rick something-or-other kissing her, *again*. Any coherent thoughts jumbled into mush. And now, Damon Wharton, of all people, had the nerve to invade her life.

All she ever desired was to make her little bookstore a success. And read. Live through other people's lives—through their words. Was that so much to ask? Well, it wasn't above her to admit defeat in Rick Whoever's kisses. Somehow they made her forget where she was, what she was doing, where she was going, what his name was. But...oh...why couldn't people just leave her alone?

Panic threatened to swallow her. Her pulse beat so erratically she thought she might faint. And she was *not* the fainting kind. Beads of moisture gathered on her forehead. She wasn't strong like Lorianne. All that tension...it was too much. She'd run out the door but for the ridiculously tall shoes she wore. No one could run in four-inch heels except...well, models and cosmetic counter women. And, possibly, women who worked in downtown areas of much bigger cities when they hailed a cab or something. And, Lorianne. But not her.

Genna just wanted to be home, in her favorite chair, in her favorite pajamas, with her current love, *When You Are Engulfed In Flames*, by David Sedaris. That's all. She might have to rethink reading that particular book. But there were plenty of others.

Regardless, it seemed she was to be inundated by unwanted emotion from every possible angle. And, almost every one of them, right in this very bar. And she never went to bars. After tonight, she vowed, she wouldn't ever again.

"Genna?"

Rick's deep masculine voice jolted her from her fog. She could feel the blood drain from her face. She spun around, hysteria so close to the surface she could hardly contain a scream. She'd almost forgotten him in her dread of seeing Damon. She yanked her arm free, and despite the four-inch heels, found herself running for Lorianne.

Lorianne, her best friend in the whole world. Lorianne, who kept her safe from unwanted people crowding her with unwanted emotions. Unwanted Damon.

But most of all, unwanted kisses.

CHAPTER 16

RICK GAPED AT THE terror on Genna's face. She'd slipped free of his grasp before he could fathom what was happening. She stumbled toward her friend sitting at the bar. Heads leaned together, positive she was enlightening her about the alleged college boyfriend, which obviously wasn't alleged any longer, based on Lorianne's reaction.

Her hostility radiated across the bar. She was a warrior, and she would fight for Genna. That thought eased his apprehension some.

Rick edged his way back to the table where Ash waited. Half the patrons in the place were gaping at him, the other half spinning tales regarding Genna and Lorianne's fevered whispers.

"What was that about?" Humor filled Ash's voice.

Rick glared at him. "I'm not sure." He kept his tone level, but he couldn't completely contain a growl, and pulled out his wallet.

"I've got it," Ash said. He wasn't laughing, but his lips twitched.

"Thanks." Rick stuffed his wallet back in his pocket.

"Hi, Rick." He started at the sultry intonation, lifted his eyes and contemplated the black tiles on the ceiling.

Ramona's husky, seductive voice made him cringe. He'd forgotten to call her. He shifted, finally settling a gaze on her. "Ramona."

"I guess your new case has had you *tied* up a bit." Her emphasis on tied had him narrowing his eyes. She had no idea. "I'm surprised to see you out and about."

Her black hair gleamed in the low bar lights. She was dressed to-the-nines-perfect. Skin-tight jeans hugged slim hips way below the actual waistline, tall sandals lengthening long legs. Her low cut blouse, turquoise satin trimmed with rhinestones, proudly displayed her deep cleavage. It was difficult to believe she was a college professor. She slid into the booth, crowding Rick.

Ash stood. "Later, Rick." He was gone before Rick said a word. Coward.

Rick shot a quick glance over his shoulder. Genna looked his way, brilliant pooled eyes narrowed on his current tablemate. Lorianne threw some bills on the bar. Self-control solidly in place, he compressed his lips and watched Lorianne storm out the door, Genna in tow.

Hell. He would kill Ash for deserting him like this. He'd vanished like the public's confidence in a bad economy.

Guilt kept him from following them—that, and the fact, that he would have had to climb over Ramona. He might as well take the opportunity to divest himself of at least one complication.

Several other customers moved toward the same goal, paying their tabs readying to leave, pretty boy included. The party had ended.

"Ramona, we need to talk..." he started.

Long, slender fingers, with French manicured tips, grasped his arm.

Her head fell against the booth. Dark, sultry eyes bore into him. Memory of Genna's soft lips brought a rare and inconceivable flush to his face. Yet, he met her eyes candidly, aware he'd made his choice. Logic, be damned.

She purred like a cat. "It's been several days since I've seen you. I wanted to show my appreciation for my birthday present." Her bottom lip poked out in a pout. He hadn't noticed how thin her lips were before. "I-I feel I must have come across somewhat ungrateful."

"Ungrateful?" He'd missed something. Her ill-timed visit seemed contrived. His gaze remained contemplative, impassive. He found himself comparing her experienced seduction to Genna's natural allurement. Heavy perfume saturated the air, suffocating. How had he stood it before?

One hand landed on his knee beneath the table, kneading his leg in a rhythmic motion. Her touch had a surprising, yet opposite, effect than he'd imagined. He tensed. Repulsed...and staggered by his reaction.

"Ramona?"

"I've missed you." Her voice resembled a velvet murmur.

His gaze rested on her, cool and detached. Then a thought occurred to him. "Who gave you the *History of the Inductive Sciences* volumes?"

Her hand stilled on his leg. "Excuse me?" An evasive tactic, he'd used it himself.

Her hand inched up his leg, but he clamped a hand on her wrist and brought her hand above the table. Nothing stirred. He closed his eyes and asked again, "Who gave you the *History of the Inductive Sciences* volumes?"

She leaned forward, her breath teased his neck. Her lips touched his neck. She ran a tongue to his ear lobe. She sucked on it. She might be sexy but all he could see was shocked hurt glittering in midnight-blue eyes.

Flicking his open, breath sharp, he demanded, "Who?"

She stopped and flung her head back in defiance. "The

Dean. It was nothing."

"When did he give them to you?" His eyes pierced hers, his voice stayed low.

"What difference does it make? I'm telling you now." Pouty lips protruded, her trademark he realized.

"When?" His voice turned cold, yet quiet.

She said nothing.

"Did they pass you on the promotion?" He asked, ominously.

Her eyes flashed fire. He slid her bodily from the booth, deposited her on the other side. He braced his hands on the table, towering over her.

His voice remained low and calm, controlled. "That's it, isn't it? Did you sleep with him, Ramona?" He let go of his breath. He already knew the answer. "You sold yourself short," he told her. He walked out, but guilt cloaked him. She wasn't the only one who had cheated. His just hadn't turned physical.

Yet.

Ash sauntered across the street and leaned next to the big oak tree on Bloomington Medical Center's lawn, northeast of Town Hall. He had a clear vision of the patrons leaving Pat's and maintained a quiet vigil.

The wait wasn't long. Lorianne and Genna were two of the first to sail through the door into the cool night air. Lorianne's hair flowed like a white stream of moonlight in the glow of the streetlamps. She had her arm wrapped around her friend in a protective shield.

Their voices bounded off the pavement like an amphitheater.

"Don't worry about him," Lorianne said. Her voice was low and comforting. They were close friends. He squelched any notion of jealously.

"I don't think either one of us should be there alone for a

while." That was her friend, Genna. "That's going to be tough for you, you know."

Lorianne's quick laugh filled the empty street. "It hasn't been too bad for the last few days. I expect I can keep up with you. For a short time, anyway."

Genna laughed too. It was sweet and unassuming. Something he found he'd missed—laughter. "Do you think he's the one who locked you in the basement?" Genna had turned serious.

Ash wasn't certain he heard correctly. He strained forward wrinkling his brow. Locked in the basement? What the hell were they talking about? Is that what Joanna Bakely meant?

"I don't know. It's hard to tell, really. It all seems so outrageous. He doesn't deal with people in a very direct manner, does he?" Lorianne said.

"What do you suppose they were looking for?"

"I wish I knew. I wonder if it could be more than one." Their footsteps clicked over the pavement.

"Don't ever make me wear tall shoes like this again if we're going to be walking on cement…"

Ash smiled.

Lorianne's gentle laughter rippled through the air again, fading as they rounded the corner towards Town Square. He started to step forward when someone else came out of Pat's.

"Well, well, well," Ash said softly. If it wasn't the old boyfriend. Genna's? He wasn't so sure. If he'd been Genna's and she was done with him, Ash wouldn't put it past the weasel to hit on Lorianne next. That's what he would do.

The boyfriend ambled along the street. But instead of heading the same direction as Lorianne and her friend, he started south, past the Community Theatre to Queen's Way. Ash pushed away from the oak tree and contemplated his next move, following slowly.

Ash reached the town square at the corner of Pine and Main and stood back out of the streetlight, in the shadows, exactly where he belonged, and watched.

Lorianne's blonde hair wisped in the wind as she and Genna crossed a grassy green in front of the municipal offices. The engine fired, and the reflection of the lights appeared.

He slowly exhaled the breath he hadn't realized he'd been holding. Movement from a block south at Pine and Queen's Way snagged his attention. Window-shopping after hours sounded just the thing. He wasn't likely to get much sleep, regardless.

CHAPTER 17

"OUR VIRTUES ARE MOST frequently but vices in disguise.'" Genna put her hands to her head. "How do people do this all the time?"

"Cut the dramatics. Hell, you only had two, and you didn't even finish the second one."

Eyeing the proffered cup Lorianne held toward her, Genna snatched it from her grasp. Strongly brewed coffee filled her senses, warmed her palms. "What time is it?" She sipped. It was perfect.

"Seven. The construction boys aren't due until nine."

Genna frowned. "What are you doing here?"

"You needed me. I slept in the spare bedroom. I love it there, anyway."

"Hmm." Genna considered her answer. "It doesn't have anything to do with the fact that Ashton Turner showed up at Pat's last night does it?"

Lorianne didn't respond.

"Yeah, I thought so." Genna took another sip. "This is good, maybe you should move in."

"Very funny."

Wistfulness stole over Genna, watching Lorianne wander to

the dresser. She examined the various pictures, stopping at one in particular. Genna knew the exact one she was looking at. The one where she stood with her parents the day she'd graduated from high school. Shoulders drawn up, her timidity belied by a huge smile, Genna's head was tilted up, her flat cap sliding off behind. The gold and black tassel dangled in her face. She'd been so happy. She'd stared at that same picture a million times.

Lorianne broke into her thoughts. "What happened last night when you disappeared in such a hurry to the ladies' room? You left Toddy hanging. Not only hanging, but hanging all over me. But not *for* me. He wanted to know all kinds of stuff about you. It was kind of embarrassing *and* disgusting. He smells. Why doesn't he take a shower or something?"

"*'What does not kill me makes me stronger.'*"

Lorianne lifted her gaze and met Genna's eyes in the mirror. She spun around, sputtering, "Oh, my God! Toddy hit on you. How long has he been asking you out?"

Genna's embarrassment turned to annoyance. "Too long, and he won't take no for an answer." Her lips thinned.

Stunned silence filled the room, followed quickly by Lorianne's burst of laughter.

"That was a nice change of subject," Genna accused.

"I don't know what you are talking about," Lorianne said, placing the picture back on the dresser.

Genna eyed her carefully. Lorianne was running her finger along the edge.

"Yes, you do. Where was he sitting?"

"In a booth by the windows." Lorianne examined her fingers. "You need to dust in here."

"You're hired. Did he talk to you?"

"No! I'm never talking to him again."

"I guess we did have to make a quick getaway because of that stupid Damon." Thoughtfully, she ventured. "Do you think he might be stalking me?"

"Probably." Lorianne turned back to the photos. "Ashton must have been there the whole time. Otherwise, I would have seen him come in." She spoke in a broken whisper. Genna strained to hear her.

Downing the rest of her coffee, Genna jumped out of bed and went to her. Planting both hands on her shoulders, she swung Lorianne around. "I'll beat the crap out of him if it will make you feel better. And I won't be afraid." Though she was teasing, she really did feel like she could kick his...his butt!

"I could feel him staring at me during the town council meeting." Lorianne sniffed.

"Well, what did you expect? You were the prettiest one there. You didn't expect him to stare at Ida Finch, did you?" Genna pulled her into a quick hug. "Come on, let's eat. I'm starving."

Lorianne gaze narrowed on her. "Did you just say crap?"

CHAPTER 18

"I think we need to clear this shelf and tear it out. That way we can widen the entry to the other portion of building. This small door to get in the coffee shop just won't be big enough. What do you think, Lorianne?" Genna stood, hands on her hips, and surveyed the shelf. It was eight feet high and at least, six feet wide. A lot of books would fit in that space.

The shelf currently housed the growing sexual awareness section. Along with the cookbooks, travel, and sale and clearance items. They would have to be stored in the basement to complete the remodel. "We need to have the carpenters repair the stairway railing while they're here, too."

"I thought all of that was settled weeks ago," Lorianne said.

"It was," she sighed. "I was just saying it to say it."

"Oh. Well, then, I think it's a great idea."

"Can you handle things here while I run next door? I want to go over the plans with Lewis."

The doorbell tinkled. It was time for Mrs. Bakely's next installment of three books.

Lorianne lowered her voice to a whisper, "I think so."

"'*He that can have patience can have what he will.*'" Genna glared at her, but Lorianne's attention was back on the computer screen.

Lorianne responded with an unladylike snort.

Genna shook her head and stalked out the front door. She rounded the corner to the south side of the building. Construction on the Turner project was in full swing. Jackhammers vibrated the ground beneath her feet, shaking up a concrete dust fog. She followed the sidewalk to the expansion space. It looked nothing like the spectacle going on across the street. The door was a block of wood with a bolt on it. Once the remodel was completed, it would serve as an emergency fire exit. Genna pushed on the door and went in.

Lewis Peale was not hard to spot. His large, black, muscular frame hovered in the corner where new copper pipes for the coffee shop's plumbing had been installed. Lewis was in his early forties. A small gap between his front teeth was further defined by one gold cap, his head shiny and bald. A virtual tower of a man, he rose over six feet, seven inches.

Genna had known him her whole life. She was a toddler when her parents began hiring him for odd jobs, back in his early twenties. They'd helped him finance his own business. That business had flourished and grown. Lewis was in great demand. But she knew she was special. Always an extra pair of eyes looking after her, whether it was making sure she'd made it home from grade school or keeping stray boy-dogs scattered and running the other direction through her junior high years. He could be quite intimidating.

"Hey, Genna-girl, how's it hanging?" he smiled, his one gold cap reflecting the morning sun. Thank goodness the rain had ceased.

"Nothing's hanging, Lewis. But that's why you're here—to make sure things get hung." Genna glanced around. Ladders were poised and ready for the painting crew. Drop cloths wadded in one corner, various tools in another, begging for skilled hands to work their magic. "What time is the crew due to start?"

"Should be here by nine."

Genna dug out her list for miscellaneous tasks, one that included the rickety basement railing.

"That's already been discussed, decided and approved, missy," he told her.

Genna stood back and looked up at him. Way up. She shoved her glasses on her nose, and scrunched her eyebrows together.

"What' chu worried 'bout, girl?"

She squirmed under his intense scrutiny. "'*A goal without a plan is just a wish,*'" she said.

"Don' hand me that quotin' stuff. Yer worried 'bout sumpnin' and I wanna know what it is."

"It's nothing. I'm just excited about the business growing, that's all."

"You don't wanna talk 'bout it to ole Lewis, that's fine. Now git on outta here so's I can git to work." Genna made an acute effort not to huff as she backed toward the door, wondering how it would all come together. There was so much to do. She stopped in the middle of the room.

Her plan to have the internet café completed by late summer needed to coincide with the fall semester for the college and high school students. She circled the area, considering walls already stripped, waiting to be textured and painted. Wiring rewired, light fixtures not yet installed, countertops and cabinetry for the coffee area. There was still the door to be widened between the two spaces. Overwhelming. An impossible task.

She had to trust Lewis would get it done. He darted an impatient look at her and she hurried outside. She paused a moment on the sidewalk to take in the cool morning air. It felt fresh and new. Things were going to be okay. Their luck would turn around. Lewis would make sure everything was safe going forward. His very size practically guaranteed it.

From the corner of her eye, she spotted Ida Finch, hands full, fumbling with the keys to her craft store. She rushed over. "Here, let me help you with that, Mrs. Finch." Genna unloaded Ida's arms of a box that was certainly too heavy for her to carry.

"Thank you, dear." Mrs. Finch unlocked her door.

"What do you have in here, Mrs. Finch? Rocks?" Genna inquired, trying to peer in the box. Clear packing tape obscured her view.

"Crafts, dear. I have a craft store." Ida held the door open allowing her to pass.

Genna grinned. "Where would you like me to set it?"

"Behind the counter is fine. What brings you out so early?"

"I wanted to meet with Lewis. He's working on the expansion. Lorianne is minding the store."

"Oh my. It's a bit untimely for her, isn't it?"

Giggling, Genna refused to deny or confirm the statement.

"I must say I am very excited about having coffee nearby, dear. I won't have to walk all the way down the block and around the corner to Plank's once your café is open."

"Yes. But you're so energetic, that stroll is nothing for you, and you know it." She left off the fact that access to the café would still be at the end of the street.

"Too true." Ida slipped behind the counter and produced a large box knife. She ripped the poor box to shreds. "Has Plank said anything derogatory about your new coffee shop? I didn't think of it at the time, but it will be competition for him."

"Oh, you know Mr. Plank, he never says much of anything. That's one quiet German. Besides, we're targeting different markets, regardless." Genna paused. "I've been thinking of something I can use for the new coffee shop."

"Anything I can help with?"

"Yes. I have an idea that I thought you could help with.

What would you think of putting the letters 'R' and 'I' on coffee cups. Maybe in different colors. You know, for Renewed Interest."

Ida tapped one finger on her wrinkled cheek. "You could take it a step further," she said slowly. "Make the 'R' and the 'I' extra-large, and in smaller letters finish out other words. Like Romantic Idol or Rarely Impractical or Really Impatient." Ida chuckled at her own joke.

"Hmm, it is a cute idea. I'll run it by Lorianne, see what we can come up with, and let you know."

"I'll fix up a couple to show you dear and drop them by," Ida said.

"Thank you, Mrs. Finch. It's a terrific idea." Genna went to the door. "I'd best get back."

FROM HIS CORNER OFFICE on the third floor, Ashton clearly witnessed any comings and goings of Bloomington's Arts and Crafts. His current offices were just across the street to the east of Ida's. The corner view was Victor Town Park. It was a handy location. He could observe the progress of his new offices south of Genna Lyndsey's property.

Ash ran a palm over tired eyes. This project had not progressed as planned. He sighed. It would have made the perfect parking lot. But Joanna Bakely's unexpected offer of the other lot, well, it wasn't a total loss.

He chuckled when he caught sight of Genna's dark wild hair. She breezed down the walk. Something seemed different he couldn't quite put his finger on. It was an unusual sight to see her on the street in the broad light of day. He glanced at his watch, and it wasn't quite nine; the store was normally open by now.

Several men in white t-shirts and cargo pants filed into her expansion space. He supposed the chances for striking a deal with her were nil. When she raised a hand, greeting the painters, the change dawned on him. Her standard attire of faded jeans and wrinkled shirt were replaced by something a bit more fashionable and—bright. She sauntered to the corner and disappeared. As a hard-assed business owner, Ash had to admit admiration for her tenacity.

His research found her building supported by wood, better held up with toothpicks. The wiring had not been updated since the twenties. The whole scenario set it up for a disaster begging to happen. Now she was expanding. The space between her store and Ida's was not much better, but would, at least, force the construction to current code by law.

His offer had been flagrantly generous. That building was about to fall down around her ears, yet she didn't care. He couldn't deny the viability of her business in a small town. It was unique and useful in a town the size of Bloomington. Due diligence showed it offered something for everyone. Adding the internet café was a stroke of genius. It would cater to both the local college and high school community. He grinned. Even the perverted, if Reverend Colvert was to be believed.

He hadn't been in the store, but he'd had it scoped out. He knew the layout—from the number of bookshelves, to each and every category housed. His research had been thorough. The only thing he didn't know was how Lorianne Gentry figured in. The property was in Genna's name. It had passed from her great-grandmother, to her grandmother, to her mother, finally landing in her lap.

He suppressed a groan and shoved his hands in his pockets as he found himself assaulted with more thoughts of Lorianne. Lewis yelled something out the door before disappearing inside.

Calling Lorianne's house late last night had proved fruitless. She hadn't answered. Plagued by dreams, he'd waken, his hard-on spilled on his belly—and that was when he'd managed sleep at all.

Jesus, he hadn't had sex since he'd left Lorianne's bed one morning at three o'clock. *That* would have to change. Silky hair streaming through his fingers had him clenching a fist. He'd given up the chance to run a tongue along her collarbone, nuzzle the hollow of her neck. Blue eyes full of mischief, as she scraped fingernails over his chest, dipping lower to pleasure him. The groan escaped with the strain of an instant and painful arousal.

Sex. That's what he needed. He shook himself back to the problem at hand. Hand, brought a whole new set of thoughts. Well, hell.

He started to spin from the windows, but for some reason Joanna Bakely's piercing blues, so similar to Lorianne's, invaded his reflection. With startling clarity, it hit him. Granddaughter! Joanna Bakely must have been talking about Lorianne. But what had she meant by business owner? And danger?

Ash jerked up the phone. When he caught sight of the short, curly haired freak that had followed Lorianne and Genna out of Pat's the evening before, he dropped the phone back in the cradle with a deceptively gentle fall.

Ash's gaze followed his path, past Ida's shop door, on past the expansion space. He slowed his pace before continuing west to the corner near Renewed Interest. Eyes narrowed, Ash kept them trained on the scene below. Toddy Wilson emerged at the corner from another direction, seeming to startle him. Ash couldn't make out their facial expressions, but from where he stood, they appeared to say their hellos then moved on.

The college boyfriend meandered on east, through the light, crossing the street alongside the church. Toddy already disappeared from view past the construction zone, headed to the park, he supposed. It was the only destination in that direction.

Rick implied he was Genna's old boyfriend from college. Was he Genna's or Lorianne's? Something primitive and violent surged through him at that man touching Lorianne. In fact, it disturbed him greatly to think of any man touching Lorianne, save himself. At least until he found himself ready to relinquish said touch.

He moved behind the desk, dropped in the chair, and contemplated Lorianne's blue eyes. How similar they were to Joanna Bakely's. And something in the way they held their hands as well. If there was one thing Ashton knew, it was people. He would bet his new office that Lorianne had no idea Joanna was her grandmother. But why would Joanna Bakely hide information like that? And, from her granddaughter? What purpose did it serve?

Joanna failed miserably in hiding her fierce emotions where Lorianne was concerned. Whether it was the hungry way in which she'd watched her at the council meeting, or the well-timed dump from his chair she'd served him up in his own office.

Yes, Lorianne had no idea. Ash leaned back and steepled his fingers. That business about her being in danger needed clearing up. The hunch that he played a large part in the entire farce crippled him.

His secretary stuck her head around the door, startling him out of his musings. "Lewis Peale, line one."

"Thanks."

CHAPTER 19

GENNA SHOVED HER HAIR out of her face and looked at her hands. Disgusted, surely having left her face streaked in dirt, she surveyed the stacks of boxes she'd completed. A couple of more and she could stop for a bit. The shelf was almost empty; all that was left to pack was the erotica.

Lorianne's tapping pen penetrated her thoughts. "I'm ready for lunch, Genna. We should just order pizza."

"Really? Pizza?" She needed the packing tape.

"I'm starving."

"Why don't you go ahead and get lunch. I'm not hungry just yet. I need to finish up here. Only two more and I can get them in the basement."

"Don't try to take them down by yourself, it's too dangerous with that railing loose." Keys jangled.

"I won't."

"Are you sure you'll be okay? You're the one who said we shouldn't stay here alone." Lorianne hesitated.

"It's not for very long. Besides, Lewis and the painters are just on the other side of this wall. I'll scream bloody murder if a serial killer comes in." When Lorianne still didn't move, she said, "I can scream really loud."

"I guess."

That settled, the bell jangled Lorianne's departure. Genna went back to stacking the rest of the books from the soon-to-be dissipated shelf. The pounding of the occasional hammer and maybe an expletive or two, sounded through the wall. The laughter and chattering of foreign tongues made her smile. It was probably a good thing she didn't understand a word.

Armed with a black marker to label the boxes, she started her task with relish. A loud crash, cry of pain, and rapid-fire Spanish ripped through her. Panicked, she dropped the pen and shoved on the door next to the shelf.

Blocked. In a frantic pace, she snatched up her cell phone and punched in 911. Genna rushed out the front door and around the corner, the bookstore forgotten.

She pushed through the expansion space door, appalled at the scene. Three wiry Hispanic men stood over another sprawled on the floor. His leg twisted awkwardly beneath him. Blood covered the ground from a severe gash in his other leg.

"No, no, no," she whispered. She shoved her way through the men, and dropped on her knees beside the hurt man. Genna ran her fingers along his arm to his hand and squeezed gently. His eyes were closed, his olive skin pale. "He's dead!" she cried.

"Don't move him, *senorita*," someone said. She nodded. Her gaze never swayed from him. She rested the back of her hand on his forehead. Warm. She could make out a slight throb on his temple. Thank God. Relief sagged over her.

"He's not dead. He's not dead. He's not dead." If she kept repeating the words, they would be true.

RICK HAD BLOWN HIS opportunity to level with Genna— *chickened out, more like*—and she was going to be pissed. He had an obligation to be truthful with her. Her startled expression at Ramona's presence at Pat's the evening before was another nail in an already flat tire. Her parting expression kept him awake half the night.

He hurried down the street, anxious to set things right. He wanted her. And he couldn't have her until she knew exactly who he was.

Sirens pierced his preoccupied stupor. He reached the bookstore and tugged open the door. He started in, when flashing lights winked through the window to the south, the one showcasing Turner Development's new office complex.

He let go of the door, he dashed around the corner where an ambulance parallel parked in front of the building between the craft store and the book store. Apprehension speared him. Rick broke into a sprint. A crowd already gathered outside. When the gurney hit the ground, rattling against the concrete walk by the emergency technicians, Rick had a vision that had his heart stopping in his chest. *Genna hurt.*

He shoved his way past the onslaught of people through the door and took in the scene. An overturned ladder, three men of Mexican descent, and a fourth, lying on the floor with Genna on her knees beside the fallen man. She had a white-knuckled grip on his hand.

"Ma'am, clear the way, please. Let us through. Ma'am?"

Rick rushed forward and knelt down. "Genna, sweetheart, let go of his hand," he said, gently. He pulled her grasp from the unconscious man's and tugged her to her feet. Her legs failed to support her. He caught her up and cradled her like a child. Silent sobs racked her small frame.

"What happened?" Rick demanded. He could barely contain the fury. Fear for her engulfed him. She was so fragile, he was afraid he might crush her.

"I don't know. I don't know. I heard them talking and laughing from the shop. And the next thing I heard was a crash."

He buried his face in her hair. The fragrance fresh and wild and *innocent*.

There were other things to take care of right now. Important things. "I need to look around," he told her. "Will you be okay?"

He held her steady, allowed her legs to slide to the ground. He tilted her chin up and met her eyes. "Take a breath," he said. Passionate anger threatened to overrule his good sense; the desire to keep her safe, ferocious. But he needed to maintain a cool resolve to accomplish that goal. The claims on his desk reinforced his suspicions tenfold.

A large black man materialized in his line of sight. One hell of a *large* black man. Rick fixed him with a wary glance, but the gentle tone he directed to Genna reassured him. "Genna-girl, it's okay." It didn't stop Rick from tightening his lips when Genna surged from his embrace, throwing herself into the giant's muscular arms, burying her face in *his* shoulder.

"Oh, Lewis. I-I don't understand. What's happening?" Rick could hardly make out her mumbling.

"That was some quick thinkin' you done, girl. You done good." His voice was deep and steady. Assuring, consoling, comforting.

Rick debated his actions, taking in Genna's familiarity with the would-be linebacker, Lewis. His arms were massive, rigid and strong. Jealously seared his gut.

He'd let it go for now. Frowning, he turned from the two of them, and kicked a stray screw on the floor. He had to get control of himself. He wasn't doing anyone any good if he let his emotions rule him like a...a woman. Disgusted with such thoughts, he surveyed the surrounding area—inexplicably drawn to the overturned ladder.

Rick edged his way in that direction. It was a start. A lone worker ran his hand over the length of one leg. Rick observed him carefully—his expression, grim. Rick peered over the rungs himself, studying them. Searching for something...anything that would signify...what?

And then he saw it. Fourth rung from the top, split in half, covered in blood. Something like that didn't just happen. Someone sawed through the sucker. The injured man never stood a chance from that height. They were lucky the ladder hadn't landed on someone's head. This was no accident, this was deliberate.

"Don't touch anything," he barked. The man next to the ladder stood slowly, and nodded. He turned to his co-workers, rattling Spanish, fast and furious. They all stepped back, Rick's implication made clear. He turned to Lewis who still murmured quietly to Genna, his tone melodic.

Genna trembled like a leaf in a brisk wind. Her pale, waif-like face, stained with tears had tracks of dirt streaking her cheeks. He wanted to snatch her from his grip.

To Lewis, he snapped, "You know her?" Rick indicated Genna.

"We goes way back." His soft voice contrasted his physical stature overpoweringly. The uneducated grammar belied the shrewd look in his eyes. It spoke of an intense protection. Lewis pulled himself up to full height. Damn, he must be close to seven feet tall. His skin was a dark golden brown, his head shiny and smooth. Someone you'd want on your side. A sense of relief floated over him. He was not the enemy.

"You're going to need to suspend work, until the insurance company determines the circumstance." Rick gentled his tone, conscious of Genna's reaction to the defensive-end. This investigation had just taken a deadly turn.

Genna nodded, yet refrained from speaking. He could hardly stand to see the confusion and disappointment in her brilliant blue eyes behind those black nerdy glasses. The police came through the door. He let out a cursed breath. The essence of a long afternoon loomed ahead.

After a lengthy interview with the police, Genna let Lewis secure the dead bolt on the expansion space, and Rick walked her back to Renewed Interest. He didn't touch her, but stayed close. The gentle wind sent wild honeysuckle wafting over him. What was it about her that made him want to lock her away? Stash her in a protective bubble only he had access to?

Sawing through the rung of a ladder was serious business. He needed, no, *intended* to find out who was behind this destruction. Pulverizing a business, hurting innocent people in the process, destroying property was one thing, but this was a desperate attempt to get a point across. The question was why? He was certain now it wasn't Genna.

Faking her devastation by the construction worker's injuries was not her style. There was still the matter of the odd note he'd seen on the counter. How had that slipped his mind? His instincts usually served him better.

She remained quiet, standing aside while he opened the door. He followed her in, bolting it and flipping the sign to 'closed.'

No getting around this talk, he decided. "This was no accident."

She turned a startled glance on him. Her face was so pale he was terrified she might faint.

He captured her hands and pulled her into him. He led her to the worn sofa and tugged her onto his lap. Cradling her head to his chest calmed his own senses. He shut his eyes, willing danger away. Because that's what it was. Danger.

GENNA RESTED HER FOREHEAD against Rick's chest, against his pounding heart. She breathed deep, reveling in the scent of sandalwood and spice. Let his strength envelope her. How many years had it been since she'd felt the comfort of someone sharing her troubles? She was not a forward person by nature but his heat tempted her as she'd never been tempted. She wanted to rest her lips on the pulse in his neck, drown in its strong steady rhythm. Her eyes drifted closed, it would be so easy...

Let someone else wrestle with the responsibility of disaster. She was tired. Warmth flooded her face when she thought of sliding her hands beneath his shirt. Maybe unbuttoning the top clasp of his jeans, sliding the zipper down to reveal...How much like Damon *was* he? It was a question she never thought she'd want to ask anyone. Ever.

"I was hired by your insurance company to investigate your recent claims," he said.

"What?" Genna jerked her head from him, confused. Her confusion was followed quickly by stunned hurt. She struggled to comprehend the meaning of such an outrageous statement. Her mind spun with dread. She sprung from his lap, horrified at the lapse in restraint.

"*You're* the examiner?" Genna asked. Incredulity laced her tone. "Y-you think I'm sabotaging ..." she couldn't finish her sentence. Incredulity turned to anger — a scalding fury. Her hands clenched into fists as she fought to keep from pounding them against his chest. *He* thought she was sabotaging her own property. "Why? "What possible reason could I have for destroying my own business?"

Attention? Surely not. Insurance money? It sounded more...more man-justifiable! A spurt of hysteria threatened to erupt. Her insurance policy would barely cover the structure—much less replace inventory or loss of business. Even if that were the case, why would she remodel the adjoining space to expand?

Her gaze bore into Rick. He wasn't looking at her though. It was apparent his mind played on the possibility that she was out to destroy all of her own hard work from the last three years. Not to mention, a property that had been in her family for over *three generations*. Were all men really this stupid? Seething with rage, unable to help steady her breath, it expelled ragged and uneven. Anger scorched her control. "'*Everyone has a right to be stupid, some people just abuse the right.*'" Furious, she couldn't keep her trembling under control, nor the stifle of her silly quotes—her only line of defense—or habit of defense. She'd work on that, she vowed.

"What?" Fascinated with this new side of a fiery bookworm, Rick just gaped at her.

She paced the floor, face hot from fury. "I'll just place little nails in the floor to tear up customer's shoes while they wander the bookshelves. *Maybe* I've fixed the roof so a person can be tortured with water from the leaks. Here's an idea! I could make a CD of Turner's jack hammering for easy listening or...or set up black lights for better reading. Better yet, why don't I just cross the wires myself and *set the place on fire!*"

Genna knew she was out of line, but she felt so...so helpless. Her—the calm one. Her—the reasonable one.

"Are you sure you didn't cross the wires?"

"Oh! You big oaf!" She rounded on him. He caught her hands up in his before she was able to plant them on his jaw. She'd never been so angry in her life. Low key, shy to a fault, non-confrontational, unassuming bookstore owner. That's how people knew her. Not this angry, scared, termagant, muddled mess she acted when Rick Johnson was around.

"Settle down," he hissed.

Before she could tear herself from his bruising embrace, he crushed his mouth to hers. Her valiant efforts were useless. His mouth softened, his tongue invaded, melting her in the swish of hot breath and moist heat. She tried pushing him away, really, she did. But she just wanted one more moment, and pulled him closer instead. Her outer body started pulling away from her inner one. Disgusting. It's just, he tasted so good. Warm, safe, sexy.

No. It was fear. Fear made people do strange things. And she had no doubt how strangely she was behaving. Her outer body observed her surrender into him without reserve.

But there was something else, too. He clung to her. *Her*. His one arm wrapped her waist, the other locked across her shoulders, ironclad. As if she *could* move regardless of his hold on her.

Oh, what was the matter with her? This was insane. *She* was insane. She didn't want to kiss him. She didn't want to desire him. Desire! What a ridiculous word. Notion. Whatever! She didn't want anything to do with him, or anyone. Anger—common sense—surged forward. Okay, maybe he did kiss better than Damon. And, maybe she wondered what else he could do better than Damon, but only a little. Her outer body merged back in, and with it, acumen. She shook her head, and broke away.

She was awarded some satisfaction when he ran fingers, which were not so steady, through his hair. His chest heaved ragged. A surge of thrill pressed through her seeing he wasn't so unaffected. But she grasped her fury, with both hands. "*'Ordinarily he was insane, but he had lucid moments when he was merely stupid.*'" If only her tone weren't so irritatingly breathy.

His eyes narrowed, fingers stilled. "I know you didn't just call me stupid."

"What do you want from me?" she demanded. She planted both hands on his broad torso and pushed him out of the way. She stomped to the door, which had been locked long enough. He was out his mind. Insanity clear in her own mind, how else could she have let him kiss her? How else could her fingers itch to dig into his shoulders for more?

She had a business to run and people couldn't buy a used book if they couldn't get in the store. He snagged her before she reached it, spinning her around. He lifted and fitted her to him tightly. So tight she could feel the bulge in his pants. Her feet dangled above the floor. "A date."

She gaped at him. "I don't want to date you. I-I don't want to date anyone." His lips touched the column of her neck just below her ear. Hot breath sent unwanted shivers prickling her skin.

"Are you sure?" he whispered. His hand splayed across her lower back, pressing her further into him. His mouth trailed her jaw line, his other hand, managed its way under her shirt. He stroked her ribs, leaving a blaze of fire.

Her nipples tightened against her shirt, her breath came in rapid shallow gasps. Genna closed her eyes, but in her mind's eye, he sprawled over her, leaving nothing between them.

Her eyes flew open. She wasn't some young, naïve college co-ed any longer. She was a grown woman with a business. Now she had another disaster to contend with, and *he* thought she was responsible.

She almost stomped her foot in frustration, but her feet didn't reach the floor. She scrunched her nose. From the corner of her eye the sexual therapy books mocked her. She pushed her glasses up, and pressed her lips together. "Let me down."

He did so slowly.

With a shove against his chest she moved back and said, "Didn't I see the 'Sextacy' girl in your lap at Pat's?"

"'Sextacy' girl?" He repeated, confused. Yet, Genna noted the small blush creeping up his neck.

She should have felt triumphant, but it was dismay that clenched her insides. She thought he might like her, just a little. He was proving more like Damon every second she was in his presence.

She planted her hands on her hips and stared him down, rather up. "You know. Tall, dark, beautiful." She'd never been so angry in her life. Or hurt. Tears pricked her eyes but she refused to back down, or turn away. She glared at him. She'd rather die than cry in front of him.

It didn't surprise her when he ignored her accusation. He stared at her for a moment. There was a single mindedness about Rick Johnson, Insurance Fraud Claims Investigator that would drive some woman crazy, some day. *Just. Not. Her.*

"We need to talk about that letter," he said.

"What letter?" Both irritated and confused by the turn in conversation.

A rattle of the door handle startled the two of them.

CHAPTER 20

LORIANNE SLIPPED THE KEY in the lock of her small doll-like house. It was painted a cheery yellow and sadly in need of another coat. Large trees shaded a wooden porch where portions of the wood could be found rotting, if one looked too closely. She hadn't been home in several days, using Genna's as a refuge. But she needed to check on things.

She stood in the middle of the tiny living room and surveyed the various pairs of shoes where she'd stepped out of them. She should probably donate some. No one should have this many pairs of shoes. Gathering up at least four pairs, she clomped to the closet in the bedroom, stepping over another six pairs.

Lorianne collapsed in an obnoxious, cushy pink and purple chair and unbuckled the Mary Janes she had on. Said chair was covered in clothes and surprise—another pair of shoes. She tugged them from beneath her and pitched them toward the closet. Lessons could be had in housekeeping from Genna, no doubt. Aside from—dusting.

Heaving a sigh, she cleared the chair of all its contents in one swift swipe. Plopping down, she faced the bed, still rumpled from the last time she'd crawled out of it. It hurt to look at it. She knew Ashton's scent would still linger on the pillow. Oh, why did the jerk have to be so...so...

"You're a hard person to reach." His voice was deep and menacing.

Lorianne let out a startled scream. Instinct kicked in, she snatched the Mary Jane from her foot, and flung it at the doorway, with amazing accuracy.

It hit its mark, dead center.

"Oooh," Ashton grabbed his chest in pain. "Nice shot."

"What the hell are you doing here?" Lorianne found her voice, and her fury. "Waltzing in my house like you own it?"

"The door was open. Not smart." He leaned against the frame, and rubbed his chest. "I wanted to make sure everything was okay."

It pissed her off to see him so cool and collected. There was some measure of comfort in that little shot she took. "Okay? Oh, I'm okay." She'd found her sarcasm.

He ignored that. "I've been trying to call you."

"I haven't been home." She leaned back down and unlatched the other shoe. She kicked it off—a little harder than she'd planned. It flew across the room. She didn't look at him. Instead, she chose the coward's way out and hid in the closet. She needed taller shoes. For advantage.

"I want to see you again."

That statement brought Lorianne's head up with a jolt. She knocked it on a metal clothes rod. "Get the hell out." She rubbed the pained area.

"I said I want to see you again."

He had some fucking nerve. She dug around for, and found, a pair of gray satin platform, peep-toed pumps. They sported four and a half inch heels. They ought to help out nicely. She backed out of the closet aware of her undignified reentry. She slipped the shoes on and stood slowly—smoothed damp palms over her jeans. She faced him, head held high. Pride was a wonderful salve.

"Now you've seen me. You can leave."

His stare bore into her.

She squared her shoulders, lifted her chin.

"I'm not leaving."

Butterflies fluttered in her stomach, but if she didn't stand her ground, he'd mow her down. She moved directly in front of him, jabbed an index finger into his chest. Hard. "Well, your actions of inactions have made me wiser. And, *I* don't want to see *you* anymore." She tapped his chest, drilling her point into him. Too bad she hadn't thought to grab one of her Betsey Johnson spiked heeled numbers.

"What kind of mumbo gibberish is that?" Genuine confusion touched his expression. "Actions? Inactions? I don't get it."

"Just get out," she grated, and tried to brush past. "I know all you wanted from me was access to Genna's building." She poked him in the chest, again. "Well, it's her building and she doesn't want to sell. You can't scare me."

"Quit that." He grabbed her wrist. "What do you mean 'scare you'?"

"Who else would have locked me in the basement and ransacked the office? Although, I can't imagine what thought you might find." This last was said as an afterthought.

"Locked you in the basement?" He frowned.

"You left me there!" She was screaming.

"I don't know what you're talking about," he ground out.

"Oh, don't play innocent with me." Lorianne's attention snapped right back. "I read you loud and clear. I was easy and willing. But now I'm not."

"I offered her a more than fair price for her property."

"Some things are more important than money."

"Like what!" he demanded.

"Like legacy," she retorted. She lowered her voice, it was a struggle to keep it even and cool but she was pissed. She could feel the pain seeping through. She had no legacy.

For a moment Ashton looked as if he would argue that statement. Instead, he surprised her by stepping back. She slipped past him into the living room.

He changed the subject. "I've seen some guy following you around."

"Following me? What are you hallucinating about now?"

"You didn't use to be such a smart ass," he told her.

"Like you would know," she hissed. "Besides, I. Grew. Up." She enunciated the words.

He ignored her and grabbed her arm. "Some short, dark haired guy. He seems to be following you everywhere."

"He's not following me," she spat. "Now, let go." She snatched her hand from his.

"Then why is he everywhere you are?" His hand fell to his side.

"He's not everywhere I am. I'm here, aren't I? And he's not." Then to be fair, she said, "He's following Genna."

"Genna!" She had a hard time believing he was that astounded. "What would he be doing following a skinny, nerdy, wild-haired thing like her?" he snorted.

"He's her old boyfriend from college, and we don't know why he's following her around, but he is." Lorianne poked him in the chest again. "And don't you call her a skinny, nerdy, wild-haired thing!"

She narrowed her eyes, which appeared almost amused, on him. He put his hands out in a gesture of surrender. "Sorry."

"Tell me why Genna's really not interested in selling." He said it softly. Disgust filled her when she felt it tug at her heart.

She spun away. "It's all she has left of her parents, grandparents, *great*-grandparents." She began to pick up discarded clothing about the room, trying to focus on anything other than him, and the tears clogging her throat. She *hated* him.

"What do you mean?"

"Her parents were killed the day she graduated from high school." The actual words said aloud sickened her. Lorianne sat on the edge of the couch. "She was the smartest kid in her school. There was no question she would be class valedictorian. But traditionally, the valedictorian gives a speech, something she adamantly refused to do."

"Why?"

"Because she's shy. What do you care?"

"Maybe I've changed."

"Right," she snorted.

"Did she make the speech?" he asked her. His voice was…coaxing.

She watched him closely, gauging his sincerity. "Yes."

"What happened?"

She hesitated.

"I really want to know," he told her.

She looked at him, gauging his sincerity. She'd allow him the genuineness this time, and answered. "Somehow they'd convinced her to make the speech." Lorianne allowed a small smile at the picture she envisioned. "She spent hours at the library doing research on the phobia of speaking in front of people." She chuckled softly. "Can't you just imagine her studying news reports of people speaking before a camera where reporters were the audience?" She shook her head. "She probably studied performers on shows taped live to see how they handled the odd questions or practiced speeches." Tenderness gripped her insides. "That girl can research anything."

"I didn't know."

"Whew! She's a perfectionist." Lorianne paused. Then her voice dropped. "Anyway, she did make that speech. But on the way home, they were hit by a drunk driver. Her parents perished in the accident. She never even remembered the impact. She had to go to the library to find the article." Lorianne stifled the emotion, but it broke her heart to think of Genna so alone. She jerked away when she felt his hand on her cheek. He brushed away a tear she hadn't realized had fallen. She was surprised to see him sitting next to her. A dangerous place to be.

She moved back, shoved his hand away. Hardening her voice, her heart, she said, "She's the strongest person I know."

Then, with scathing accusation, she spat, "Men! She had *him* as a boyfriend. He did a real number on her too. She became more introverted. Now she uses these ridiculous quotes to keep anyone from getting too close. Sometimes I get really annoyed. But sometimes it's funny, and I understand. She's tough, and she's strong."

Ashton edged closer.

She saw the maneuver and stood, stepped back. "Now, for some reason he's popped up out of the blue. Weird stuff is happening to our business." She studied him for a moment. "It's almost like someone's hired someone to sabotage…" Her voice faded, suspicion filled her.

"Weird stuff?" He repeated. But he was drawing a deadly caress with his finger down the front of her shirt. Her breath caught when the top button flicked open…and with such expertise. Lorianne stilled. Dared not move when he leaned toward her. When she felt his tongue touch her between her breasts, she swayed forward—but snapped to her senses before she fell under his sorcerer's spell.

She jumped back, anger returning full force. "It's time for you to leave."

"I've missed you," he whispered. He sounded like he meant it, but she knew better. Why now?

"Get out," she sneered, pointing to the door, irritated with her shaking fingers. She kept her voice hard and cold.

He stood too and pulled her to him for a quick hard kiss. "We're not done," he told her.

"That's what you think," she mocked. He let her go so suddenly she stumbled back. But he wasn't watching—he'd barged out the front door.

Her shoulders hunched at the slam. How would she survive another onslaught of him? The snake would just sliver out of her life again, and she had no intention of putting herself through that misery a second time.

She kicked off the ridiculously outrageous pumps she no longer needed, stomped to the closet, and dug around in the closet for some flats.

She skipped lunch.

ASH WINCED WHEN WOOD hit wood. God, he'd wanted to throw her on the bed and fuck her brains out. More like fill his hands with perfect breasts, use his tongue for more than mere kissing. When he'd found himself sitting next to her on the sofa, he'd scarcely been able to resist such allure. He wanted to spread her wide, dip his head, and stroke her inside out with his tongue. He *would* have that...*her*...again.

It had taken everything he'd had to go through that door. One thing had become blatantly clear—she wasn't completely immune to him. He'd have to devise an attack. He needed a clear concise plan.

Disgusted, he wondered when she'd penetrated that deeply under his skin. She hadn't really gotten over him. But when he couldn't sleep, eat, think without her image devouring his mind and other senses every waking moment, he definitely needed a plan.

He frowned. She was a cool one. Well, he was experienced, and he had a decided advantage. *He* knew what she liked. And she'd be begging for him before he was finished with her.

He cut off the thoughts with an ax. Right now there were other, more important, matters to attend to. He wanted answers, and he knew where to get them. He flipped open his cell.

"We need to meet," he said tersely. "Fifteen minutes. Pat's." He snapped the phone shut.

Daylight or no, he needed a drink.

CHAPTER 21

"GENNA, DEAR, ARE YOU okay?" Joanna's surprise couldn't have been greater.

Her dark blues eyes sparkled with something Joanna couldn't define. Cheeks flushed, stance rebellious, hair unruly—well, she'd seen her hair like that before. But it was the fierce defiance in her eye and heightened color that drew Joanna's curiosity.

She'd discarded the scruffy jeans with holes, and the bland colored tee for a ribbed, button-down sweater in a vibrant hue of mulberry. She looked...well, beautiful.

"Is everything okay, Genna? Dear?" she asked again, keeping her tone mild. Something stirred up a hornet's nest. The young man who'd just stormed out was the likely culprit. He appeared to be suffering from the same affliction. She wanted to smile, but managed to contain it to a twitch of her lips.

"Of...of course."

She watched Genna struggle with...*temper*? That didn't seem very likely. Genna was the most *even*-tempered young person she'd had the privilege of knowing. Her steady influence on Lorianne allowed Joanna peaceful sleep at night.

"Is there something I can help you with?" Her smile

threatened again, but knowing it would offend Genna, she stifled it back.

"N-no th-thank you."

Joanna started as a thought took hold. She narrowed eyes on Genna's pressed lips. "Did that Reverend Colvert come back and harass you?" she demanded. She would personally strangle the good Reverend.

"What! No. Nothing like that, Mrs. Bakely." Genna's genuine surprise reassured her.

Joanna let out a slow breath. "Then what is it, dear?"

Genna strode to the counter. "I found another author you might enjoy, Mrs. Bakely."

Though Genna's breathing still labored, Joanna accepted the change in subject like the good sport she was. "Who is that, dear?"

Genna exhaled slowly before answering, "Sabrina Jeffries. She has a really cute line of stories on school heiresses."

"Oh, yes. I've read her. She's excellent. Conflict, conflict, conflict. Up to the very last page. Makes for a terrific story, of course."

Genna disappeared from view, rummaging beneath the counter. Once she emerged, it looked as if her usual even-keeled self was securely in place except for the slight flush dotting her cheeks. All that was needed to complete her normalcy was an appropriate quote, which somehow never came forth.

Joanna reached for the two paperbacks, thumbing through them with experienced nonchalance. "Thank you, dear," she murmured.

She burned to confide Lorianne's parentage to Genna, but the courage failed her. She yearned to know how much Lorianne divulged to Genna. Joanna wondered how much Lorianne knew of her father, or her father's family. Doubt plagued her as deep as the ocean. Bridging the chasm with her granddaughter was as unreachable as touching an actual star. For all Joanna had in her life, Lorianne's trust and love were the things she knew her money couldn't buy.

The door signaled another customer, startling Joanna. She withdrew to the historical section. Regency. She loved Regency. It reminded her of Victor, and a sense of melancholy settled over her.

"Hello, Toddy," Genna said. "I have a new Sci-fi for you. *Nature of the Beast*. It's by Richard Fawkes. Part of a military series..." Her voice faded. She didn't sound too enthusiastic.

"That sounds good, I guess."

Joanna listened to the exchange with half an ear. She had to find some way to tell Lorianne. She wanted to be a grandmother to her granddaughter. It was long past time to set things right. They were all each other had left.

"...out soon." Joanna tuned them out, trying to decide the best way to approach Genna regarding the dilemma with Lorianne. "...in common." If Lorianne trusted anyone, it was Genna. Somehow Joanna had to enlist her help. Genna had a level head on her shoulders. If anyone could aid in the silent war Joanna had waged on herself, it was Genna. "...not good enough..." Joanna browsed the shelf without seeing anything, just her own doubt and fears.

"...enough, Toddy. I've already told you, there is no tomorrow." Genna's sharp tone jolted Joanna out of her fog. She frowned. Hearing Genna raise her voice was an unusual, disturbing occurrence.

The bell jangled again. "Oh, not now!" Genna's natural calm resembled an apparition. Gone in a puff of smoke. Her frustration reached a new level.

Joanna peeked around the corner in time to witness Genna's annoyance before she turned from the new character. He was new in town, she'd never seen him before. Toddy Wilson, whose hair was almost as wild as Genna's, wore baggy jeans that were dirty and wrinkled, his black t-shirt, the same. He still wore wire-framed glasses held together with tape. They slid down his nose. She wondered why his mother didn't appeal to him to dress better.

Joanna cringed. That's what had gotten her into trouble with her own son all those years ago—trying to manage Peter, whether he needed it or not. She made a silent vow to give Beatrice Wilson a break in the future. After all, Toddy had to be nearing thirty.

The new customer, dressed impeccably, was attractive, though he lacked height. Not a hair registered out of place. Surprising, when you considered his curls. A childlike smile struck her as boyish affection. But the intensity of his eyes on Genna disturbed Joanna.

Joanna sensed a façade that hid something dire. Yet, the contrast between the two men separated their differences on the spectrum. The dark end of the spectrum.

Genna spun from the new customer back to Toddy. Lips pursed, hand on her hip, her eyes glittered dangerously. Her fists were clenched so tightly, Joanna thought she might punch one of the two men in the nose. This was a side of Genna most people did not witness, and it surprised her. She felt almost sorry for them. Almost.

"Genna, dear," Joanna started. Both young men, clearly startled, jerked their gazes her way, simultaneously. She stifled a grin at their dismay. Directing a pleasant, questioning tone toward Genna, she asked, "Have you heard of this Eloisa James? These look awful intriguing," she said, waving two books. Joanna had read almost all of Eloisa James and loved them.

Relief in Genna's shoulders was palpable.

"Oh, yes, Mrs. Bakely, she's quite terrific. I believe I have several more of hers that have yet to be logged. She usually has two heroines. In her latest one, there is a ten-year-old child, quite precocious." Her eyes narrowed at Genna's babbling.

"Would it be much trouble to see them, dear?"

"No, of course not," she breathed. Genna darted around the counter a second time and disappeared below.

Joanna kept an open, blatant gaze on the young men. She took some pride in making them uncomfortable. Just her little contribution. Something was off about the whole situation. Lorianne may be her legitimate granddaughter but she happily absorbed Genna as a surrogate. Whether they knew it or not these girls needed her, and she meant to be there for them. Both of them.

The attractive, shorter man swung his gaze from Joanna to Genna, then raised his hand in a quick wave, and backed out the way he came in.

Hesitating for a brief moment, Toddy moved to the door as well. "I'll come back later, Genna. We'll work out that date." His face contorted with an unnatural anger that gave him a silly dwarf-like appearance.

Joanna was especially proud when Genna stabbed her gaze on him like a sharp blade, and said with firm resolve, "There's no date, Toddy. Not now, not ever." Once the bell indicated his departure, Genna turned a blinding smile on Joanna.

Joanna smiled back. Yes, she was very proud.

ANGRY NONE OF HIS tactics worked, he stepped outside and squinted in the bright warm sunshine. How could Genna treat him like he didn't exist? It had taken him years to step up and let her know how he felt.

She hadn't said anything about his note either. He *was* the choice for her.

He swiped damp palms down his shirt. Maybe Lorianne threw it away. She was probably getting even with him for locking her in the basement. He hadn't even realized she was frightened of the dark. Secretly, it gave him a thrill like he'd never known. A sense of power.

He loved Genna. If he could just talk to her. *Really* talk to her, he knew she would understand the mistakes he'd made. He'd be ready for the next opportunity. Panic swarmed him, creating another consuming hunger. What if there wasn't another opportunity?

He fought down that hunger—it would sink him in the end. He needed *ice*. *Ice* was his friend. He'd managed without it for almost a week now. His mouth watered, and he shoved his hand in his pocket to still the sudden trembling. He closed his eyes as the power he'd felt a second ago descended into an endless black elevator shaft. His heart rate shot up. Sweat gathered along the edge of his shirt. He tugged it away.

Experience told him he did not have much time. The fix. He wanted, no needed the *fix*. It was the only way to silence its physical hold. But he could handle it.

With strained effort, he placed a bland smile on his face and raised his other hand in greeting Selma Stotts, and strolled north toward Town Square.

CHAPTER 22

PAT'S WAS DARK, THOUGH the sun glittered brilliantly outside. The lunch crowd long gone, too early for happy hour, the place was practically deserted. Save for old Amos sitting in a far corner of the bar.

"What the hell is going on?" Ash demanded.

Seconds passed while Rick waited for his eyesight to adjust to the dark interior after the blinding sunlight. Ash lounged in a booth, both hands wrapped around a mug of beer. "What are you talking about? And keep your voice down."

"Lorianne locked in the basement at the bookstore, for one thing," he growled. "She accused *me* of locking her in."

Rick marveled at Ash's outrage, thrilled. His reaction deflected guilt, right?

"She told you that?" He pierced Ash with reservation, not ready to lay his cards on the table.

"And, what the hell is this business about a stalker?" He sounded almost afraid, further dispelling Rick's suspicions. "She said he was stalking her friend, but I find *that* hard to believe. I mean, look at the two of them. Which one would you stalk?"

"Watch what you say, *friend*." Fury surfaced to the threshold, but Ash's reaction to Lorianne's incident held his wrath in check.

Ash stopped. "You're an investigator, you must have some idea." His voice lowered in volume but couldn't retain the hard edge completely.

Emotions surged through Rick. Fear for Genna and Lorianne's safety. Guilt-ridden, believing his friend capable of less-than-honorable actions, frustration in convincing Genna—

Rick pushed air through pursed lips, irritated no answers came to his many questions. He grazed Ash with an impassive look.

"It's no secret you want that property," Rick finally said. His tone matched his expression.

"You can't believe I'd hurt those girls to get it?" Anger glittered in Ash's eyes, but Rick knew it was masking hurt.

Rick knew how Ash felt. He hated himself for even doubting his best friend's integrity, but his reservations climbed higher. There was a wall ten feet high and a mile wide between them. Rick could see the anger choking back the other indefinable emotions in Ash's expression besides the hurt. Now, that was interesting.

How much could he confide? Rick glanced away, and pushed a hand through his hair. He turned back to Ash, and leveled him with a stare. Could he trust him? They'd been through a lot, starting from high school.

Ash stared back, gray eyes, hard chips of crystal.

"There have been several occurrences. Somewhat unnerving," Rick conceded. "Alone, they don't amount to much, but when you step back, it's a disturbing picture."

"Maybe you'd better start filling me in."

"All right. Let's start with an easy one. Do you know Lewis Peale?"

Ash's lips tightened. "Of course I do. He's a great general contractor. Intimidating, too."

"What do you know about him?"

"He's a hard-ass worker," Ash spit out. "You cannot possibly believe *he* locked Lorianne in the basement."

"I don't know what to believe." Rick kneaded spread fingers on his temples. "Someone is doing something. The insurance company hired me to check into the possibility of fraudulent claims."

"Like what?" Ash demanded.

Rick told him about the faulty wiring, flooded basement, recent roof collapse…

"Are you trying to tell me that Genna Lyndsey is doing these things for insurance money?" Ash snorted. "That's impossible."

"What? You think she's not smart enough?" Rick barked out a sharp laugh, if you could call it that. Wisely, he kept the story of his search for the *History of the Inductive Sciences* to himself. He smirked. *From the Earliest Times to the Present*. It didn't escape him that his thoughts lent credence to her guilt.

"You're calling her a scholar?" Ash questioned.

Rick chuckled at the disbelief in his tone. "She has a PhD in Library and Research Sciences," he told him. Bits and pieces of her file strewn across his desk popped through his mind.

"You're kidding. A PhD?" He truly looked surprised. "That wild-haired thing?"

Rick ignored that remark. "*Someone* is sabotaging the building. But it's gone beyond the building now. They've branched out." He stopped. Then, "Did you know that Lorianne was afraid of the dark?"

The scowl on Ash's face sealed it. He'd had no idea.

"She's absolutely terrified."

A SHADOW OF A smile touched Ash's lips. "You wouldn't know it, would you? You should have seen her ready to tear into the mighty Reverend Colvert at the town council meeting."

Lorianne's fierce stance at that meeting, fists clenched, ready to strike, had him biting back a grin. Blue eyes spitting fire—identical fire that radiated from Joanna Bakely's eyes moments before she tipped him out of his chair, knocking him to the floor threatening to cut him up and send him back—what was it she'd said? *Send him back to his daddy in a box?*

There was no question in his mind now 'who' the mysterious granddaughter was.

"The Reverend," Rick repeated, drawing Ash back to the present. "What was it he accused Genna of? Selling pornography?"

"Yeah. I thought Lorianne was going to punch his lights out. Genna grabbed her arm and pulled her out of the room. It was quite a sight." A laugh squeezed through his tight throat.

"I'll bet," Rick snorted.

"I gotta tell you, the place is not up to code to begin with. Regardless, how do we go about finding out who's damaging their property? That's the place to start."

"We? There is no 'we'!"

"You obviously need help. How long has this been going on?"

Rick froze. Ash and Rick had been friends a long time, and Ash was counting on that fact to weigh in his favor.

It did. Relief filled him when the fight went out of Rick. He told him about the flood and crossed wires. Rick finished with, "The first claim was filed two years ago."

"Two years! You think it started that long ago?"

"I think it's possible. Not only did someone lock Lorianne in the basement, they turned the office inside out while she was in there. There was a chair wedged under the doorknob."

Ash's mouth tightened. "What else has happened?" Ash sat through Rick's cool, assessing gaze. He gave it right back and waited, all the while, the rage building into an inferno ready to blow.

"Someone sawed through a ladder rung in the new expansion space. One of Lewis's contractor's fell and busted up his leg, but good, along with a nice hardy concussion. He was hurt pretty badly."

"But, why?"

"That's the question, isn't it?"

Ash sat in silence, digesting this information. It bothered him he hadn't known Lorianne was scared of the dark. He'd just thought her insistence of the light on in the bathroom meant wanting to see him in all his glory. His ego had reveled in it. Ha! Evidently, he and Lorianne would be having another, more intimate, little talk—and the sooner the better. "Has anyone else offered to buy the property?" Ash threw out.

"Not that I know of."

"Well, we're missing something."

Rick's sardonic expression caused Ash some discomfort. "You need a beer," Ash told him and signaled Josh.

CHAPTER 23

"WHERE HAVE YOU BEEN? I've been worried sick," Genna demanded when Lorianne stormed in the bookstore some hours later. "It's almost closing time."

"I know. I'm really sorry." Lorianne pitched her purse and a shopping bag on the settee, falling back next to it.

"You went shopping? For shoes?" Genna could tell by the shape of the bag.

"I couldn't help it. I was upset."

Genna examined her openly, noting her pouting lips and furrowed brow. She reached for the bag, and peered in the box.

"Oh, Lord. You really are upset, aren't you?" Genna dropped down on the sofa beside her. "You already have a pair of those strappy pumps. They must have four and a half inch heels."

"These are fuchsia. The ones I already have are hot pink," Lorianne sighed. "Fuchsia has a bit more purple in the tone." Her monotone demeanor did not fool Genna. "I need height."

"You're already five ten," Genna muttered under her breath. "More Betsey Johnson's, too." It was a statement, not a question. Oh, something was truly wrong. If it wasn't Jimmy Choo or Dior, it was Betsey Johnson. This was bad.

"Yes, Betsey Johnson." Lorianne's deadpan answers filled

her with growing dread.

"You got them on sale, right?"

"Sale?" Lorianne seemed confused by the question.

Genna grabbed Lorianne's hand. This was getting worse every minute. "What's wrong? Did something happen?"

"Happen?"

"Yes. What happened?"

"I'm getting too predictable," Lorianne choked out.

"Oh, you're not predictable. Definitely, not predictable. We know each other, like sisters. Please, tell me what's wrong?"

"I went home for lunch, to check on things. You know." She sniffed back tears.

Genna waited.

"And *he* came by."

"He?"

"The fucking Greek God of Bloomington."

"Rick?" Genna gasped in surprise. "What was he doing there?"

"No!" Lorianne snapped.

An unwelcome blush crept up her neck. Luckily, Lorianne did not seem to notice.

"Ashton!"

"Did he hurt you?"

"He wants to start seeing me again." Lorianne's eyes flashed in anger, but her fingers shook when she swiped at a tear.

Relief rushed through Genna, surprising her. "What do you suppose brought that on?"

"He's just using me to get to you. He wants this building. He asked me why you wouldn't sell."

Sudden anger flared, driving away any compassion for Lorianne's resurfaced suitor. Was that so? Well, they would just see about that, wouldn't they? "You think he's behind the destruction of our business? He's already made two offers for this property," Genna bit out.

Lorianne's slight hesitation did not escape her. "I don't know."

Genna took a breath to steady her rapid pulse.

"But it wouldn't surprise me," Lorianne spat viciously. She was angry, and her statement rash, but it wouldn't alter the facts.

Someone *had* sliced the rung on that ladder. Rick had to know she wouldn't have had the strength to do it personally. Maybe he thought she'd hired someone. But who would she have hired? Lewis? He was big, he was strong. They were friends. And though he wasn't educated in the traditional sense...actually...he was the perfect fall guy. Wouldn't he have had the ideal opportunity? A sudden need to speak to Lewis swarmed her. She needed to warn him.

"Lorianne," Genna said with urgency. "I think we have a problem."

CHAPTER 24

AFTER THE THIRD DAY in trying to reach Lewis, Genna was in a panic. "He's not answering his cell phone." Genna told Lorianne. The impelling need to hurry compressed her chest, making it hard to breathe. "I've been trying to reach Lewis for three days. Can you close up? I need to drive out there."

"Yes. Go ahead."

Genna stopped at the door and faced Lorianne. "I'm sorry he upset you, but is he worth the anguish?" She spoke softly. Then, with a lift of her lips, "Try not to wear the Betseys, maybe you can return them."

Genna may have been furious with Ashton Turner, but she had a feeling it had taken everything he'd had to face Lorianne on her own turf. A slight groan rumbled in her chest. She didn't want to give him a break. He was threatening her livelihood. To think of him as human would have her forgiving him in doing their business harm.

She steeled her resolve. Lorianne was right to steer clear of him.

Genna stepped outside through the door of the shop, poised to dart across the street when Damon stepped in front of her. Her eyes rose to the sky in aggravation.

"Hello, Genna." His dark curly hair gleamed in the sunset, his smile tentative. Two high spots of color appeared high on his cheeks.

"Damon. Don't you have *anywhere* else to be?" Her sensitivity toward him had long since evaporated. And thanks to him showing up everywhere, the shock of seeing him, as well.

"Can we talk?" His voice winded like he'd been running to catch her.

"Sorry. I'm in a bit of a hurry." She stepped around him, then stopped. She spun and slipped her key in the lock of Renewed Interest. They still didn't know who'd torn up the office and locked Lorianne in the basement. Not to mention the crossed wires and plumbing problems, the leaky roof...

It was inconceivable to believe someone had deliberately crossed the wires and jacked with the plumbing. Could it not have been just a coincidence? The building *was* old.

He still blocked her path. "Damon, I'm in a hurry," she reiterated.

He reached for her arm. Panic seized her. Startled, she jumped back out of his reach.

"Is there trouble, Genna?" She was never so glad to see anyone in her life. Even if it was Toddy Wilson's scraggly self.

"I was just going to my car, Toddy." She gave him a brilliant smile.

"I'll walk you." He sounded distracted, but she'd take help from any quarter.

"Thanks." She felt breathless. Pain flashed across Damon's face and she hardened her resolve and latched onto Toddy's arm. She had to drag him across the street. Foreboding flooded her, urging him on.

Just as they reached the parking lot behind the church he slowed. "Genna," he started. Oh, not him too, she winced.

"What!" She yanked her arm from his grasp.

"Ms. Lyndsey," Reverend Colvert called out. Would she never get away from here? She had to talk to Lewis. She ran for the car, but the reverend was quick. She schooled her features into a blank mask, and faced him.

"Any chance you've burned the pornography you have stashed on the top shelf at the back of your shop?" His self-righteous tone grated on her. Anger rose in her chest like the rush of a tsunami wave. The lowering sun helped cool the heat she felt flaming her cheeks.

"On the top shelf? At the back of my shop?" she repeated, sweetly. "I don't recall your being in my shop before, Reverend." An electrified silence followed, but Genna stood her ground, shoulders squared, gaze direct. *How dare he.*

"The wraths of hell, girl!" His voice thundered in the quiet of the empty parking lot.

"Thank you, Reverend." Ducking in her car, she managed a clean escape from Toddy, the Reverend and Damon, who was running across the parking lot. She hit the power locks.

She didn't exactly peel out, but satisfaction surged when gravel kicked up in the rear view mirror. Genna sat at the light, shaking with elation. She'd stood up to him. Stood up to the great Reverend Colvert. She breathed deep trying to still her racing heart, while her hands trembled on the steering wheel, the shock reverberating through her. She let out a sharp laugh.

She'd stood up to all of them. It was a heady, euphoric sensation.

But something about the reverend's words bothered her. How on earth could he know where she shelved the erotica section? It wasn't like they were at eye level for just anyone to see. He was tall, but she would have known if the Reverend would have entered her bookstore. It would have been all over town in a half a minute of his arrival.

Someone would have to *know* where they were. So he had a

spy of some sort, she supposed. And now they were boxed up. That though triggered visions of the young worker's broken body. Her need to talk to Lewis magnified.

She eased through town, careful to stick to the posted speed limit until she found the turnoff to Farm Road 653. Lewis lived eleven miles north of town. She recognized his desire for the tranquility. The trees were flush with different shades of green thanks to the recent deluge of rain. It wouldn't be long before the warmer days of summer were upon them.

Genna turned onto the gravel drive, marked by a mailbox on a rickety post, leading to Lewis's small wood-framed house. It was a winding quarter-mile trek. His truck was parked at an angle blocking the view of the front porch.

She switched off the engine and pulled the key out of the ignition. A nervous laugh escaped when she looked at the keys in her hand. She dropped them in her purse, but then pushed her purse to the floorboard.

Apprehension shrouded her. She opened the car door and stepped out. She loved the quiet his property afforded, but at the moment it felt more oppressive, ominous, isolated. Maybe it was thoughts surrounding the injured man; or her run in with the Reverend, or...or Damon showing up everywhere. Whatever it was, right now she would gladly welcome Mrs. Finch's constant girl-like chatter, even Wanda Buford's outrageous gossip.

Genna circuited his large F250 pickup and stepped up on the porch. The screen door clattered when she knocked, its fit ill-slotted from age. The clatter of the screen caused the door behind to part slightly. It hadn't been completely closed.

"Lewis," she called. "It's Genna. Are you home?" She banged again. Louder. He surely couldn't sleep through that, she thought. Besides it was early evening. She supposed he could be out back. There was a small pond on the property, and he loved to fish. He'd taught her how to thread a worm on a hook. Of course, she'd only been ten at the time.

Genna started her descent from the porch when a small sound caught her attention. Fear touched her spine, goose bumps raising her flesh. She moved back to the creaking screen, and pushed opened the front door, she called out softly, "Lewis?"

"Genna-girl? Is that you?" His voice sounded more like a moan.

Genna poked her head through. The house was small, the living, dining combo area sharing most of the entire space, along with the tiny kitchenette. The blinds were drawn but it didn't keep out all of the light. A chair was overturned at the small table, newspapers strewn about the floor. Completely out of Lewis's neat-shaven character. She somehow refrained screaming his name. It sounded loud all the same. "Lewis?" Alarm seized her insides. Something was truly wrong.

Just when she said his name a third time, she saw him—stretched out on the floor near the door that led into the bedroom. "Lewis!" she cried. "What happened?" Bile rose in her throat.

"Someone broke in," he whimpered. He didn't move. "I guess it wouldn't be breakin' in, if my door was unlocked."

She dropped to the floor, hovering over him. His head lay in a pool of blood. "There's blood. Do you know where it's from? How long have you been like this? I need to call the police." She couldn't seem to keep from babbling like an idiot.

"No. No police," he bit out.

"Lewis, you're hurt. Tell me who did this."

"I dunno, but they said, no police."

"Okay," she conceded, "we won't call the police. Yet."

"Thank goodness I have such a hard head." He tried to laugh, but his voice was breathy with a pain she could only guess.

"I don't see anything on the front or the top," she said, running fingers gently across the smoothness of his shaved head. "Having no hair here is going to help, considerably," she said with a lightness she didn't feel at all.

He tried laughing again, but it came out as a groan.

"I'm sorry." Her gaze darted about the room to find something, anything that might make him feel better.

"Don' go makin' me laugh, girl."

"Can you move?"

"Maybe." She grimaced at his wince, but he managed to struggle to his forearms.

"Let me get a cloth. Stay put."

"In the kitchen." It terrified her to see Lewis like this. His very size should have kept him safe.

Her feet echoed on hardwood floors as she dashed across the room. She rummaged through the drawers looking for a hand towel or dishrag. Anything to dampen. The metallic scent of blood assailed her nostrils, threatened the contents of her stomach. Reading about blood was okay, she reasoned, because you couldn't *smell* it. Oh, why couldn't she be home just reading? She was not cut out for subterfuge. Jerking open the third drawer down on the left, she found what she was looking for. She splashed cold water on a cloth and hurried back.

"Here, let me see," she demanded, settling behind his head. He was sitting now, leaning forward.

"Lordy, girl." His voice had dropped to a whisper. "What's going on?"

"Surely, you see we have to call someone." She ran the cloth over the back of his head. "There's quite a gash here, you may need stitches. Who did this?" She asked again.

"Dunno. They caught me from behind."

"Did they take anything?" She asked the question, but she already knew the answer.

"Nothin." He took the cloth from her, and wiped the damage on his hard head, himself. She moved to a chair across from him and waited. Her eyes met his. She could see the uncertainty in his expression. He spoke slowly. "There's a card on the TV with a phone number. We can call him."

A chill touched the nape of her neck. She moved to where he pointed. An expensive card with embossed script read Ashton Turner, III. Turner Development. Genna felt an absurd sense of panic start to choke her. She stared at the card, unable to touch it. She struggled to get hold of herself. Doubts raged through every facet of her mind.

Was Lewis working for Ashton Turner? Worse...*could* Lewis have sabotaged the ladder? She'd known him her whole life. Everything screamed it wasn't possible. But what other explanation could there be? She reached for the card as if it were a cobra ready to strike. Swallowing hard, she picked up the card.

"Ashton Turner?" She had trouble verbalizing his name. Fingers trembling, she looked at Lewis with effort.

"I'm GC for him on several jobs. I trust him."

"GC?" She swallowed, hard.

"General Contractor, girl."

"Oh, right." Her brain was mush. "How can he help?"

"I dunno, but he can. He's got connections."

"Connections?" she squeaked. Terror rolled over her in waves. She didn't know whom to trust. How much could she tell Lewis now? She stared again at the card in her hand, then at him. What should she do?

Her first instinct was to drop to the floor in tears. But crying never solved anything. Neither did hysterics. What did she usually do when she was upset?

Read. She would lose herself in a book. Something obscure and unconventional. Like *Thomas Jefferson and Sally Hemings: An American Controversy* by Annette Gordon-Reed. Anything. The next time she was able to sit down and read, it would be something *not* bloody, she vowed.

Her next instinct was to call Rick, her handy dandy

insurance claims fraud *investigator*, who kissed really, really well. Lean on him. Let him find the answers.

Trust him? Right. Kissing well didn't solve crimes. Not to mention the fact *he* believed she was sabotaging her own business for insurance money. Investigator, her foot!

No. She was on her own in this. The story of her life. "'*Each man is the architect of his own fate*,'" she whispered.

"Wha'chu you sayin,' Genna-girl?"

"No-nothing," she stammered, coloring.

"What are ya waitin' on? Git the phone."

She could scarcely manage one foot in front of another as she crossed to a table next to the sofa where an old fashioned, dirty, beige-colored, push-button phone glared at her in the dim light. She punched in the number with a shaking finger. She could feel Lewis's chocolate eyes boring into her, where he still sat on the floor. She would explode, waiting for someone to answer on the other end.

What would she say? All she knew of Ashton Turner was his less-than-chivalrous treatment of Lorianne. How hurt she was when he'd never returned her call, and his chilly gray eyes, staring them down across the room at the town council meeting. When the Reverend started berating her on selling porn, he'd started to stand and...a recorder picked up.

She let out a relieved breath she hadn't realized she'd been holding.

"No answer," she told Lewis, breathless, fear allayed.

"Hang up."

She slammed the phone down, hoping her eagerness to disconnect wasn't so apparent.

"You need ice," she told him. She ran to the kitchen and jerked open the freezer.

The action coincided with his, "check the freezer." There wasn't any, so she grabbed a bag of frozen corn and hurried back.

Lewis was on his knees trying to stand.

"Wait. Let me help you." She tossed the corn on the coffee table.

"A little thing like you? You'll be crushed." She tried to appreciate his humor, but it was difficult.

Regardless of his protests, she grabbed onto his massive arm and offered what weight she could. A ridiculous notion. A hysterical giggle threatened to erupt, while tears stung her eyes.

With concerted effort they made it to the chair. Genna reached for the cloth she'd handed over earlier. It was covered in blood. Holding it out with the tips of her fingers, she darted back to the kitchen and dropped it in the sink. In the third drawer down, she found a dry towel.

"Lewis," she started, walking back toward the sofa. "Someone sawed through the rung on that ladder."

"Yeah?"

Genna carefully wrapped the towel around the frozen bag of corn. She stole a look at him, and moistened her lips. She handed over her makeshift package.

"You think it was me," he stated.

"No! No." She hastened to assure him. "But I tried to call you...I-I wanted to warn you that..." her voice trailed. How could she tell him her suspicions? She tried again. "Some things have been happening, and the insurance company thinks..." She sighed in frustration. Nothing was coming out right.

"You think I been doin' stuff." Again, the resignation of defeat. It broke her heart.

"No! Please. Hear me out. I'm not saying anything right." She took a deep breath. "There have been some wiring and plumbing problems over the last couple of years, even the roof."

"The roof was replaced three years ago, girl. You don' need no roof."

She plowed forward. "The insurance company is having the

claims investigated." She looked at him, but he was looking down. One hand held the covered corn to the back of his head.

"They think that it's me—or at least I think they thought it was me until your employee fell. They have to know it couldn't have been me now, unless..." She swallowed. "...unless they believe I had help," she said bitterly. "And...and that's not all." Sucking a in a deep breath, she blurted out the rest. "Someone snuck into the store. They locked Lorianne in the basement. Then they tore up the office inside out—looking for something. We just don't know what..." She held her breath, and waited.

"Locked Lorianne in the basement?" He raised his eyes to meet hers. Alarm registered in his gentle face. "But she's scared of the dark."

"Yes. It's occurred to me that someone may be trying to set *you* up. I couldn't have damaged the ladder myself. They have to believe that someone else did it, or that I had someone do it for me."

"Me?"

She took another breath. "Unfortunately, you're the next logical choice." She paused. "And when you didn't answer your phone, I got worried," she finished on a whisper.

"That was a good thing," he told her. He stopped and stared at her.

She squirmed under the scrutiny.

After a terminable silence, he said, "There's a cell phone number on the back of that card. Hand me the phone."

CHAPTER 25

RICK HADN'T REALIZED HOW late it was when he and Ash finally emerged from Pat's and saw how low the sun had dipped. The odds of Genna still working were in his favor. He refused to analyze his need to make sure she made it safely to her car. Their little misunderstanding earlier had him on edge. Anticipation had him cranky and...excited. Set his pulse in motion to slightly above normal. Not enough to signal the alarms, like lighting flares or anything, just enough to make him uncomfortable, physically.

She was fine.

If she didn't walk to her car.

Alone! Hell. He picked up the pace.

"What's the hurry?" Ash said.

He didn't know how she'd managed before she'd met him. The sun sunk lower in the western sky. Broad strokes brushed pastels in pinks, oranges and blues like a watercolor worth millions. "Uh." Rick shortened his pace. "No hurry."

By unspoken consent, he and Ash walked south and rounded the corner on Victory. Ida Finch was juggling a box in her tiny arms, trying to stab a key into the lock of her corner store.

"Ida, you need some help?" Rick relieved her of the box. It

was surprisingly heavy.

"Thank you, young man." She batted her eyelashes at him, shamelessly. Ash smirked.

"Where are you parked?" Rick asked, ignoring Ash.

"Behind the church," she chirped.

"That's two blocks away," Ashton frowned.

"Oh, I'm spry, you know."

Rick bit back a smile when Ida grabbed Ashton's arm. He barked out a laugh when Ash turned a helpless look toward his office—the opposite direction. They had to slow their steps to match Ida's, but at least they were heading in the direction of the bookstore.

"What the devil is in this box, Ida? This is too heavy, no matter how spry you are," Rick said.

"Oh, I ordered some things for Renewed Interest and wanted to drop them off. I do hope they haven't left yet." Her voice was young and sweet, like springtime, despite her age, which no one knew, of course. "Genna is usually there all hours of the day and night."

Rick's mouth tightened, but he held his tongue. Didn't he know it! That would stop, if he had to lock *her* in the basement. He wasn't sure when he'd adopted the role as self-appointed chief protector, but it occurred to him that's exactly what he'd become. And it was high time she cooperated.

They sauntered past Renewed Interest's expansion when Rick spotted Pretty Boy jogging from the direction of the church parking lot. Rick shot Ash a warning glance. Rick picked up his pace to the corner.

Surprisingly, Damon ran right by the bookstore, past Plank's coffee shop and darted into Selma's Beauty Salon. Rick waited at the corner for Ida and Ash.

Box still in hand, Rick let Ash reach for the door. Ash rattled the door, it was locked. *Thank God*. Through the beveled glass he could see Lorianne hurrying over. Her expression darkened when she saw her visitors. He was almost positive she would have walked away had Ida not stood there. In any event, she took her time unlocking the door, Ida or not.

"Mrs. Finch, what a surprise." Lorianne smiled. It was pasted on strictly for the old woman's benefit.

Rick bit back a smile, her eyes never touched Ash. Whatever their disagreement, he probably deserved every jab she threw his way.

"Hello, dear." Ida smiled brightly. "These nice gentlemen were kind enough to walk me here. I have cups for the new coffee shop I wanted to show Genna. Is she here?" Ida said, glancing around.

Apprehension flitted across Lorianne's features, but it was so fleeting it could have been his imagination. Regardless, his hackles rose.

"Not right now, Mrs. Finch. What cups? May I see?"

Where in hell was she? She never left before Lorianne, and the whole town knew it.

"Of course, dear. Where can we set them?" Lorianne indicated a small table between two chairs in front of the windows. Rick set the box down.

Ash wandered the store, restless, not quite managing to keep his gaze diverted from Lorianne. Rick studied her, them. She kept a wary eye on Ash, while Ida busied herself divesting the box of its contents.

"Where is Genna?" Rick asked. Unease crossed her features. Alarm bells rang in his ears.

No. Just Ash's cell phone.

"I told her I would close tonight," Lorianne evaded. "Oh, these are adorable, Mrs. Finch." She snatched a pink cup out of Ida's hand. All Rick could make out was a large 'R' and 'I' stenciled on the sides of the cup. Lorianne was hiding something.

He glanced around but nothing appeared out of the ordinary.

"Does this say Racing Icicles?" Lorianne's delicate laugh permeated the air. She picked up another cup—blue. "Rambling Intellect? Oh, that's rich. We should save that one for Genna. Whose idea was this, Mrs. Finch?" She reached for another.

"Genna stopped by and we just brainstormed a bit."

"You know, she doesn't really like 'i' words," Lorianne told her in a conspiratorial tone.

"No? Why is that?"

"I think it has something to do with her over-the-top *intelligence*." She laughed. "Sometimes she's quite sensitive about it. Or my *in*sensitivity to it."

Rick coughed to cover a bark of laughter.

Lorianne shot him a quick smile. He glanced at Ash over his shoulder. Ash talked low in his phone. With a flick of his wrist, he snapped the phone shut.

Ash sauntered back to the group, but his light demeanor didn't deceive Rick for a moment. Tension surrounded him like the fog from a movie set in 1940s London—mouth drawn tight, shoulders tense. Rick's instincts sharpened.

"Are you ladies about ready?" The edge in Ash's tone solidified a knot in Rick's gut. He heeded the warning. Time to go.

Rick turned to see Lorianne puff up, spoiling for a fight, if he was any kind of judge. "I'm not quite ready to leave," she informed them. Rebellion flashed like a neon sign. It was directed at Ash.

Rick compressed his lips.

"Rick, if you'll walk Ida to her car, I'm happy to help Lorianne gather whatever she needs," Ash rebutted. His eyes bore into her like a drill bit in metal.

Any other time Rick would have loved to sit back, enjoy the entertainment, watch the fireworks this little scene would have offered, but for the forewarning Ash portrayed. He still had no clue where Genna had disappeared, hedging up his dread.

"Come on, Ida," he said, taking her arm. "Sounds like these two have something to work out."

She let out a girlish giggle and flitted out the door he held.

"WHO THE HELL DO you think you are?" Lorianne rounded on Ashton even before the door sounded behind Rick and Mrs. Finch.

"Get your stuff, Lorianne." His calm façade really pissed her off.

"Don't give me your highhanded bullshit, Turner." Fury almost choked her. "I told you to *leave me alone.*"

He ignored her. *Ignored her!*

"That was Lewis Peale on the phone. Someone walked into his house and smacked him on the head."

Lorianne paled. "Genna..."

"Is fine," he finished for her. "For now."

She gasped. "I'll get my purse."

"Excellent. I want to make sure you make it to your car okay. You're going home."

"What the fu..."

CHAPTER 26

"I THINK LORIANNE AND Ashton Turner make a very engaging couple," Ida Finch told Rick.

Despite the tension asphyxiating him, a burst of laughter squeezed through. Her conspiratorial tone dispelled some of his suffocation. Rick held her arm as they waited for the light to change. He glanced over his shoulder. Lorianne was screaming at Ash. "I think you may be right," he agreed.

"I declare, I think there may be some kind of funny business going on," she said in her sweet, singsong pitch.

Rick's senses went on full alert. "What do you mean?"

"Well." She tapped him on the arm. "You should know, dear. You were there in the thick of it today."

"I'm not sure I follow, Ida."

She flung out her other dainty hand, and said impatiently, "That poor worker. Why, the whole town was standing on the street when the ambulance carried that poor fellow off."

"Ah."

She slid a sly glance over him. "Nor did I miss you practically carrying Genna Lyndsey back to her shop," she said. "I smell romance in the air. And not just for Lorianne and Ashton, mind." She batted her lashes at him. "I can sense these things."

The light changed and he forged ahead. Dusk was the only thing hiding Rick's warm cheeks. God forbid she witness his blush like a schoolboy. He needed a distraction. "Ida, don't tell me you park behind the church over here every day," he chastised.

"My goodness, you boys are worrywarts." She actually tsk'd.

Rick considered coming clean to Ida's question, but pushed away the thought before it could fully form. The idea was ludicrous. "Ida," he started.

"Now, sweetie, don't try telling me not to worry my sweet little head about anything." What was she, a mind reader? No just a reminder of his own mother. *Who was trying to marry him off.* "I'll ferret the information out of you, regardless." She squeezed his arm, affectionately.

Right.

Still, she was observant; her guileless manner deceived anyone who didn't know her. Surprising himself, he confided, "Someone is trying to entice Genna to sell her property. And it's not, in what you would call, a forthright approach."

Her brow furrowed a frown. "What exactly do you mean?"

He studied her outright for a long moment. "Someone locked Lorianne in the basement and wreaked havoc on their office."

"Oh, my," she whispered. "Lorianne is deathly afraid of the dark, too. The poor dear." She shook her head, gray curls bouncing. "She must have been beside herself."

Her remark brought them to a halt. "How common is that knowledge, Ida?"

"What knowledge, dear?"

"That Lorianne is afraid of the dark."

"Why, I'm not sure," she shrugged. A shiver shook her delicate frame.

"Come on. Let's get you to your car."

GENNA HAD TO GET out of Lewis's small house. There was no place to hide. She had no intention of running into Ashton Turner, so that meant now. An unfashionable lamp gave the room a soft glow, allowing Genna to consider Lewis's pale face.

"How do you feel?" she asked. "Maybe I should take you to the emergency room."

"We'll wait." He lay back, head resting along on the back of the chair, eyes closed. Genna started gathering strewn newspapers, setting overturned chairs upright, unable to sit any longer. "Feels like I got hit by a two-by-four."

Genna turned to him in horror. "Is that what they used?" Her gaze swept the room. There! In the corner. She scrambled to the far end of the room, near the bedroom door. The handle of a hammer was propped against the wall. "This is what they used, Lewis. A hammer. There's blood on it," all thoughts of fleeing gone.

"Don' touch it, girl."

"I won't," she said softly. She squatted, careful not to disturb anything. The handle was wood and worn. She didn't know much about forensics—just what she'd read—but even her inexperienced eyes realized lifting a fingerprint would be difficult. She could easily make out the blood. An involuntary tremor shook her. "I'm going to call the police, Lewis."

"No." He said it firmly, decided.

"Lewis, we have to tell someone."

"We will, girl. Mr. Turner will help us."

Panic went through her. How could she have forgotten *him*? "I've got to go."

"Go?"

Oh, how was she supposed to explain? She glanced over. He was looking at her like she was crazy. Maybe she *was* crazy.

"Somethin' you not tellin' me, girl?" His eyes narrowed on her. She'd never been a good liar, especially to him. He was practically a substitute father.

She groaned. "Lewis..." Her voice trailed. She spun away from that intensive stare, looking anywhere else.

Gravel crunched the drive outside and she started. She felt dizzy. Hand on her chest, a sense of impending doom shortened her breath, as if someone had covered her head with a blanket and there was no oxygen. Maybe she could dart through the kitchen. Yes! She could make her way around front, jump in her car, and...and take off.

She'd have to mind the speed limits, of course. She fanned her face. Oh, who cared about speed limits at a time like this? She didn't want to hurt anyone; she just wanted to sneak out. Quietly.

The car door slammed. She jumped. Oh, Lord. She edged her way to the kitchen.

Footsteps echoed on the wooden porch just outside. *Lots* of footsteps. Oh, Lord, *he'd brought goons*. She glanced at Lewis. She couldn't desert him. If he could just walk...fast... "Lewis, if we hurry—"

A quick knock pounded the door, but the intruders didn't bother waiting for an invitation—the door crashed back, banging the wall behind. Genna slid to the floor and hugged her knees to her chest, eyes squeezed tight. They probably had guns. They might even use the same weapon on her. *The bloodied hammer.*

She wheezed, now she was hyperventilating. If they brought her a bag, all they had to do was suffocate her...she was going to die...

"Genna! Are you alright?"

Relief spilled through her. Suddenly, lightheaded, she opened her eyes. Rick was squatted down before her. She met his eyes, dark with concern.

"Rick?" But behind Rick, Ashton trained a hard gaze on her.

Keenly observant. "Yes," she whispered. She gathered her wits and struggled to her feet with Rick's help. His hand was large, strong, capable.

"Mind the hammer in the corner," Lewis said. "That's what they used. Lucky, I have such a hard head."

"Yes, lucky," Ashton repeated. He sounded so cold, distant.

The need to escape was crucial. She drifted to Lewis, keeping an eye on Ashton Turner, placed a hand on his massive shoulder, drawing strength from his warmth and familiarity.

"I'll check the bedroom, you check the kitchen," Ash directed. They each went separate directions.

Genna seized her chance. Squeezing Lewis's shoulder one last time, she leaned over and kissed him on the cheek.

"You'll be okay now," she whispered. Before he could question her motives, she sent him an apologetic glance, darted out the front door and jumped in her car. Luck was with her. She opened her purse, keys right on top right where she'd left them. She didn't even care about the thrown rocks when she spun out on the gravel road. Speed limits be damned...*darned*.

CHAPTER 27

LORIANNE WAS LIVID. ASHTON Turner was a jerk, a hot, sexy, bastard-jerk! She couldn't think of an adjective that would adequately describe her rage *or* her hatred for him. She sat in her little red Honda, sorely tempted to defy Ashton's direct *order* not to drive out to Lewis's. She tugged her cell from her purse and called Genna.

No answer. What the hell was going on?

Genna was fine. She had to be. Annoyed to see her hands shaking, she channeled her anger toward the one person who really deserved it. Who was he to tell her what she could and could not do? In a fit of rebellion, Lorianne bolted from the car. She wanted coffee. He couldn't stop her from getting coffee, the big...jerk.

She was so furious she couldn't enjoy the sun making its final descent beyond the horizon, or the late spring air's slight nip. She stomped back around the south end of the Baptist church. Back towards the store. She waited at the crosswalk, arms folded over her chest. Waited for the light to change, fuming.

AS WAS HER HABIT, JOANNA found herself driving by Victor Town Park. Nostalgia assaulted her. Truly, it was times like these she really missed Victor. Lorianne would have loved her grandfather. He'd been a strong, silent man with a heart of gold and a ready hug. Joanna never deserved him. She choked on the guilt. Her actions had cost her Lorianne *and* Victor. It was her fault they never had the opportunity to know each other.

But Victor would have allayed her doubts. But Victor was gone. Years, now. Every day the urge to confess grew more and more difficult to contain. Lorianne was the spitting image of her father, Joanna's son, with her blonde waves, stubborn chin, slim build, and blue eyes.

As if conjured from her imagination, Lorianne appeared in the crosswalk in front of Joanna. She shook her head at the image when she realized it was Lorianne. Her granddaughter's gait was very determined. Fury emanated from her. She looked magnificent, head held high, back straight. She was quite angry, Joanna realized.

She marched passed Renewed Interest's storefront to Plank's. *Opportunity*? Joanna didn't hesitate. Without allowing a change of mind, she turned abruptly into the church parking lot.

A minute later she practically jogged across the street. Thank goodness for Tai chi. She stopped for a breath, one hand on the handle. She paused, and inhaled deeply. Victor would encourage her to set herself free. Truth. Could she do it? Could she unsettle Lorianne's life? Take the chance on a granddaughter's hatred for all she'd missed in her young life?

Yes. No question. But to have Lorianne come to her for future needs, she'd risk it.

She counted to ten. Chanted her daily affirmation, "I will be calm and collected." Breath. "I always find the right thing to say," Breath. "I can meet successfully all the challenges I encounter..." Ah, the hell with it. She opened the door.

Lorianne stood at the counter, her back to Joanna. Every muscle contracted. She was enraged.

Doubts swarmed Joanna. Had Lorianne already learned the truth? Was Joanna doing the right thing? Lorianne might never forgive her. Throat constricted, she hesitated...

Lorianne spun and faced her. Joanna froze, certain that Lorianne read her every thought. But Lorianne's own face, pale, eyes puffy, looked as if she'd been crying. Joanna rushed to Lorianne and pulled into her arms. "What is it, dear?" Her voice soothed.

"Oh, Mrs. Bakely. Something is terribly wrong," Lorianne sobbed.

"What is it, dear?"

"It's Genna." Panic reeled from her.

Joanna led her to a nearby chair. "Why don't you start from the beginning?" Another delay. She never denied being a coward. Life would change quickly enough when Lorianne learned the truth.

Between gulping hiccups Lorianne explained how Mrs. Finch happened by with Rick and Ashton Turner to deliver some new promotional coffee cups. Then Ashton's phone call from Lewis Peale, and, how someone had hit him on the head. "Genna drove to Lewis's house because she was worried about him. Rick and Ashton are there now. He wouldn't let me go," she wailed. Yes, a bit dramatic but, oh, she loved this girl.

"He?"

"Ashton!" she sniffed.

Joanna let out a silent sigh of relief at this piece of information and handed Lorianne a napkin from the dispenser on the table. She glanced up. Plank watched the two of them with a stern intensity, his face shadowed. His hard features appeared concerned. Joanna gave him a small smile and turned back to her charge.

She wasn't sure if Ashton's actions were due to her threat to his person, or for some other reason. For whatever reason he made her stay behind, she was thankful.

A blast of cool air sent their startled glances to the door. Genna burst through, breathless and antsy.

Lorianne knocked her chair over to reach her friend. Joanna glanced around the small shop, avid curiosity in every look.

"We need to talk," Genna whispered. "But not here."

Inspiration struck, providing that perfect opportunity, if her courage did not fail once again. Joanna refused to let it. It was time. She motioned for the girls to follow her out. "We'll go to my home," she told them. She bustled them through the door and to her car before either one had a chance to object. Or she lost her nerve.

Joanna's home was nestled in the hilly, lush addition of Blackberry Hills Estates- large homes on small acreages established back in the sixties. She and Victor were one of the first families to build in the area. Joanna pulled to a stop before the massive electronic gates that framed her sizeable home through black aluminum slats. She punched in the security code and waited for the gates to welcome them through.

She couldn't help wondering how Lorianne would react to seeing this opulence after having grown up with nothing. Her only hope lay in Lorianne's generous spirit of forgiveness for Joanna's many egregious sins. And there were many.

She never thought she'd be ashamed of her home, but in that moment, when both girls came to an abrupt silence, she felt just that.

GENNA'S ASTONISHMENT STRANGLED HER. They pulled into the circular drive of Mrs. Bakely's mansion and there was no other way to describe it. A soaring brick façade lined with huge columns, boasting a stark whitewashed balcony. Two separate stairways curved upward to a great porch, surrounding a large flourishing bed of flowers in lively spectrum of pinks, purples, and yellows.

Climbing from the car, she knew Lorianne's shocked gaze mirrored her own. She was hit with another surprise when the door swung open, held by an older man—erect and formal. Mrs. Bakely handed over her keys and instructed him to move the car. By the shock on Lorianne's face, Genna clapped her own gapping mouth shut.

How had they never known Mrs. Bakely lived like a queen in a fortress? When she thought about it, of course, it made perfect sense. Mrs. Bakely *loved* historicals. Regency, she clarified, silently. Maybe she fancied herself as one of Julia Quinn's dowager duchesses out of the Bridgerton series. Her home certainly fit the part.

An open foyer had a ceiling as high as fifteen feet or more. The elaborate Waterford crystal chandelier swayed gently. Hardwood floors gleamed with a shiny wax, and a grand staircase, complete with curving balustrade, rounded to an upper level. Genna felt as if she'd stepped into a scene from *Gone With The Wind*.

Mrs. Bakely ushered them to a library off the entryway, stopping briefly to confer with a young woman. Genna swallowed. A library? She stepped over the threshold, stunned by bookcases lining three out of the four walls, from floor to ceiling. They were filled with books of all shapes, sizes, colors, and subject matter. Books everywhere, save for the mantle topping an ornate fireplace. She could easily die happy at this moment.

Not a speck of dust was in sight. A grand piano in polished black ebony, laden with family photos taken through the years, graced one corner, partially blocking a window.

A feeling of anticipation —no, more like foreboding—stole over Genna. She glanced over her shoulder toward Mrs. Bakely. Anxiety colored her expression. Genna was confused. What would she have to be so frightened about?

Her left hand circled her collarbone, eyes never straying from Lorianne. She never noticed Genna's glance in her direction. Genna flicked her gaze to Lorianne. She was looking at the photos on the piano. She had no idea what to make of the tension that suppressed the air. But just the same she edged closer to Lorianne, feeling the need to grab her hand.

"Look at this, Genna," Lorianne spoke softly. She pointed to a picture of a young man with gold curly hair and bright blues eyes. He was down on one knee. Next to him, stood a proud, very large English Mastiff hound. "Isn't he cute? The dog, I mean."

Genna leaned forward for a closer look. Astonishment kept her voice whispered. "Yes," barely escaped her tight throat. She spun around and met Mrs. Bakely's terrified eyes. Genna's hand flew over her mouth. How had she not seen it before? The same blue eyes, the same tilt of their heads, the curious questions about Lorianne? It should have been obvious.

"Why is there a photo of my mother?" Lorianne's voice was puzzled.

The young woman Mrs. Bakely had addressed in the foyer hastened through the door carrying a tea service. Genna still clasped Lorianne's hand. The atmosphere took on a surreal quality.

Genna's out of body experience tugged at her once again. She noticed the soft sconces decorating the wood panel. They separated the bookcases into symmetrical columns throughout the room. Sheer muslin linings were framed with heavy brocade drapes in reds and browns, roped with braided gold cords. Her fingers tightened on Lorianne's. The books were sorted by author, alphabetically.

"There's a picture here of my mother," Lorianne said again. She turned slowly and faced Mrs. Bakely. "Why?"

"'*Faith is the antiseptic of the soul*,'" Genna whispered, squeezing her hand.

"Not now, Genna." Her voice was devoid of emotion.

"Have a seat, dear. W-we need to talk." Mrs. Bakely was surely in need of sustenance. But Genna could see the determined resolve, and admired her for it.

She let go of Lorianne's hand.

RICK THOUGHT THEY WOULD never finish with the police. By the time Lewis's place was dusted for fingerprints, more questions had been raised than answered. Three and a half hours had come and gone before they'd deposited Lewis at the emergency room.

"If I were a betting man," Ash grumbled. "I'd bet Lorianne didn't go straight home like I suggested."

"Suggested?" Rick would have laughed but his odds, regarding Genna, were likely similar. And he would hunt her down. What the hell was she thinking, running out like that?

Ash hadn't complained once about the gravel dinging his BMW—a couple of nice little gifts on the finish of his car.

"What now?" Ash broke into his thoughts.

"The first thing I'm going to do is make sure the bookworm isn't hiding in her bookstore." He ground his teeth. "I wouldn't put it past her."

"That's as good a place to start as any," Ash agreed.

Rick admired the quiet of the BMW, respectful of its silent power. One great thing about guys, they didn't require a lot of unneeded chitchat.

Bloomington was a small town, a bit sleepy most nights of the week. This night was no exception. Under Ash's skillful guidance, they pulled into town from the east by the church parking lot—coinciding with Ash's colorful expletive.

"Son of a bitch. Her car is still there! God forbid she do the smart thing and go home like I asked."

Asked. Right. "Like you would, you mean."

It was difficult not to grin when Ash's response was a

heartfelt scowl along with another muttered word unfit for most others. Ash swung the car onto Victory and waited for the signal to change. He had a clear view of Renewed Interest. To Rick's relief, it appeared closed up for the night. He ground out an expletive of his own. "That's Genna's car in front of Plank's," he bit out. "Turn left."

Ash made the turn, pausing in front of the bookstore front. It damned sure was. Her little white Camry sat there, front and center, covered in dirt—evidence of her visit to Peale's.

"Well, wherever they are, you can bet they're together." Ash's voice held steady. The tension in the car soared, as did the silence.

"That's something, anyway," Rick muttered.

CHAPTER 28

VIOLENT, STORMY WEATHER STARTLED Genna awake the next morning. A bolt of lightning lit up the room. She shot straight to a sitting position, panting and disoriented; nothing was familiar. She expelled her breath slowly, remembering. She and Lorianne were at Mrs. Bakely's nice little *mansion*.

There'd been no way to extricate herself gracefully the evening before, whereupon Mrs. Bakely's...Joanna...as they were asked to call her now, blurted out the whole sordid story. Lorianne sat in stunned silence for over an hour. An hour! It wasn't possible for Lorianne to not say anything, ever, for an hour, proving just how truly upset Lorianne was.

As soon as was politely possible, Genna made a murmur of getting to her car. Mrs. Ba... *Joanna*...had insisted they stay the night, and had instructed the maid—the *maid*, there was a *maid*—to set up a room for each of them. Lorianne had not looked very happy about that.

By the time Genna was shown upstairs, the luxuriousness of her room was no longer a surprise. It did not keep her from stunned admiration, however. Elaborate, shimmering embroidered squares, reminiscent of Byzantine mosaics, were stitched on chenille bedcovers of thyme green and antique white.

Genna reveled in the softness of the mattress. No expense had been spared. Matching curtains, drawn back with a loop, draped floor-to-ceiling windows. A sheer coverlet fell free in a style similar to the library. Who wouldn't thrive in the natural light and privacy it offered?

If this was her room, Genna couldn't help wondering how Lorianne's compared. A clock on the bedside table showed five-thirty a.m. Genna pulled herself from the comfort of the massive bed and padded into an adjoining bath, which had left her mouth hanging open the evening before. She looked around with a degree of regret, knowing she would have to give it up soon. Her tiny bath at home definitely left much to be desired.

She marveled at the large tub with clawed feet, the showpiece of the room. It had brushed nickel finish on the removable faucet head, and an old-fashioned vanity against one wall. The room was large enough to sport two floor-length windows overlooking some kind of courtyard. But the hour and the rain obstructed the view. A chair and small table rested between them. A lovely Persian oval floral finished the effect on wood floors. It was a dream.

Genna hoped Lorianne could see past her...confusion...to accept Mrs...*Joanna*, she corrected. Genna would happily accept Mrs...errggg...Joanna...

She knew Lorianne just needed time. Genna had never known her own grandmothers. Her parents were much older when she'd been born and they'd been gone for years. She would *happily* accept Joanna as a grandmother.

Unable to resist the fabulous tub, Genna started a bath and added bath salts from the vanity. Still, she could understand Lorianne's shock. When Mrs...Joanna...started explaining how her son had married Lorianne's mother, Lorianne froze. Not a word passed her lips. An hour, she thought again. It boggled the mind.

Joanna's story was compelling. And sad. It didn't paint Mrs...Joanna...in a very nice picture. She'd told them the truth, sparing no detail—nor any of the harshness. Genna felt her pain as clearly as her face portrayed. She'd aged ten years in that hour. She placed Lorianne's mother's demise squarely on her own shoulders.

Even though they'd lost years, Genna admired Joanna for trying to set things right. How hard must it have been to find Lorianne's mother, only to discover she'd died leaving a child behind? Her regrets must feel monumental.

Genna sighed, sinking down in the bath—both in bliss for the tub and sorrow for Lorianne's dilemma. It was a strange turn of events. Almost perfect, actually. Lorianne was always searching for Prince Charming. And by the slightest twist of fate, she ends up with long lost 'fairy *grandmother'* who was rich as Croesus.

A laugh escaped her at the irony.

It was rich. Oh, Lord. That was funny too. She laughed so hard she slipped under the water.

Lorianne may be upset right now, but she wasn't one who stayed angry for long. It took too much effort. Genna would bet the store that she and Joanna would be real family in a matter of days.

Genna reveled in the hot scented bath another twenty minutes before struggling out with regret. Between the bathroom, the bedroom, and the library, she might never venture to leave again.

But she had a store to run.

She descended the grand staircase, determined to locate the kitchen, or a person, whichever she found first. The foyer, lit brightly the evening before, was in total darkness, despite the large windows framing French doors. Stormy gray clouds soaked up any light from outside, thunder rumbled noisily.

Genna looped behind the stairs, just because in her imagination, the kitchen should be there.

It was. Even better, the aroma of warm bread filled the air. She paused in an arched entry. Of course, this would be the dream kitchen of a lifetime. How could it not be?

Oak cabinetry covered the room from top to bottom. A large gas grill with at least six burners, trimmed in stainless, had large red knobs on front. Genna couldn't tell where the refrigerator was. Cabinets, short, wide, tall, were everywhere.

Dark granite covered the counters, and she counted three sinks, a moveable butcher block on wheels, and an opened brick oven, already flaming. It smelled like heaven.

Realistically, a dream kitchen would be wasted on her. She liked to read too much to spend her time in a kitchen—but she was not above admiring, much less eating, in such a place. What she'd really like right now, besides the freshly baked bread, was a phone book.

She wanted to get to the shop. She'd had enough drama to last a lifetime. The urge to sit down and read a nice lengthy book—something interesting along the lines of *Laughter of Dead Kings* by Elizabeth Peters. It had been ages since she'd read a mystery, and that one was fourteen years in the making. There was also *The One Hundred: A Guide to the Pieces Every Stylish Woman Must Own* by Nina Garcia and Ruben Toledo. Not that she was all about fashion. It just sounded interesting, that's all. She frowned.

"Can I help you find something, Ms. Lyndsey?" Genna started, heart pounding. The young woman they'd met the evening before, appearing out of nowhere.

"Um, I'd like to call a taxi," she told her. When the corners of the young woman's mouth turned down, Genna hastened to assure her, "I wanted to let Lorianne and Mrs. Bake...I mean...well." Genna stumbled over her explanation, "I thought they might want some time. Together. To visit."

"That's no problem, miss. But would you like to wait a bit? It's storming something fierce out. I could make you a nice breakfast, quiet like, while you wait."

Genna started to deny the need for food, when her stomach answered for her. Before she could stop herself, it, of course, slipped out, *"The belly is a commanding part of the body."* Luckily, it was under her breath. Sometimes people just didn't understand Homer or her.

"Excuse me, miss?"

"Thank you. That would be nice."

CHAPTER 29

"FINALLY." RICK WAS BREATHING fire by the time he saw Genna leap from the only available cab in town in front of Renewed Interest. Writhing fury, after having sat for over two hours in her driveway late the night before, finally admitting she wasn't coming home. Fuming when he found himself out of ideas to find her, knowing someone meant her harm.

He punched out a quick call to Ash, who was trying to chase down Lorianne, found his situation much the same. It occurred to Rick, not for the first time, women were a pain in the ass.

The rain returned in sheets. It did not improve his mood. He took a last swallow. A few choice words burned their way down his throat along with the hot coffee, but he was out the door and at her side before she could lock herself in. She was nothing if not predictable.

He grasped her arm before she slipped inside, startling her. Her instincts served her well, however, when her purse flew at his head. He managed to duck in time, but it clipped him on the shoulder. "Stop, it's me," he bit out. Relief flared in her eyes, replaced quickly by fury, hair dripping with rain.

Pushing her through the door, he spun and flipped the deadbolt. Hell, it was only six-thirty in the morning. Quick shallow breaths heaved in the dark.

"'*The only morality the tyrant recognizes is obedience to him.*'"

"Oh, please!" He almost laughed but suspected books weighted down her purse. He'd wager his shoulder would be blue by noon.

A flash of lightning pierced the sky, illuminating the store in an odd iridescent glow. The shaft of light showed her chin raised defiantly and her hand reaching for the light switch. Tossing out any rational thought, he snagged her wrist. "Not yet," he whispered. He caught her about the waist and tugged her into his body. He felt her stiffen, unsure of his next move. Understandable, since he couldn't tell her what his next move was to save his life. Rain pummeled the roof.

He brought her hand to his lips—kissed the tip of each finger.

Early morning gloom added to the intimacy. Eyes closed, he breathed in a fresh scent he didn't recognized. It wasn't wild honeysuckle. He planted a kiss in the hollow of her neck, damp with rain, and breathed her in. Her purse thumped to the floor.

Danger abated. It was a hopeful sign—it missed his foot. Her pulse throbbed beneath his lips. He paused, reveling in its wild pounding. Another hopeful sign. When she drew a quick breath, he scooped her up and set her on the worn sofa—safely away from the door.

He pressed a kiss to her forehead, skimmed a fingertip over her jaw. When she slipped her arms around his neck, he uttered a groan and took her mouth with a reckless abandon.

Her lips were full, sweet, and soft. His tongue met and chased hers. Diving, plummeting, sinking helplessly into her. She tasted delicious. He traced her jaw with his lips, feathered her closed eyes, cheeks. He moved back to her mouth with an impatience he hadn't felt since his college days. Wet, moist, hot.

Slender hands slid under his shirt to his chest. The silky touch on his bare skin pushed him over. In a single motion, he rid her of her glasses, dropping them on the table behind. He shoved her sweater over her head, pinning her arms—a helpful weapon.

His mouth moved over the lacy contours of her bra. A desperate squeak erupted. He smiled and glided his tongue over her ribs, nipping her in places with his teeth. He teased her belly, dipped his tongue in her navel, and chuckled softly when her muscles jumped in anticipation. How long had he been waiting for this? For her?

When a moaned ecstasy slipped through her lips, he stripped her of her jeans in one swift motion, divesting his own just as quickly. Adjusted to the dim wash of daylight, Rick could see her eyes widen with surprise, lips quivering with her unspoken passion.

In a moment of clarity, he realized he'd been waiting for this moment his whole life. This…this bookworm. When had she stolen his heart? The first obscure quote she'd spouted? The museum, when he couldn't drag his gaze from her peach-tinted lips?

And how? With those adorable sturdy-nerdy glasses? Or the wild crazy hair and brilliant brain? Whatever it was, the combination created a package that threatened to unman him.

Trying to still his rapid breathing, he moved up over her. Freeing her arms from her sweater, he covered her mouth in a hungry, desperate kiss. Her arms, delicate and tentative, slipped around his neck. He lifted her, and unhooked the clasp of her bra. He brushed a thumb over one nipple, licked and suckled the other. Luscious. He swirled his tongue over it, peaking it to beaded attention.

He couldn't stand it, he needed more. His arousal was so hard it pained him. But he didn't care. Looping his arms beneath her bent knees, he held them in place.

"No," she whispered.

"No?" He breathed against her.

"Yes."

He felt her shock. Just like the honeysuckle flower on those lazy summer days, plucked from the base of the petals, he spread her gently. His fingers applied pressure in a spot he hoped she'd never experienced before. Her gasped surprise confirmed it. He sucked at the nectar inside the petals to collect at the tip…over and over, never relenting, until she writhed beneath his mouth, screaming her release.

Her pleasure, sure and explosive, bounded from every hard surface in the shop. He drank sweet nectar, every exotic drop—holding her tight. Once her passion migrated to something more manageable, he pulled away.

Genna lay panting, chest heaving. "Oh, my. You're nothing like Damon."

"Damon!" he roared. He'd just given her the thrill of her life, and she compared him to…*Pretty Boy*?

"Oh, I-I didn't mean…I mean…'*I am indeed amazed when I consider how weak my mind is and how prone to error…*'" She trailed off, flushing. She tried to scoot away but he moved up beside her. Grabbing her hand, he placed it on his swollen flesh.

"This is what you do to me. You," he choked in a cracked whisper. "Just touch me."

Her hand brushed him with light soft strokes. She cupped his scrotum then raked her fingernails in an upward motion. Groaning, he raised his eyes to meet hers.

He clasped his hand over hers, showing her how to increase the pressure, his pleasure. To his astonishment, she dropped to her knees on the floor before him. Hot breath touched him.

His gasp was overcome by the blood pounded in his ears. She fondled him, awe lighting her expression. He fell back and squeezed his eyes tight. When her tongue explored the tip tenuously and her thumb traveled the rim in a light motion, he almost exploded.

That was for another time! In a prompt, efficient move, he had her straddling him, her protest stifled with his mouth. Slipping deep inside, he held her in place fighting for control.

"Don't...move," he begged.

But she shifted, testing him, moved side to side, back to front. He couldn't wait. With the cry of a warrior he let himself go, spilling himself into her. He crushed her into him, claimed her lips once more. A message skirted the back of his mind, something important, but forgotten. But he couldn't seem to make himself care right now.

Holding her to his chest, unwilling to let go, the sanity of the situation seeped through in small stages. The storm inside waned while the one outside still raged. Finally, awareness of their nudity crept into his mind. Awareness of the passing time.

Fighting his reluctance, he moved her to one side, and found her bra, her sweater, and her jeans and pitched them to her. "Put these on, before I come after you again," he growled,

She dressed in silence. A violent crackle of thunder rattled the building. She jumped.

"What time do you open this place?" he asked her.

"Nine-thirty." It came out in a croak. She cleared her throat, averted her eyes.

He grimaced. "Then why are you here so early?" He ran his fingers through his hair. Hell, he'd almost forgotten her disappearance. He demanded, "Why did you run out of Lewis Peale's house like that?" The more words that spilled from his mouth, the angrier he became. "And where the hell were you all night?"

GENNA ZIPPED UP HER jeans, body still throbbing with desire. She'd never felt anything like that in her whole life.

What did you say to a person after you had...had, well, done it that completely? How did you look at them? What did you say? And, had she really compared him to Damon? *Out loud?* Though Damon had nothing on Rick. How did he learn to do that stuff with his tongue? In retrospect, Damon had been a clumsy, awkward lover. Gosh. Apparently, she was practically a virgin. Or, rather, *used* to be practically a virgin, if what she'd just experienced was anything to go by.

It was obvious she had things to learn. In addition to researching lessons in art form and theory, she needed something regarding the social reform in handling oneself after an onslaught of intimacy. Maybe she should consider examining the pleasures of sex for anatomy. She cast a coveted glance toward Rick. Better yet, the male anatomy. Even better, Rick's anatomy.

She sighed. There probably wasn't a book on Rick's anatomy. A shame.

Lightning flashed, casting his face in harsh shadows. He was glaring at her. Heat flooded her face. Her heart pounded, competing with the rain on the roof.

She turned away embarrassed.

"Oh, no, you don't," he growled.

She squeaked when he snagged her from behind, pulling her back into his chest. He spun her around and devoured her mouth. His tongue invaded her, again. She couldn't think when he did this. She floated up, her feet leaving the ground. She clasped him tightly about the neck, and melted into his arms.

"Now. Tell me where you were last night," he whispered against her lips. "I watched for you all night."

"Last night?" she asked, confused. "Last night. I was at Joa..." she shook her head. "At Mrs. Bakely's."

"Mrs. Bakely? Victor Bakely's widow?" He let her feet touch the ground, only by sliding her down his hard body, rousing her passion again. "Why?"

She pushed at his shoulders. "This sounds suspiciously, like an inquisition," she accused.

He let her go.

She stepped back, tried to gather her muddled senses, pushed fingers through her damp hair. She must look a wreck. Her hair was crazy on her best days. She dreaded turning on the lights. "Where are my glasses?"

He reached around her to the table beside the sofa. He deposited them on her nose, adding a light kiss that spelled anything but chaste. "Stop that," she said, irritated at the thrilled current moving through her. She adjusted her glasses.

He grinned.

Stalking to the door, she flooded the room with lights. He winced at the sudden assault.

Her lips twitched.

"Why are you here so early?" he asked her.

"I always come in early."

"Six-thirty?"

"Sometimes." She leaned down and picked up her purse. The contents covered the floor.

"Where's Lorianne?"

She looked up and saw him glaring at her. She scooped up her wallet, loose change. "Lorianne hardly ever comes in early."

"She didn't go home last night either," he said.

She flashed him a startled glance.

"Ash was looking for her."

"Oh." Genna stood and moved behind the counter. She set her purse below. Still unable to meet his eyes, she said, "She learned last night that Mrs. Bakely is her paternal grandmother. I wanted to give them time to visit." She lifted a shoulder, feigning indifference. "So I called a cab."

"She didn't know her paternal grandmother?" He sounded confused.

Genna sighed. "It's complicated."

"Granted," he conceded. Then, "you've answered two of my three questions. Why did you run out of Lewis Peale's last night?"

"I don't have to answer your questions, you know." She pierced him with a stubborn look. "I'm here to work. If you don't want to help, then you need to leave." As if to punctuate her sentence, God helped out with a blinding bolt of lightning, followed by a blast of thunder that brought her hands over her ears.

The lights flickered, then winked out.

BY HIS ESTIMATION, THERE was over an hour before anyone was due at the bookstore. Even if Genna came in early, as was her normal habit, there was still time to take care of business. No lights had appeared in the store within the last half hour. He'd watched.

Genna's car still was parked at Plank's, but she and Lorianne were seen leaving with Joanna Bakely the evening before.

This rain was a killer. But it might end up being more of a help.

He edged his way around the corner, convinced normal people were snug in their beds, where they ought to be.

If he didn't get this job taken care of, all would be lost. He scowled. Someone had suspected the circumstances of his father's death. He was running out of time. He had to stop Genna's expansion plans.

Whoever *they* were, and whether *they* knew it or not *they* were in over their heads and *they* would pay. When he completed this job, he would be free. Free to love. He savored the word. Free to…

His mouth started to water with the familiar craving. It had to be the stress.

CHAPTER 30

LORIANNE STRETCHED HER ARMS over her head. Arching her back, she pulled in a deep breath then let it out in a big whoosh. She sank back into the large comfy bed, let her muscles go limp, reveled in being covered in pink and white pillows. She loved pink!

A grandmother! It just didn't seem possible. After the news hit her all she could manage was to sit on that silly-looking red and gold settee, processing everything Joanna Bakely said with a stone face. How Joanna chased her mother away, not realizing she was pregnant. Then her biological father had died. Died! At twenty-one.

The story was fantastic at best. Mrs. Bakely had started crying. Oh, not big sobs, like Lorianne was apt to do, but huge silent tears. And Lorianne sat there and let her. Totally lost, with no idea what to say.

Genna escaped just before the first tear spilled. Oh, it all sounded so hopeless.

How could she have a grandmother who lived in such a monstrosity of a house? With so much money? While Lorianne and her mother lived on the streets. Never knowing where they would sleep or eat from one day to the next.

On the one hand she felt ecstatic—*she had a grandmother*.

But guilt stabbed her with a sharp blade. The suffering her mother went through. How ill-treated. How they'd struggled, the places they'd slept, lived.

And, now Mrs. Bakely, now to be called Joanna—she could think again! New anger swept over her. Lorianne had managed without a grandmother all these years, she could continue to do so.

She rolled over and closed her eyes. She would think about it, *her*, later. For once, the rain offered an isolated comfort. Well, that and the bathroom light, door slightly ajar.

ASH PICKED UP HIS cell on the first ring. "Any luck?" he barked into it.

"Apparently, they stayed at Joanna Bakely's mansion last night."

"How did you find that out?" Ash slumped in his chair, hardly believing the relief soaring through him.

"Genna showed up to work at six-thirty this morning. We've...uh...been talking."

"I'll bet," Ash grinned. Rick's hesitation hid nothing.

"Look, I just wanted to let you know she's okay. There have been some revelations."

"What? That Joanna Bakely finally had the guts to inform Lorianne she's her grandmother?"

"Jesus. I thought I was the investigator. How does everyone know all this stuff before me?"

Ignoring that, Ash said gruffly, "Thanks for letting me know." He snapped the phone shut and pulled himself from the chair which protested loudly. He took up a stance before the window. The gray clouds matched his morose mood perfectly. The rain had slowed to a steady drizzle— Slow and depressing.

Ash had checked all the windows and doors at Lorianne's

house—not that she would appreciate it. Once it dawned on him Lorianne wasn't hurrying home, he'd gone to his office and paced the floor the remainder of the night. It hadn't hurt to make sure no one was lurking about. Knowing she and Genna were more than likely together eased his fears a little, and, yes, damn it all, his jealousy.

He'd managed a little sleep, evidenced by the wrinkled throw on the sofa. Though it was only psychological, he felt better when he could see the store. Playing watchdog helped in a small way. He'd never admit it to anyone, however.

This strange sensation in his gut was unfamiliar territory. Now that Lorianne knew Joanna was her grandmother, he had a feeling it would not be easy to rein her back in.

He had to face a tough fact. He might have really blown it.

Ash touched his forehead on the glass. As clear as he could make out in the pouring rain, some guy stalked alongside Ida's craft store and turned down the alley.

JOANNA SAT IN HER massive kitchen gazing out at the gloomy weather. She'd handled things all wrong with her granddaughter. She pulled in her resolve. She was finished with crying, however soothing it might feel. She had a granddaughter to win over. She would not buy her. There was plenty of time for that once Joanna filled her time allotted on this earth.

No, what Lorianne needed was—acceptance, strength and love—that only a grandmother could fill. Unconditionally.

She sipped the tepid tea, barely aware of its lack of warmth. Elbows resting on the table, fists supporting her chin, she continued her contemplation beyond the windows. She started at Lorianne's warm presence.

"This kitchen is something." Lorianne planted herself directly across the table.

"Tea?"

"Is there coffee brewing somewhere in this gargantuan of an eating place?"

"Gargantuan? Is that what they taught you at that fancy college?"

"Fancy college?"

Joanna flushed at Lorianne's narrowed eyes.

"You paid for my college?"

Joanna paused, wondering how much to tell her. In the end, it wouldn't matter. Honesty was the best policy from here on out. "Yes."

Her heart broke in more pieces when Lorianne shifted an unreadable gaze around the kitchen. How she must feel seeing how Joanna had lived while she and her mother…she might as well come clean.

"Well, you have to admit, your grades were not the best." Joanna issued her best disciplinarian tone. It helped in hiding her anguish. "The scholarships weren't forthcoming in droves, if you remember."

Lorianne acknowledged the remark with a small shrug. At least she hadn't stalked out.

"When did you find me?" Lorianne's voice was quiet, controlled.

Disguising the pain as best she could, Joanna hesitated, and then sighed. "I'd hired an investigator several years before, trying to locate your mother. When your father died, I was devastated. By the time I'd realized how arrogant, obnoxious, demeaning, monstrous…"

"Okay, okay. I get it. You were a bitch," she concurred. "I'll take some tea."

Joanna nodded to the maid, who immediately presented a steaming cup.

"I'll admit my mother was not the easiest person to live with. But that's all I'll admit."

Joanna continued, "Well, she appeared to fall off the face of the earth." She took a deep breath. "I'd dismissed the investigator a good five years before you were seventeen. Then one day he called out of the blue, said he'd run across an article in the St. Louis newspaper and did some checking…the rest, they say, is history…" her voice trailed.

The confusion on Lorianne's face was torture. "But why wait so long to tell me? Didn't you want me?" Her voice broke.

"Oh, darling. Of course, I wanted you. More than anything." Joanna's own voice cracked. She ached to take Lorianne in her arms, but Lorianne had to know everything. "The only reason I found you was *because* you'd just lost your mother. Afterward, I kept in very close contact with the school counselor." She paused. "You were in such a fragile state. Rebellious state. She was able to convince you that college was something productive."

"She also made me realize, had I stepped in at that moment with all of this." She flung out an open palm toward the elaborate kitchen. "You weren't ready for such a change. Not at that crossroads in your life. So I-I took her advice. I stood back, watched you. Waited for you to settle." Flinging out another restless motion of her hand, she said, "Time made it harder to disclose the truth. You were doing so well. Your friendship with Genna. Your business. You needed each other. I couldn't hinder that…" Joanna broke off, raising her eyes, to meet Lorianne's exact match.

"Genna." Lorianne's lips quivered with emotion, eyes dropping. "Genna would say something ridiculous like, '*Our great illusion is to believe that we are what we think ourselves to be.*' Then she would punctuate it with 'Henri Amiel, blah blah blah!'"

"Yes, she would," Joanna agreed with a soft smile. Joanna waited, clenching her impatience through hands hidden in her lap while Lorianne contemplated her. It was agony.

Before Joanna could blink, Lorianne was out of her chair, on her knees, head in Joanna's lap, sobbing loud, gulping sobs. Joanna dared to breathe, smoothing her hands over Lorianne's hair, thanking God for this wonderful gift she surely did not deserve. She lifted her granddaughter's chin and faced her tear filled eyes.

"I *do* love you. You will never know the regret that fills me for all we've lost. I know there is no excuse for how I treated your mother, except for my own petty jealousy." She frowned and cupped Lorianne's face with both hands. "But, know this. I tried to make it up by seeking what advice was at hand. I'm not sure what I could or should have done differently, but I will make it up to you somehow." Her own tears fell free. Joanna leaned forward and placed a kiss on her granddaughter's brow.

"Joanna," was Lorianne's whispered response.

CHAPTER 31

GENNA LOCKED THE DOOR behind Rick, unable to stifle her grin. Her face hurt from wanting to smile so much. Then laughed outright thinking how Rick insisted she follow him down to the basement.

He was just showing off how men understood junction box wiring better than women. She knew the wiring was faulty. She did need to call an electrician. She would do it today. She would. She smiled again. It was kind of nice being worried about.

The lights flickered again, sending her into another aggravating darkness. This infernal rain was going to put her out of business. She jerked up the flashlight for her second trek down.

So this was what it felt like to be in love. *Love*. That wiped the grin off her face. She was *not* in love. How could you fall in love with—number one, a man whom you'd known less than a month? A man who was tall, strong, and...okay, attractive.

A man who—number two, thought one could sabotage their own business for insurance money, because that is surely what he thought. Or could conspire such a thing. The idea was ridiculous. That did not constitute love. She was not the one who fell in love at the drop of a hat. That was Lorianne's specialty.

And, three. Just because he knew how to do those really

strange and exciting things with his tongue…well, it didn't mean she was in *love* with the man.

She was all wrong for someone like him. She'd seen the woman who had landed in his lap at Pat's. All sophistication and glamour. While she, a little known used bookstore owner, tried to expand a small business with disaster after disaster plaguing her.

She had crazy hair, not sleek, black, and glossy. Goofy glasses that covered not-so-spectacular eyes—certainly not mysterious exotic ones. Nor long sleek legs. Just skinny, short ones that could fall open... She plopped down on the bottom stair. What could someone like Rick Johnson possibly see in someone like her? Genna's cheeks burned in sudden humiliation. Especially when she thought about those wicked things he'd done. How could she look him in the face ever again? Elbows on her knees, she dropped her face into cool palms. Salve on hot cheeks.

Anyone would have nailed the rickety railing back into place, like he'd done before he left. She would have laughed thinking how he'd stopped at the base of the steps, causing her to stumble into him. He'd turned so quickly and sucked the breath from of her with sinful kisses in the dark. He was certainly experienced with firm lips and a busy tongue. Teasing her wrists, her neck, her earlobes. Sensitive earlobes might be something worth researching. But she didn't feel like laughing. If it wasn't love, it was something just as devastating.

Genna coughed. She felt choked up. Unguarded emotion took a toll on girls like her. Burning tears stung her eyes. She swiped them away and reached for the flashlight. She pointed the beam up where dust moats danced in a hazy swirl, then shined the light towards the junction box, the effort difficult. Time to get busy.

Inhaling another deep breath, she stood, but the burning sensation that had her eyes watering now scratched her throat.

Genna coughed as realization punched her in the gut.

It wasn't dust floating in the air, but smoke.

RICK STRUTTED DOWN THE street past Ida's craft store, intent on Ash's office, where the rain had finally lessened to a steady drizzle. He grinned, satisfied his little bookworm had finally started to understand the importance of contracting a qualified electrician. Satisfied, that…hell, just satisfied. For the moment anyway.

"I thought you were going to call an electrician." Rancor sharpened Rick's tongue. "At least the rain is starting to taper off."

"When have I had time?" Genna retorted. "It was just yesterday." He snatched the flashlight out of her hand. She had her hand on the doorknob, the one that led to the basement, the one with a broken railing. "Give me that! It's my shop and my responsibility."

"Come on. I want to show you something." He nudged her aside and started down the stairs. "Be careful, the railing needs work."

"Are you kidding me?"

He grinned at her sarcasm, knowing she couldn't see his face. He might have laughed outright if he wasn't afraid she'd help him the rest of the way down, the easy way—with a small shove on his back.

He stopped at the bottom. She plowed into him like he knew she would. Steadying her with a firm hand, he stole a quick kiss. Well, maybe it wasn't so quick. She was delicious. Succulent and juicy. It was dark. It was private. If her jeans—correct that, if their jeans were gone, he could just lift her up. Have her wrapped legs… He touched his lips to hers again. It sounded like fireworks going off in the background. The heat crackled between them.

Yes. Satisfied. He could hardly wait until later. Now that

he'd had her, he wouldn't be letting go anytime soon. His pocket vibrated. Ah, his cell.

"It's Ash. I can see you from my office. You'd better get here. I see something a little strange." Something in Ash's tone had trepidation prickling down his spine.

"Two minutes." He clicked off, and took off like the devil was at his heels.

Rick followed Ash's voice to his office when he opened the door from the stairwell, panting from the three flights he'd taken in a dead run. "What is it?"

"Check this out."

Rick hurried to the windows where Ash had not budged.

"There," he pointed. "At the back of Ida's."

Rick squinted, the rain hindering his vision for a moment. Then he saw it...or rather...him. "Who is it?" He made out a figure in a gray zipper front, hood covering his head, oddly positioned in the alley.

"I can't tell. The rain isn't helping." Ash's tone reflected his confusion.

"What the hell is he doing? Breaking a window?" Rick had a bad feeling. "That's the back of the expansion space. He's crawling *out* of the window." It made no sense. They watched in silence as their quarry looked around quickly before darting through the back door at Plank's. "I don't understand," Ash said.

Rick shook his head, equally puzzled. Just as he started to turn his head, something else caught his attention. Something dire. "Is that..."

"Smoke?"

"Ho, shit." Rick ran for the door. "Call 911. Genna's in the store. Fuck." He took off. Raw, primitive terror seared through him. Only the thought of her suffering kept him from succumbing to anguish strong enough to drop him to his knees.

GENNA'S THROAT ACHED, HER eyes burned. She knew you were supposed to keep your cool, act fast, yet with caution. Stay low. That was one of the rules too, right? But what the heck were you supposed do that when you were already underground, that was low, right? Keeping cool? Impossible, it was a fire! Act fast. Act fast. *How? What else?*

Okay. Caution. Caution. Caution, she chanted silently. Why would nothing else come to mind, she wanted to scream?

What about panic? No! No, you weren't supposed to panic. Crying. Was crying allowed? What if you couldn't help crying? You probably shouldn't cry. That might entice panic. Frightened? That was more a feeling. She was frightened. There was nothing you could do about how you felt.

Where were these stupid thoughts coming from? Funny. She felt like laughing. How could you feel like laughing, when you were about to cry or die? She gasped, which started a bout of coughing. Oh, right. It was that outer body experience thing again. It seemed to be taking over quite a bit lately. She could see the smoke clearly now. Dust particles hung heavy in the air. If you rose out of your body in the outer body experience, you rose out of the smoke, right? Or did it put you in the thick of it? She felt a little like crying. No. She felt like laughing.

Which was it?

No one knew she was here. No one—except—Rick. Oh, no, she was slipping. She tried to stifle back tears. If she started crying, she wouldn't be able to stop, and then she wouldn't be able to see. Which made her want to laugh again. It was dark, she *wasn't able to see anyway.*

How did you act fast, yet with caution, when you were underground, in a fire, and no one knew where you were? If panic was not okay she was in a lot of trouble. *Because she was about to lose it. She screamed.* A blood curling scream with every ounce of fear, frustration, and yes…panic…devoured her.

She dropped to the floor. Defeat? She'd left a note for Lorianne and Mrs. Bak...Oh, wait...they were supposed to call her Joanna. Joanna. If Joanna got the note, she was going to be their grandmother, right? A grandmother. She'd never had a grandmother before, at least not one she'd known. She'd never had a sister either. But Lorianne and she were sisters, in the ways that mattered. She couldn't leave behind a sister.

The sink in the corner! Did it even work? She didn't know but she could try. She reached for the flashlight. She jumped to her feet before remembering you were supposed to stay low. Yes, she had the flashlight. She might not need the flashlight. Fire was light, who needed a flashlight in a fire? Another hysterical laugh choked out, scraping her raw throat.

Sirens. Were those sirens? She'd heard sirens the other day. Next door. Was that glass breaking?

Yes. "I'm down here, I'm down here," she screamed, but her voice, already spent, only croaked. "I'm down here," she whispered, falling to her knees, eyes stinging with tears. "Down here…"

Someone yelled her name. Didn't they? Genna crawled to the stairs. She pulled her sweater up, in an effort to cover her nose. She couldn't do it, she was too tired. The smoke was asphyxiating. Just for a minute. She'd close her eyes, just for a minute.

Dark brown eyes met hers, comforted her. She reached out—nothing. It was a dream. It was okay, she just needed a minute…seconds…really…she slipped away.

Her out of body experience again, she supposed.

THE FIREFIGHTER REACHED FOR Genna. Over Rick's dead body.

"This way." With an amused grin the firefighter led the way to the truck. "We need to check her vitals."

Yes, they needed to check her vitals—that made sense. Rick

hurried after him to the ambulance, but they'd have to kill him to make him relinquish her. Her limp body hung from his arms like a rag doll. The emergency tech reached for her.

"No. Just do it," Rick barked.

"Sir?"

"Check her vitals."

"W-we have a gurney..."

"No." He tightened his hold. Her hair stood straight out, black soot covered her clothes, face, hands. Volcanic rage roiled below the surface, but the vein ran deep.

"Please, sir—"

"Rick, put her on the gurney." Ash stood there, next to the stretcher.

Slowly, Rick lowered her on the makeshift bed. The tech slipped an oxygen mask over her nose and started with her blood pressure. A small cough erupted from Genna and tears pricked the back of his eyes. He'd never heard such a welcome sound.

In a surreal fog, Rick looked around. The fire was under control now. The plate glass window was broken out to the south of the storefront. Quite a crowd had amassed in the street from both Victory and Elm.

Mrs. Finch leached onto Ash's arm, her impish face creased with worry. Construction personnel poured from Ash's new office project along Victory. Many of the shops in town were unopened just yet. The bank clock put the time at close to nine. Most opened at ten.

Plank stood outside his coffee shop with his standard grim expression. Did he ever not have a grim expression? Rick didn't think so. But, the perpetrator had slipped in through the back door of Plank's and it bothered him. A coincidence?

Pretty Boy stood next to Plank. Not surprising. He was too well put together, considering the messy weather—poking a hole in the theory that he was their guy.

Sara Pendergrass had come out of her bakery, bearing gifts of pastries; one of her employees followed carrying coffee.

Frustrated, *scared*, Rick knew he was missing something. His glance swept the area for a second time. Something. Or *someone*.

He started when one of the emergency techs said something. They started to load Genna into the ambulance. "What are you doing?" he snapped.

"No burns, but there's smoke inhalation. We're admitting her to the hospital for observation," he repeated. "Who is the emergency contact?"

"Me," he growled. His confident tone brooked no argument. He turned to the closest firefighter. "We need to get her bag. It's on the counter. Just inside," he added when the man turned a skeptical probe on him.

Rick turned on his heel, content to let him follow.

CHAPTER 32

GENNA GROANED. HER CHEST hurt, her head hurt. The light. She tried to tell someone to turn off the lights, but nothing emerged.

"Don't talk."

She recognized the voice but for the life of her she couldn't put a name to it. A warm large hand engulfed hers. Her eyes, too heavy to open, felt swollen shut.

"Water?" she croaked. A second later her head was lifted from the pillow and the rim of a plastic cup touched her lips.

"Slow. Take it slow," he commanded.

"Lights. Can you turn down the lights?" She could whisper now. At least a little. She squinted but she couldn't focus. The florescent lights winked out. Gray overcast sky flowed through tinted windows. "Better," she sighed.

"Can you tell me what happened?" His voice was deep, strong, familiar…Genna's head fell back, she closed her eyes.

"I-I don't know. I…can't remember." Her voice sounded far away.

"It's okay. We'll figure it out." His voice soothed her ravaged thoughts. "Get some rest. I'll be here when you wake up." She sunk into oblivion, those last words comforting her.

"Where is she?" Lorianne screeched. "What did you do to her?"

Ashton blocked the door to Genna's hospital room. She pounded her fists on his chest. "What did *I* do to her?" He manacled her wrists, immovable.

His voice was cold and stoic, but she didn't flinch. Joanna caught her upper arms from behind and pulled her gently from his hold. It didn't offer much comfort.

"Lorianne, I'm sure Ashton had nothing to do with this," Joanna said.

Lorianne turned narrowed eyes on Ashton Turner. He looked as if he hadn't slept in days. It served the bastard right. Once she would have reveled in running a soothing hand over his tired eyes, held him to her breast, kissed the scar on his cheek. But now? He'd lost his fucking chance.

"I had nothing to do with this."

Lorianne returned his insolent gaze with a vile one of her own. She was immune to it…*him* now.

"She's going to be okay," he said.

He was placating her, surely designed to invoke reassurance—it infuriated her.

"But keep your voice down, she's resting."

They stood in one cold, stark wing of three at Bloomington Medical Center. The blue wing of the hospital was just that. All the doors were painted blue, against a drab dungeon of beige walls. Lorianne glanced around wildly.

Tears threatened to spill. "Where is she?"

Rick poked his head out of the nearest room. "In here. Can you keep it down?"

Lorianne shook off Joanna's hold and brushed by Rick. The sight on the bed would not let her contain her tears. She tried her best not to heave big gulping sobs by shoving her fist in her mouth. It almost worked.

"Lorianne?" Genna croaked.

Lorianne rushed to the bedside grabbing her hand. "Oh, my God," she whispered.

"Do I look *that* bad?"

Lorianne, so relieved to hear her speak, blurted, "I'm afraid so."

"Is it okay to come in?" Joanna Bakely rounded the door.

"Of course, Mrs...I...I mean...Joanna," Genna stammered.

Joanna slipped through the door followed by Rick, then Ashton. Lorianne could feel the fear grip Genna. She squeezed Lorianne's hand, cutting off the circulation. Her eyes plastered on Ashton.

Lorianne glared at Ashton. "Get out," she hissed. But Ashton ignored Lorianne, and focused his scrutiny on Genna. Contempt inflamed her.

"Someone crawled out of a window from your expansion into the alley." There was a hard edge to his voice Lorianne hadn't witnessed before. She froze.

"Who?" Genna croaked.

"Try not to talk, dear," Joanna told her.

"Who?" Lorianne repeated. She eyed him with suspicion. She wouldn't put it past him to lie.

"We couldn't tell. He ran into Plank's." He raked an indifferent glance over Lorianne, which raised her skin into a million tiny pinpricks. She hoped he could feel the daggers she shot him. If looks could kill... "Then all hell broke loose," he finished with annoying detachment.

"But, if you saw...then you..." Genna's voice was broken, raspy. It hurt Lorianne's throat feeling Genna's fight for breath.

"Don't talk, dear," Joanna told her again.

"But..." It was a whisper. She turned pleading eyes on Lorianne. Lorianne compressed her lips, stubbornly. She knew what Genna wanted her to say, but Lorianne didn't want to say it. If Ashton had really seen someone lurking…escaping…running, then it eliminated him as the saboteur. Lorianne tugged her hand from Genna's and crossed her arms over her chest. She did *not* want to let him off the hook.

He stood there waiting in that exasperating way of his. Lorianne glanced at Genna, begging her—*don't make me say it*. Too late. Lorianne blew out a frustrated breath at Genna's softening expression.

Lorianne turned to Rick. "What is your consensus?"

"We did see someone come out of the store in the alley," he confirmed, "I suspect it might have something to do with Plank, but I can't imagine what. It's worth checking out."

"Shouldn't we be letting Genna get her rest?" Joanna asked them.

A resounding three nos and one croak made Lorianne want to laugh. Hysterically, at least. Hysterics should be allowed.

CHAPTER 33

"HOLY SHIT!" ADRENALINE PUMPED through his veins. He fell to the floor on his knees. The cravings consumed him. He had to get control, remain focused. Black spots swarmed his vision, turning the room into a freakish funhouse one might find at a traveling fair.

A hairy ball of fur pressed its head against his thigh. He pushed it away, then scrubbed away the perspiration that had gathered at his upper lip. He'd had no idea Genna was in the bookstore. He'd almost hurt her. His head fell in his hands. He loved her! He closed his eyes rocking back and forth, before drawing in a shaky breath.

"Meow."

None of the other minor things had hurt anyone, well, if you didn't count the ladder.

"You know, Kitty? I risked my life getting on that roof. Loosening those shingles wasn't easy. In the dark. In the rain! I've snuck in through that stupid window a hundred times. Why was she there? *It was six-thirty in the friggin' morning.*"

The cat rubbed his leg. He ran a fingertip behind its ears.

"I know she loves me," he told the ball of fur. She responded with a soft purr. Unless Genna found out he'd almost killed her, he scowled.

"I know she's not as pretty as her friend, but she's nice to me," he said. "Everyone else treats me like some stupid nerd. But when she looks at me, she really sees me." Not some goofy idiot like his father used to say. He couldn't even form the words aloud. Of course, his father wasn't a problem any longer. He'd been gone for over four years.

The cat, impatient with its head rub, jumped in his lap. "We've known each other for years. I-I'll talk to her—tell her how much *I* love her. That's what I'll do."

Willing his pounding heart to slow, he brought himself to his feet and dropped the cat to all fours. He locked the door and pitched his keys on a nearby table. They slid off, crashing against the wall behind. He ignored the miss and paced the small lobby area. His mother would be in soon. It wouldn't do at all to be agitated.

"Come on, Kitty. You're probably hungry." He made his way down the short hallway to the tiny break room. Toddy checked the cat's dish for water and food.

She hopped on the counter in a graceful leap. "No one saw me climbing through the window." He blew out a breath. "But when I heard the sirens before I got out…well, it was a close call." He touched his nose to the cat's; nuzzled its head in a rhythmic motion. "I didn't dare come in through the alley," he told him.

The back entrance to the photo studio connected to the alley that separated the museum's parking. There was too much risk of being seen. Darting through Plank's kitchen was a risk as well, especially when he'd almost knocked the old man down. Maybe he'd do something about Plank. No one would miss him anyway. He was a mean old bastard.

But Plank scared the crap out of him. The malevolence in his face when he'd stepped back is what sent his adrenaline surging.

Now that he'd calmed down, he couldn't help but wonder if Plank wasn't the one blackmailing him. But why? What reason would he have for not wanting Genna to expand her business?

"Could it be Plank? No one knows him very well," he told the cat. She gave another purred response, louder this time.

Once in a while the old man showed up at a town meeting or at Pat's like he did the other night. The more Toddy thought about it, the more plausible it seemed. He tapped his chin with blunt fingers. But how had Plank learned his secret?

He pictured the little colorless crystals he ached to smash to powder. Closing his eyes, he inhaled deeply, feeling the tickle of powder in his nostrils. His hands trembled with the force to follow through in reality, but Toddy pursed his lips with grim determination.

The drive had already started to build. He grabbed hold with chains of unbreakable steel. He wanted to fight it, but it was already too late. Plank and Genna retreated from his mind. He pushed the cat away and made his way past rooms set up for the next shoot. Graduating students and first babies. The cat, anticipating his destination, darted in front of him to the back of the shop, and shot into the dark room before Toddy slammed the door to lock out the world.

With a shaking hand, Toddy Wilson reached for the stash of crystals hidden in a ceiling panel.

"THE FIRST THING WE need to do is determine why the bastard ran into Plank's," Rick said. His mellow baritone was edged with teetering control. His body vibrated with a fury he hadn't known he possessed.

When he thought how close she'd come to…it didn't bear thinking about.

"You're going to bust a gasket if you don't get hold of yourself," Ash said.

Rick responded with a clenched fist. He wanted to hit someone, and Ash looked like hell. He didn't need to lose it on the one person he trusted. He took a measured breath. It helped.

Rick stood at the window while Ash sat across his desk reading the dossier on Wilhelm Plank. "Second generation emigrant from World War II Germany. Widowed after thirty-three years of marriage to one Ilse Katrine Plank. One daughter, Liesl Katrine, deceased, age twenty-six. One granddaughter, Richelle Ilse, deceased, age eight. Good God." Ash breathed.

Rick ran fingers through his hair. "Yeah. The whole family was lost in the Rhine Floods in Köln, Germany twenty years ago. Can you imagine? It certainly explains the hard expression he wears."

Ash cleared his throat. "It says here 'Wilhelm Plank, small business owner, was in London when the storms hit. An estimated fifty thousand people in Köln, and tens of thousands more from eastern France to the Netherlands, were driven from their homes over the Christmas holiday; Jesus! Over Christmas. I can't believe I'm going to say this but his life was worse than mine."

"Just in a different way." Rick's heart sank as Ash went on.

"At least five people were killed in Germany. Three of which were Plank's family." He stopped and Rick turned around. "None of this has anything to do with Plank setting the fire," Ash told him.

"No, but it gives insight to the man himself. Think about it. He comes to this country to start over after a catastrophic loss-not just monetary. Builds a somewhat thriving business. In the interim—or rather, late in his life— two young women just out of college open up a bookstore that steadily grows." Rick paced the carpet, laying out his thoughts. "Luck and opportunity meet when trends change in their favor. Bookstores all over the country start diversifying businesses by adding little coffee shops, and *voila*! Competition."

"It's not *that* farfetched. But what you are suggesting is cold-blooded," Ash agreed, but shook his head.

"The question is," Rick went on, "does competing for the premier coffee shop in a town of 11,000 people lead to murder?"

Ash ignored him. "There's more."

"You're not going to like it," Rick said, turning back to the window.

"I already don't like it." Ash flipped to the next page. "'The estimated damage ranged in the hundreds of millions of dollars. The river, normally a quarter of a mile wide, coursed through Köln, swelling to more than half a mile across, inundating roads and cellars.'"

"Yeah, his family was in the basement of their sweet shop," Rick finished for him.

"Shit. According to this, the granddaughter was scared of storms and hid in the basement. Ilse and Liesl were trying to find her when the floods poured through. Their bodies were located when the waters receded." Ash set the report aside.

"The thing is," Rick admitted, "I didn't see anything indicating criminal behavior." He ran his fingers through his hair. "Hell. God only knows what I would have done if I'd lived through something like that."

"Where's the story on Damon?" Ash asked. "I'm sure you ran one on him as well."

"You're so sure?" Rick meandered back to his desk.

Ash snorted.

Rick picked up the phone. "Lillian, did Officer Godwin drop off a report for me?" Lillian marched through the door holding a thick manila envelope. "Thanks."

Rick sliced open the envelope and pulled out the sheaths of paper. "All right," he started. "Damon J. Wharton, height five nine, weight one seventy, eyes brown, hair brown, place of birth, Orange County, California. That figures," he smirked.

"Citizenship...blah blah blah," he scanned. "Okay. Reporting Agency, Pima County Sheriff's Department. Scars, marks, tattoos, amputations. Well, I know what I'd want amputated," he muttered.

"Just stick to the report," Ash retorted.

Rick threw him a scowl, but complied. "Convictions. Here we are. Two Felonies: Sexual Conduct with a Minor, Selling Alcohol to a Minor."

"What about prison? Did he go to prison?"

He ran a finger down the page. "Custody and Case Information. Incarceration, eight months, Yuma State Prison. Participated in the Impact of Crime on Victims program, Thinking Straight. Huh!" he grunted. "Apparently, he did the 'diddy' with a seventeen-year-old. Daddy found out and turned him in."

"Hope he learned to keep his pants zipped," Ash commented.

"He also sold alcohol to minors." Rick pitched the papers to Ash in disgust.

"Well, with a record he would be smart to watch his step. It could certainly backfire," Ash said, head down, continuing the read-through. "Has Genna said anything about him stalking her?"

"No. Nothing." He gritted his teeth. "He's worth keeping an eye on."

"Just makes you want to beat the crap out of the little peon, doesn't it?"

Rick scowled at Ash's little disguised humor. It sure as hell did. But he wasn't about to say it aloud. That would point to premeditation.

Rick stood. "I need to get to the hospital."

"I WANT TO GO HOME." Genna knew her bottom lip poked out in a pout, but she couldn't help it. Her whole life had just gone up in smoke, literally.

"You sound a little better. How is your throat?" Rick bit back a smile.

Irritated, Genna curled on her side away from him. "Still scratchy." She was *not* going to cry, at least not in front of him.

"It's only overnight." His gentle tone almost did her in. She did not want pity. She hated that he felt sorry for her. All the more so after those embarrassing things he'd done to her. How pathetic.

"'*One night awaits all, and death's path must be trodden once and for all.*' Horace."

"So we're back to that, are we?"

"What?" She was *not* going to look at him. Blinking back tears, she rolled over and looked at him. He was sitting in the hospital's brown vinyl recliner, feet propped up, arms folded over his chest. She didn't know what to make of his frown. He had his eyes closed.

She couldn't resist the opportunity to study him. His brown hair was in disarray, deep circles under his eyes. She'd forgotten he hadn't slept the night before. He must not have gotten any rest.

He was so attractive it hurt, reinforcing her reservations about their tenuous relationship. Honestly, she couldn't believe it had gone as far as it had. He seemed to be everywhere. She cringed and new tears blurred her vision. Only because he thought she was sabotaging her own property. The thought was a bitter pill.

It must be clear by now that she wasn't, unless he believed she was suicidal. His breathing deepened. Lord, he'd fallen asleep. Genna sighed and closed her own eyes and reveled in the sound of the slow and even pace.

Surprised—because for the first time in weeks, she felt…safe.

CHAPTER 34

LORIANNE WAS A BUNDLE of nerves. She wasn't sure what else could happen in their lives, her life, to shock her more. Mrs. Bakely...Joanna Bakely...*Joanna*...

Lorianne hadn't even known she had a grandmother before yesterday, and now she was supposed to call her something completely different. Lorianne sucked in a breath. A grandmother—who was a *freaking* millionaire. She could hardly fathom the thought. Granted, she seemed pretty nice. How little-orphan-Lori-*Annie* could you get?

Oh my God. She started laughing. It didn't take much for such hysterics to turn it into tears. In fact, it took nothing, because they were free-flowing. She sank to the floor in her little living room. One shoe poked her uncomfortably on her bottom. She dug out a spiked-heel gladiator sandal and pitched it towards the bedroom.

Joanna had wanted her to stay at 'The Mansion' but she needed space. Space and time. Rick was at the hospital with Genna. So she grabbed the opportunity to get out…and away.

A knock sounded on the door, startling her. She was tempted to not answer, but her car was in the driveway, so there was no way she could get away with not being home. Dragging herself to her feet, she swung it open.

"Oh, for God's sake. Why do *you* keep popping up?" she demanded of Ashton.

"We need to talk." He didn't wait for her to invite him in, just opened the door and strolled in like he owned the place. Jerk.

"I'm not talking,"

"Good. I'll talk, you can listen." He sat on the couch, making himself at home, stretching out his long legs.

She narrowed her eyes. He had all the motions of someone in complete control, but she sensed the underlying tension that belied his supposed ease. She lowered herself across from him into a large poofy chair with big armrests and an ottoman to match, mirroring his ease. And waited. For a minute, she thought he'd lost his nerve.

"I know you're angry with me."

"Brilliant deduction." She said this under her breath. Was that hurt glittering in his eyes? Ha. Lorianne clenched her teeth, pushing away any softening thoughts regarding Ashton Turner. It had to be her imagination. He was the one who hadn't respected her enough to call. She owed him nothing.

"I did offer to buy Genna's property, you know."

"I know," she clipped. That seemed to irritate him. *Good.*

"But I did not do anything outside of having Van Horn contact her."

She kept silent.

He let out an exasperated sigh. He pulled his legs up and leaned forward, knees supporting his elbows. "I would never have done such a thing."

Lorianne considered him in a frank and direct manner. "I think that's true as well," she relented. "Now. If that's all?"

"No. That's not all," he growled.

She pursed her lips. "Then get to the point. I'm tired."

"Aren't we all?" He shoved a hand through his hair. He did

look tired. She stifled the tiny ache to offer him comfort. That was just a habit she had with men, a *bad* habit. The one that led to all her troubles.

She decided to let him off the hook. "Look," she started, "I'm not angry with you anymore. It was clear this morning at the hospital you aren't the one who's been doing…" She waved out a hand. "…stuff." His eyes drilled her. She pulled in a deep breath, determined to get through this. "You don't owe me anything."

"I'm not here because I think I *owe* you something," he rumbled. His frustration confused her. But, again, she pushed it away.

Genna was right about one thing, some things were *not* her fault. For the first time in her life Lorianne clearly saw how fear, driven by Clark's abandonment, ruled her life. She did cling to men for all the wrong reasons.

Well—she was done.

Her throat closed up. Ashton would not draw her in again. That was not desolation in his gaze boring down on her. "There is no need for you to feel any obligation to…to us."

"Obligation," he repeated. He made the word sound ominous.

"Whatever. There is nothing. Do you understand? Nothing—you and I have to discuss." She was trembling now, aggravating her further. "I think you should leave," she whispered, terrified of her actions, should he choose not to.

"Lorianne."

She steeled herself against the softness in his tone.

"No!" She took a breath. "It's time for you to leave. I have *nothing* for you," she reiterated, assailed by a terrible sense of wretchedness. Somehow she managed to force back the tears. It was pointless to deny the attraction, but she would die before she'd let him know about it. She was not that six-year-old child any longer.

Lorianne somehow found the strength to walk calmly to the door. She held it open. He stood, his height dwarfing her small house. Her breath turned rapid and shallow when he advanced toward her. But she remained steadfast in her passivity. Refused to back away.

Her heart pounded. His hand reached out. She flinched, squeezing her eyes shut, but still she held her ground. In a touch as gentle as a soft breeze, he tipped her chin up and pressed a light kiss to her forehead. The screen door clapped against the frame before she braved opening her eyes.

She gulped hard. Hot tears slipped down her cheeks in an unusual silence. She'd done it. She'd made him go. It was over. Now she could get on with her life.

So why did it feel like her life just walked out the door?

"...AND YOU'LL LOVE ME like I love you."

Genna stirred, her fogged mind trying to grasp consciousness. She tried to pull her hand from a clammy grip. It tightened.

"You'll see. I'll look out for you. We don't have to even date." He stroked her hand.

"Not have to date?" She struggled to open her eyes. Oh, Lord. "Toddy, what are you doing here?" Glittering passion emanated from glazed-over eyes.

Fear swamped her with the depth of his passionate pleas.

"I...I was worried about you." He pushed the taped wire framed glasses up on his nose. His shirt was more crumpled than normal. And he smelled funny. She wrinkled her nose. The tape on his glasses showed dark smudges. He was *crying*.

"I'm going to be okay, Toddy." She yanked her hand from his, fighting panic, the bile rising in her throat. He truly creeped her out. She flung her gaze to the recliner where Rick had been sleeping. Empty.

"I'm going to look out for you, Genna. I promise I'll never let you get hurt again." He choked on the words. He reached for her hand again.

She strained to stay out of his reach, head pounding. "Toddy." She tried to get his attention, but her voice would not cooperate. He seemed lost in another world. Her croaked voice was hardly audible.

"My father was wrong. I'm not a loser." His gaze distanced. "I can take care of you. It was all a mistake."

"A…a mistake?" She felt a hand close around her throat. "What are you talking about?" Her voice was a hushed tone.

"I'm certain it's Plank. You know? I just can't figure how he found out about—" He stopped abruptly. And smiled, surprising her with its warmth.

Sheer black terror swept through her. Where was Rick? Lorianne? Even Damon would be welcome at this point.

This time Toddy's reach met its mark. He patted her hand with his clammy damp one. She resisted the urge to wipe away his touch. "Don't you worry," he reassured her. "I'm looking out for you. We'll be together soon." He leaned forward as if he were going to kiss her.

"I-I'm tired, T-toddy." She turned her head.

"Okay. I'll see you later, sweet thing," he said, and slipped from the room.

Genna reached for the nurses call remote but in her panic couldn't find it. She shook the covers. It clattered to the floor.

"Hello, Genna." A nice cheery nurse entered. Her name tag read Justene. How did you even pronounce that? "How are we doing today?" Justene pulled the chart from the foot of the bed, never once having glanced at her. "Are you ready to go home? As soon as the doctor comes by for one last check up, he'll sign the release forms." Her over-the-top optimism had Genna almost screaming hysterically. Justene dropped the chart in its holder and reached for her wrist. "My, your pulse is rapid. I expect you're excited about getting out of here," she said, checking her watch.

Genna's voice stuck in her throat.

Intelligent, concern roamed Justene's face. "You're a little pale," she frowned.

"I...I'm okay. I...I do want to go home." She was trembling.

"You're shaking, too." Justene placed a hand on her forehead. "No fever. But we'll take your temperature just to be certain," she smiled.

Genna closed her eyes. No more smiling. She was about to be sick.

RICK BALANCED TWO COFFEES and pastries while trying to push the elevator button. The cafeteria, located on the ground floor, was just off the visitors' entrance. He glanced over the lobby while he waited. Shit! The Pretty Boy, ex-con, had just slithered through the revolving door. Pretty Boy sauntered over to the information desk, where a couple of elderly volunteers sat.

The elevator dinged and Rick stepped back allowing the occupants to exit. He changed his mind about entering and fixated his gaze on *Damon*. That was the name she'd thrown out to him yesterday, after a particularly satisfying bout of lovemaking, right? That still stung.

An instant later, Lorianne flew through the same revolving door, bearing a large hot pink shoulder bag, almost ramming into guy-nerd. Her fierce gaze had Toddy stepping back. That drew a smile. The place was hopping.

Lorianne rushed to the elevator and jabbed the button—several times—as if that would force the doors to open sooner.

"Thanks," Rick told her.

She jumped. "Why aren't you in Genna's room?" she demanded.

He responded by jerking his head in Pretty Boy's direction.

"Ah, hell," she said, rolling her eyes.

"Why are you in such a hurry anyway? I came down here to get us some coffee. She was sound asleep when I stepped out."

She seared him with a calculated gaze.

"What?" he demanded. Hell, she was making him feel guilty. The door dinged open, again.

She stepped in and turned on him in a heated blaze. "She just called me. Something about Toddy Wilson, loving her and wanting to take care of her."

"Who? That nerd-guy?" Unable to do anything about his gaping mouth, the elevator closed, leaving him standing there staring after her. Dumbfounded.

Pretty Boy marched up and pressed the button.

CHAPTER 35

RICK MAINTAINED A POINTED gaze on his elevator mate during the short ride up—didn't suffer at all when the ex-con, cowered in the corner. Not even a tiny bit of remorse pierced his conscience when he encouraged his stay in the waiting area once the doors parted. Just helped it along with a stern glower. Satisfied, Rick ambled down the hallway. Too easy.

He pulled up outside Genna's room. "Do Not Disturb" was written in a blue marker on a little white board just outside the door. What the hell!

He frowned, until he realized the door was slightly ajar.

"...didn't have to date. I don't know, it was just weird." That was Genna. It didn't bother him to eavesdrop, either. Though he couldn't see her, he felt her shudder.

"What do you suppose he meant?" That was Lorianne. Rick heard the water running from the attached restroom. It was close to the door. *Splash.*

Genna's voice came back muffled, through a towel, he guessed. "I don't know! He said something about his father being wrong, and that he wasn't a loser. Didn't his father die in the photo lab about four years ago? Inhaled some kind of poisonous fumes? I can't remember."

Rick filed away that tidbit and set Genna's coffee and the pastries on a ledge. He had a feeling they might be a while. Crossing one arm over his chest, Rick lifted his coffee with the other. Legs crossed at the ankles, he leaned against the wall and prepared to wait. Could he help it if their voices carried?

"…and when he told me we'd be together soon…" A brief silence followed. Had she shuddered again? Rick sipped his coffee. "Then he said something really strange. Like, it was all a mistake. Ow. Watch it."

"Sorry."

Rick wasn't sure what that was about.

"A mistake? What kind of mistake?" Lorianne sounded puzzled.

Rick didn't blame her and shrugged.

Genna's voice lowered. He leaned forward and strained to hear. "He said he was worried about me." Rick frowned, and took a large gulp. "—that he loved me. And…and that we'd be together soon."

It was only a coincidence when his coffee spewed. He scrambled for the napkins beneath the pastries and dabbed the front of his shirt. "Honestly, Lorianne. It was the biggest '*bilateral miscommunication*' I'd ever had the misfortune to be part of in my life."

"Bilateral miscommunication? Don't you think that's a bit dramatic?" Lorianne let out a sharp laugh.

Then Genna grumbled something like, "Albert Wheeler."

A sense of rustling followed, and before Rick could assume any kind of nonchalant stand that appeared remotely convincing, the door flew open. Two pairs of accusing eyes accosted him.

"Uh, I got you some coffee," he mumbled, feeling the heat on his neck. It was lame, but at least he had coffee for her, "and a pastry."

Genna's hair had been caught up in a nape at her neck, her

face pink, scrubbed clean, wearing a fresh change of clothes.

"Oh," Genna said. "I thought you left."

Before he could give voice to his irritation, Lorianne saved him the explanation. "He was keeping an eye on *him*." She inclined her head toward Pretty Boy, who was hustling over. Genna's lips compressed in frustration…directed on Pretty Boy. There was a measure of satisfaction.

"Thank God you're okay," the little twerp gushed. Seriously, he gushed. Rick pulled himself to full height. It might not be wise to say anything, but intimidation was a viable option. "Can I talk to you?" Pretty Boy took her arm, but dropped it when Rick threatened him with an arched brow. "Over here," he motioned, eyeing Rick.

Pretty Boy started to the waiting area, beckoning Genna to follow. After a slight hesitation she did. Rick started after them, but Lorianne grasped his arm halting him midstream.

"What are you doing?" He hissed.

"Let her go. She needs to do this."

He tossed a frown over his shoulder, amazed at her fierce tone.

She shook her head, looking impatient. "Haven't you ever wondered why she throws out those silly quotes when you try to talk about something…anything…remotely serious or personal?"

He waited. Maybe she had something. Rick moved next to her, but kept his eye on Pretty Boy. "What do you mean?"

Lorianne lowered her hand, apparently trusting him to stay by her side.

"*He's* the reason she hides in books. Hides behind her glasses." She crossed her arms over her chest but trained her eyes on Genna. "Oh, she's always had a head for really bazaar trivia. But the quotes began after their little affair ended. She throws them out when she's nervous or to keep people from getting too close. Sometimes, it's annoying as hell."

Rick tightened his lips.

Her voice softened a fraction. "She'd never had a boyfriend before college, you know. I didn't know much about it at the time even though we were roommates from our first year. We weren't close friends until after he'd pulled that little stunt after his graduation. I was too busy partying when she'd met *him*." The look of contempt she cast toward the unsuspecting jerk surprised Rick with its vehemence. He had a feeling some of that contempt was directed inward. "I guess he worked…bartending or something."

"He did." That drew her sharp gaze. "Uh…bartend." She wouldn't let that one pass.

Yet surprisingly, she did. "Genna did all his homework, coached him for his tests. She's really smart, you know."

A soft smile touched Rick's lips. "I know."

"I doubt the jackass even took her on a real date." Hostility radiated from her.

Rick wanted to tell her to take a deep breath, but opted for silence.

"Well, to make a long story short, when he stepped off the stage during the graduation ceremony, he apparently walked right by her—to his *real* girlfriend. Probably had big boobs, big hair, and no brains…if *he's* anything to go by." She pointed toward him with her thumb sticking out of her fist.

She let out a sigh. "Graduation was on a Saturday. I'd come back for a quick change of clothes after having been gone a couple of days. I was supposed to go with a group of friends down to Mexico. Genna was a wreck. I don't think she'd eaten in two days. She was curled up in bed, the curtains closed. It was really stuffy in there." She wrinkled her nose, remembering.

Rick moved his gaze over Genna, imagining her hair all strewn across the pillow, eyes puffy from crying. Or worse, total indifference. His lips thinned in rage. Pretty Boy reached for

Genna's hand, but she quickly clenched it in a fist. Rick leaned forward ready for action. But Genna jerked it from him.

"When all this is over, everything about that girl is screaming she'll run for the hills."

Rick's head snapped back to Lorianne. She'd answered his unasked question.

"All she sees when she looks in the mirror is a short, skinny, brainiac mess with crazy hair who either buries herself with work or has her head in a book." Lorianne gave a short pause. "Which, to her, is the same thing."

Admiration filled him. How could she think she was so unattractive when fringed lashes framed eyes so deep, dark blue, shimmered with intelligence? The little black glasses enhanced her savvy and insight. Her stature might be small, but she was proud, and full of fire and passion. Those plump lips were irresistible. And he should know. Only yesterday he'd devoured her inside out.

Lorianne turned back to Rick. Her tone took on an all-businesslike demeanor. "You seem like a halfway decent guy, but I'm no judge." Her laugh held a contemptuous self-mockery.

He lifted a brow in question, quickly shifting to unease when her tone turned chilly.

"But, you listen to me." Her voice dropped to a low growl, and he couldn't possibly misread the etched steel. "If you hurt her, I'll come after you and whack off your pecker with a sharp knife."

Caught off guard, he stared, then narrowed his eyes on her. Oh, he read her loud and clear. Particularly, the blue eyes freezing him out and the sarcastic tilt of her mouth.

He would *not* be lured into something he may or may not be ready for. "Leaving my…umm…*pecker* out of this for the moment…" " His defenses were reflexive, and with effort, controlled. "I believe Genna and I can work this out without your help." He was pleased he'd kept his voice cool and even.

A shadow of annoyance passed over her face. He waited, though, to see what she would come up with next.

"Now." She let out a stream of air. "Suppose you tell me how you know he tended bar." It was a demand, not a question.

Rick regarded her for a moment then shrugged. "I did some checking into his background."

"Is that so?" she said softly.

Deciding he'd said enough, he clamped his mouth shut. The battle lines were drawn. Best friend against possible beau. A frown threatened but he kept his face devoid of expression.

"Hmm," she mused. "Maybe my *grand*mother will send us on a little vacation after all this drama. She's rich, you know."

He regarded Lorianne so intently it startled him when Genna walked up. To his satisfaction, he was not the only one.

"'*No man has a good enough memory to be a successful liar.*'" Exasperation left her in a rush. "Abraham Lincoln. Appropriate, don't you think?"

"What do you mean?" He asked carefully. He wasn't quite sure he was ready for the answer.

But a slow grin crept over her friend's lips. "You told that sucker off, didn't you?" Lorianne accused Genna.

She blushed.

Rick glanced over his shoulder. The sight of the closing elevator doors filled him with relief.

"Well, he didn't remember anything like it actually happened," she said smugly, even though her voice trembled slightly.

Lorianne engulfed her in a hug, effectively walling off any contact from him. It was a good old-fashioned standoff.

Genna made no effort to move out of Lorianne's protective guard. "Rick," she said.

He narrowed his eyes on her and waited.

"I appreciate everything you've...uh...done." Two high spots of scarlet stained her cheeks. "Lorianne will take me home. We...we need to check on Lewis."

Rick wanted to laugh, but Lorianne's dour precipice loomed over him. Not to mention losing his pecker! He had to admire her audacity.

Lorianne's eyes bored into Genna. She took Genna's arm in a possessive grasp. The smile Lorianne tossed out didn't quite reach her eyes.

"You should probably get some rest," Lorianne told him. "You look like shit."

"Lorianne!" Genna choked.

"She's right," he conceded. He *was* tired. Besides he needed to rest up for the next battle installment.

Lorianne started to tug Genna down the hall but he had a few words of his own he intended on relaying. He stepped in front of them, halting their progress.

"Lewis is in the orange wing," Lorianne announced.

He gritted his teeth, annoyed. "In a minute," he grated. "I want to talk to you first. *Alone*," he said to Genna.

Her eyes widened with uncertainty. "Well...I...we..."

"It'll only take a minute." He disengaged her arm from Lorianne's and pulled her back into the room.

Just as suddenly, he found himself at a loss for words. He slipped the glasses from her face and took in her wide eyes, her lips quivering and unsure. Lorianne's dissertation flooded his mind. He hated that his gut twisted in doubt. He could keep her safe, but was that enough? Could *he* keep from hurting her?

Resentment cascaded over him. Demands to marry from his mother, Lorianne's threats on his *manhood*. He felt short of breath. There was no doubt he felt something—but *was it enough*?

Rick sought to reassure her, but how? With what? He shut

his eyes, trying to do the same with his thoughts. Instead, he leaned forward, touched his lips to hers. Nothing invasive. Nothing ardent. Just a feathery touch that made him feel better.

"Go," he whispered. "I'll talk to you later." He dropped his arms to his sides. He wanted to promise, but for the first time in years, *he* felt...uncertain.

"What did he want?" Lorianne demanded, keeping her voice low.

"Nothing."

"I didn't hear you say anything."

"You weren't supposed to," Genna snapped.

A sense of inadequacy swept over Genna. Ha! He thought she was just some nerdy librarian type who liked to kiss. But she couldn't help it. It turned out she *did* like to kiss. And, and she was a *librarian-type*. She had a PhD in Research and Library Sciences. How could she not be a goofy *librarian-type*? She felt ill. Elation in blasting Damon, in being such a jerk all those years ago, deserted her.

Lorianne marched her down the hall. They turned the corner and entered the orange wing. Well, what else had she expected? A picture of Mabel Jones floated before her. Gray streaked hair, pointy nose, beady eyes, and a double chin— Bloomington's old-maid-librarian. Genna sniffed.

With a sudden yank, Lorianne managed to jar her back to the present. "What!"

"Keep your voice down." Lorianne ducked them into the closest room.

Genna swallowed the last of her tears. "What is it?" she whispered, glancing around. "There's someone in the bed!"

"Ashton."

"Ashton's in the bed?" Her head snapped back to the bed.

"I saw him in the hall."

"Is that all?" Genna reached for the door, Lorianne had pulled to.

"No!" Her panic seeped through, and Genna realized how pale she'd gone.

"But, we know it wasn't him. It's okay." She reached for the door again.

"No. Please. I can't talk to him. I don't want to see him. I...I'll wait for you in the car." Lorianne was begging her.

"But, Lori—" What was wrong with her?

"—no," she whispered again.

"Okay. Okay. Let me see check on Lewis though. And I have to stop at the business office for the rest of the paperwork before I leave."

"I know. Just don't say anything about me. Promise me." Lorianne's whisper became more hushed.

Genna did promise. She flicked her gaze to the sleeping occupant, and slipped out. She frowned. Had something happened? Lorianne sounded terrified.

She saw Ashton, his back to her, head cocked to one side, cell phone resting on his shoulder. He'd started to pace a small area when he caught sight of her.

Cold gray eyes met hers. The bleakness within shocked her.

He flipped his phone shut and smiled. His smile was...grief-stricken.

She drew in a sharp breath. "Lewis!" She glanced wildly about. Which room was it? She'd forgotten to ask.

"He's okay," Ashton reassured her.

"But, your face." She brought her hand up to her throat. "I thought he must have died."

"No." He smiled again. It turned warm, genuine, and for her. "You look much better than yesterday."

"I'm ready to be home. Have a nice long, hot bath," she admitted. He was quite an attractive sort, wasn't he? When he smiled like that, he wasn't scary at all. He and Lorianne would make a terrific couple. If he would *call her back*.

"I realize this is not the most appropriate time to mention this, but I'm sorry about your store."

She drew a quick breath. She hadn't thought of the shop once. His sincerity touched her.

"I'll do everything I can to help you set it to rights."

"Thank you. It means a lot." She blinked back sudden tears. Then, with determined optimism, she asked, "Where's Lewis? I've been concerned about him."

"In here." Ash pushed open the glaring orange door behind him. "You've got company, old man."

CHAPTER 36

"OH, MY." GENNA WAS shocked to her core. There was no other word for it. She stood next to Lewis flabbergasted by the sight before her. The walls were blackened with soot and stained with water where the firemen had aimed their powerful hoses. The expansion space was ruined.

"Is it fixable?" she whispered.

"I don' know, Genna-girl." He ran a hand over his shiny bald head. "How does the other part look?"

"Smoke damaged," she replied, pushing her glasses up on her nose. Placing her hands on her hips, she turned in a slow circle. "I just wish I knew what they were after. I mean, will they be happy stopping with this?" She spread an open palm indicating the mess. "Or, is it to be obliterated completely."

"I don' know, girl." His tone reflected every ounce of regret surging through her. "Have you talked to the insurance guy?"

"Y...you mean Rick?" It came out in a husky tone. She'd sort of managed to put him from her mind. She hadn't talked to him in three days. Well, that was later wasn't it? "No."

"I mean the insurance company."

"Oh." She blushed and spun away from his sharp gaze. "I...I've called, yes."

"Surely, they'll cover this."

"I hope so," she whispered.

"It's okay, girl. We'll git it done. Somehow."

RICK PACED TO THE window, seeing nothing in particular in his line of sight. No, what he saw were wide, dark blue eyes behind nerdy glasses and parted lips. He hadn't seen Genna in three days. Well, not in person. Not since she and Lorianne had beat a path to Lewis Peale's hospital room. Who, Ash had informed him, had been released and was back on the job.

He rubbed the base of his neck trying to ease the tension. Three days. It seemed like forever. How did you disregard a waif who melted at your touch? Bombarded you with ridiculous quotes no one in their right mind could pull out of thin air?

The short answer? You didn't. She just inundated your every waking moment. And every *unwaking* moment. Was that even a word? Who cared? He knew what he meant.

He wanted to wake with her beside him. Breathe the honeysuckle in her crazy hair. Fight her for the covers. Pull her body onto his. What didn't he want from her? And why the hell was he fighting it? He huffed out an irritated sigh. Because he'd never committed to anyone to that degree before, that's why. His mother's pestering was playing havoc with his common sense. He shook his head, and went back to the matter at hand.

There was something strange about the conversation he'd overheard Genna and Lorianne discussing at the hospital. He spoke to the empty room, ticking each one off with a finger:

"One: They didn't have to date." He'd have to ask her about that one.

"Two: His father was wrong and he was not a loser." Matter of opinion.

"Three: They'd be together soon." He frowned. Over his dead body.

"Four: It was a mistake." Very interesting. But *what* was a mistake?

"Five: He was worried about her." Well, he wasn't the only one, that one was a wash.

"Six: He loved her." Again, a wash. Whoa! *He* loved her. He loved her. Rick stumbled to his chair. He. Rick. Rick. Loved. Her. In one fell swoop everything fell into place. Rick loved *her*. Ho, shit, now what?

He forgot seven: They'd be together soon.

TODDY LOCKED HIMSELF IN the darkroom. The single red bulb gave off a subtle glow. He barely noticed the stench of chemicals. This was the only private place without his nosy mother delving into his business. If she wasn't careful, she'd end up like dear old dad—in an unventilated locked room.

Even the cat couldn't bother him in here.

He couldn't help feeling a little pleased. In the big picture, setting the fire had turned out to be ingenious. A chuckle escaped him. He smashed the powder in a repetitive motion, over and over.

But she'd still never mentioned his note. He frowned. It would have been stupid to sign it, of course. He'd confess that later. He just had to manage Mother. It usually wasn't that difficult.

Toddy set a small wooden board on the table away from the chemically filled sinks and carefully dumped out the contents of the bowl. With a small knife he lined the powder into two strips, hands sure and steady, for the moment. With a tiny plastic tube, open on either end, he snorted the stream of one line with his right nostril. He took a moment and sat back, reveled in the euphoria before moving to the left, hand less steady now.

Warmth flooded his body—heightened his senses. This was how he wanted to feel with Genna, *in* Genna. A giggle sounded through the room, his own. And he would. Warmth settled through him, over him. He had to be careful or Mother would surely be able to tell he was up to something. He giggled again, but clapped a hand over his mouth.

After the initial rapture of high glided over him, he reached for the camera bag and checked off the contents: rope, tape, blindfold, handkerchief, vial. No, it wouldn't be long, they'd be together soon.

Just as he'd promised.

CHAPTER 37

"ARE YOU SURE?" GENNA'S heart was breaking.

"Yes. Joanna and I think it will be good for the two of us to get to know each other better." Lorianne sounded distant and vague.

Genna plopped down. "When are you leaving?"

"Within the week." Lorianne stood at the front window looking out over Genna's quaint neighborhood.

"Oh, Lorianne. But Europe? That's so far away. From me." Genna whispered. "Are you ever going to tell me what happened with Ashton?" She knew she was on shaky ground.

"I never want to talk about Ashton Turner again. For once in my life, I don't need a man. All I need is a break." Her voice broke.

Ashton's sad gray eyes fleeted through Genna's mind, but Lorianne's sadder blues hurt as if the pain were her own. "'*What would life be if we had no courage to attempt anything?*' It's Van Gogh."

"He died at thirty-seven, and spent most of his life in a mental institution." Lorianne let out a choked laugh. "I'm going to miss you so much."

"I'll miss you, too." Genna closed her eyes, heart aching for her friend. But she knew that whatever happened, Lorianne was not the only one affected. Ashton hardly wore his heart on his sleeve, but the pain was there, deep. Not that he went out and bought shoes. She didn't know what men did when *they* were upset.

He never asked after Lorianne. It was an unspoken agreement between them. But on the off times when he did not see Genna glancing his way, his anguish was stark and apparent. She had a feeling Lorianne was all wrong about him. His feelings where Lorianne was concerned were a hairsbreadth away from plunging over Niagara Falls.

His desolation tore at her. Keeping himself busy was the way to mend a broken heart, she'd decided. She should know. She'd kept very busy.

Tears pricked her eyes. She understood exactly how Ashton felt because every day she worked to restore the damage in order to reopen, and Rick hadn't come by once. She wondered if Ashton had talked to him, but felt too awkward to ask him or Lewis. So every night she went home exhausted and crawled into bed. Too tired to eat, too tired to read. Unfortunately, not too tired to relive the morning before the fire when they…when he…

"I'm sorry I haven't helped at the store," Lorianne said, finally sitting. "I just…"

"It's okay. At least when we reopen, the inventory will be up to date." She'd had Lorianne updating the database with additions and deleting new and damaged books from home. "Just feel better."

TWO WEEKS AFTER THE fire, the store was almost ready for business. Spring storms were turning into warm and breezy summer days. Lorianne and Joanna had already been gone a week.

With Ashton and Lewis's help, Genna was finally ready to

fling the doors wide open. Ashton's construction crews were relentless. She'd almost achieved her goal.

The store cleaned up nicely. The new café had been delayed, but that was for later. The wiring had been brought up to code with a stern lecture from the electrician. Ashton stood beside him, nodding an agreement through the entire thing. Genna suffered through that lecture with stoic aplomb. The plumbing had passed its new inspection, and the roof re-replaced.

Still no word on who set the fire. Or why.

RICK SPENT DAY AND night going over every detail he could think of from the day of the fire. No one had seen the hoodie-guy who'd darted into Plank's Coffee Shop. Bloomington's Historic Museum Curator, Josephine Phillips, had appeared almost intoxicated, sitting with *Reverend Colvert*.

He shuddered reliving that interview. Of course, they'd had trouble staying focused on the actual event, God prophesying the evils of porn—foretelling the Reverend how *it* was the actual cause of the fire.

Plank was no help, as hard-assed as ever. Rick acknowledged he may have treaded more lightly, having read Plank's sad dossier. At least he understood why the man harbored such an unyielding façade. In retrospect, it was anguish, not sternness. He just hadn't felt right accusing him. Until further evidence of an involvement was forthcoming, Rick was bound by duty to treat it as a coincidence.

The back door of Wilson's Photography studio also shared a parking lot with Selma's Beauty Salon, Plank's, and the Historical Society.

And then there was Genna.

He missed the soft scent of honeysuckle, her full lips, and silly quotes. He let out a sigh. He told himself if he stayed back, the hoodie-guy would make a move and he'd have him. But so far that hadn't happened.

And he had stayed back, for the most part. Well, except for making sure she got home each day…from a distance. And well…for watching her house from the end of the street—only until the lights went out for the night. And…for dreaming about her undressing for bed…taking a bath…washing herself…crawling into bed.

Then of course, he'd have to wait for the heat to subside so he could actually drive home. At least, he hadn't taken to relieving his tension in his car. Yet. He saved *that* for when he reached home.

It was time to tell her. Time to confess the depths of his love. If the guy hadn't made his move after two weeks, then chances were he wasn't going to. Rick glanced at his watch. He refused to wait another day. He'd take a quick shower then knock on her door.

GENNA WAS TIRED.

Opening day, the next day, would be bittersweet with Lorianne traipsing about Europe with Joanna. Fresh paint filled her nostrils, drop cloths gone, *lights* working. Ashton's crew had even covered the batts of insulation in the basement, creating storage areas. With walls! Now it looked less like a haunted house and more like a utility area.

She'd shooed Lewis home thirty minutes ago. They'd worked hard. But now they needed much deserved rest. Guilt threatened but she pushed it away. Ashton had needed this as much as she had. Too bad she couldn't turn into a melting pot over him. He was attractive and sexy. He just wasn't—Rick.

Yes, they were all tired.

Genna slipped the key in the lock, thankful the glass she'd heard breaking during the fire was not her precious front door. Seems the firemen found it easier to break the window to the south, facing Ashton's new development. Her mind flittered in anxiety thinking of that life-changing day. It still had the propensity to send a chill up her spine. She rubbed her hands over her arms despite the warm weather. Her glance swept the area. Ida was leaving her shop, as well. Genna lifted her hand in a brief wave.

For the first time in days she would be home before dark.

Maybe she could even read something. Anything. Maybe a book with pictures. *The Design Continuum: An Approach to Understanding Visual Forms* by Stewart Kranz and Robert N. Fisher. It had come in the mail last week and was still sitting on the kitchen table in the box. Shaking her head, she crossed the street in a quick jog, not stopping until she reached her car. A cold knot formed in her stomach. She groaned in frustration. She was so tired and ready for things to be normal again.

Tomorrow. Tomorrow was a new start.

Genna hit the automatic locks and started the car. It was an effort to make the short drive to her home in a calm manner. Her telepathic powers were playing havoc with her over-the-top clairvoyant senses. Neither of which she trusted.

She turned down her quiet, tree-lined street and drew in a deep steady breath to calm her nerves. No one lurked in the rear view mirror, a couple of kids played in their front yard four houses down, no sinister monsters waited to jump out at her when she pulled in the driveway.

Just Toddy Wilson leaning against his car with a big smile on his face. She winced.

CHAPTER 38

RICK PAUSED UNCERTAINLY AT Genna's door, puzzled. Why she wasn't answering? Flowers in one hand, he banged on the door with the other. He hadn't called her in two weeks, and that was reason enough to test anyone's patience. But hell, it had been for her own good. And if she would open the damn door he would explain that to her.

He circled on one foot, hand on his hip, and scanned the area from her wooden porch. She *had* to be home. Her white Camry was right there in the driveway. The hood was still warm. She'd surprised him by leaving the store earlier than usual, just when he'd stopped for flowers. So he wasn't right behind her on the road. With Lorianne out of town, she should be at the store or home.

He swung around and jerked the screen door. It flew back, unlatched, startling him. He drew his brows together, irritated. He'd give her a few choice words as soon as he had her in sight. Unease trickled through him—a lecture on safety, after a heartfelt declaration of love and a deep satisfying kiss. Where the hell was she?

Silence loomed in the air like a fine mist. No sounds stirred from inside the house. Wouldn't she have turned on the television or a radio? His stomach dropped a couple of notches. Something? Of course, he hadn't been in her house, for all he knew she didn't have a television. He barked a laugh. Who didn't have a television? How could you watch sports without a television?

He tried the doorknob, more curses falling from his mouth. Locked, thank God. He hammered with his fist. First, in aggravation, but when dread pulsated through him, he thought it would splinter under the assault barely aware he'd crushed the flowers he held.

She should be in his face—irate, right? Though according to Lorianne, she avoided confrontation and hated 'i' words. But she'd never been afraid to confront *him*.

No. Something was wrong, his instincts screamed. His doubts grew fierce. Fear had his heart threatening to land on the wood porch.

Rick looked down at the damaged spray in his tightened fist. He dropped the flowers, and jumped the railing. He circled to the back of the house, and tried the back door. The screen was locked. The windows were locked. No sound penetrated from anywhere inside.

In a slow tread, he rounded the front. Drawn by an irresistible force, he moved toward her car. Reluctant steps, shifted in urgency. A white hanky, slightly wadded, lay on the drive near the driver's side tire. He swept it up in one quick motion and shook it out. He wrenched the car door—it opened.

Terror struck through him like a knife. Her purse, knocked over, splayed contents across the passenger seat and floorboard. He stared at the items, speechless. Alarm, then rage rippled down his spine, each fighting for the forefront of his emotions when he saw the one thing Genna could not or would not be without—

Her glasses.

Swooping them off the seat, he squeezed his eyes shut. The son of a bitch had done it. He'd gotten to her. He flipped out his cell.

Genna struggled to clear her mind. Her head pounded, she felt like throwing up. Where were the lights? She tried lifting a hand to her head, but something was wrong. Confusion engulfed her, spinning her senses in bewilderment. She groaned. Arms weak, she struggled again. Finally, it dawned that her wrists were bound. Adrenaline surged, sharpening her senses. She appeared to be on some kind of futon or twin bed. It was very uncomfortable. She tried to lift her head but nausea churned.

The dark was unnerving. A shuffle sounded; she froze. Someone was moving around. A second later her eyes adjusted to a stream of light coming from an open door.

"Oh, thank God!" Toddy exclaimed. He dropped beside her, rattling her makeshift bed. He didn't smell so good either. Her stomach roiled. "I thought you were dead."

"D-dead?" She choked out. "Toddy, can you help me? My hands are bound. D-did someone take us?"

"You've been out for almost thirty minutes," he blurted.

He sounded funny. Agitated? Fearful? Not so…so *normal*. For Toddy, she amended.

"Thirty minutes?" Twisting her wrists, she found them quite secure. "Toddy, these are tight." Panic started to set in, she could feel tears in a throat so dry, it scratched. She tried to sit, but her feet were restricted too. "Toddy?" she whispered. Horror pulsed through her. Choking her. It was Toddy…this was worse than seeing Damon. Was she going to die? Would he…he…she couldn't form the thought.

She squelched the possibility of rape the way she kept all fear at bay. But this was Toddy. Geeky Toddy. Sh-she c-could handle him. "Are y-you an e-economist, Toddy?" Her voice squeaked past her cracked throat.

Shifting, he pierced her with glittering eyes that drank her up, sending a nervous skitter along her spine. They almost glowed in the dark, like a cat's, increasing her panic. "An economist?" He was confused by her question. She could tell.

She was unable to make out his expression with the low light, just the outline of his head tilted to one side. Where were her glasses?

Breathing deeply, she strove for a normal tone. More for her benefit than his. "*'An investment in knowledge always past the best interest.'* That's advice from Benjamin Franklin. Can you loosen these ties, please?" Her voice sounded shrill to her own ears, but at least it was coming out.

"Of course not, Genna. You're my prisoner." He laughed and shook his head. "You're funny."

Oh, Lord. She swallowed. His movements were agitated, a little on the wild side. Unnerved by his scrutiny, she forged on. "*'Strong reasons make strong actions.'* That was William Shakespeare, but for the life of me, I can't remember where it came from. Must be a general comment from him, or…or something."

She couldn't seem to stop. Surely, he'd made a mistake. "Oh, I know others from him. Like, *'A deed without a name.'*"

Genna hated this about herself. Why, when these silly quotes popped into her head, could they *not* have any bearing on the irony of the situation? "And, uh, *'Few love to hear the sins they love to act…'*" Breath held, she hoped the meaning escaped him. If she could just keep her mouth shut. But, noooo. "*'I am tied to the stake, and I must stand the course.'* At least that's how it feels…" her voice died away.

"Why didn't you say anything about my note?" He sounded hurt.

"N-note?"

"About making better choices. I'm the better choice, you know."

"*You* sent that?"

He smiled.

She gulped.

His mood turned buoyant. He stroked her cheek. She jerked away. How she held back a scream was beyond her.

He frowned.

Her pulse went erratic.

He leaned forward, pushing his wire-framed glasses up on his nose. Lips puckered.

She ducked, and blurted, "'*Character is that which reveals moral purpose, exposing the class of things a man chooses to avoid.*' Th-that includes you." She breathed in shallow, quick gasps.

"Sometimes you say the dumbest things." He stood abruptly, and started to pace.

She sat as still as she could. Tears were close, but what good would they do? She needed a good old-fashioned Regency-era rescue. The problem she faced is that there wasn't anyone to give her an old-fashioned rescue. Regency or otherwise. Damn that Rick. Yes! She thought it. *Damn* him.

She was in love with him and he *hurt her feelings*. It was enough to make her really angry. She didn't want t-to be Toddy's—Toddy's, she swallowed again. Girlfriend, or…or anything.

She had to do something. But what, when her hands and feet were tied? She was not a victim. "Toddy, where am I?" she demanded. "And…and why am I tied up like a…a hog!"

"Oh, Genna." He shook his head at her, like she was just silly. "I want to keep you safe."

"Safe from what? Who?" Her frustration should have been clear. Honestly, she bit her tongue to keep from shouting. But she needed information, and she was confined. It was hard though.

"You were almost killed in a fire," he said. He started to

fidget.

Something in his tone, alerted her, sent her senses reeling. "Were you there?" she asked her voice low and determined.

His head shot up. "I...I wanted to keep you safe. I've been trying for days..."

She waited, not sure where he was going with the direction of this conversation. Her heart lodged in her throat.

"But, I couldn't. That insurance guy was always there. And, I love you so much, Genna." He sounded angry.

"Insurance guy?" she whispered. It wasn't possible.

"He followed you home every night. I...I just wanted to talk to you...alone. Tell you how much I loved you. Let you know that...you know...that you'll love me too. You'll see," he finished, sounding awkward.

She gasped.

He pursed his lips, turning angry. "But, he sat outside in his car a few houses down from your house—*every night.*"

While sick feelings swarmed her, his words touched her with a sense of thrill.

Toddy smiled and said, "It was sheer luck that you left early yesterday."

It wasn't possible. Rick? Watching her? But why? Why didn't he...Why didn't he what!

"'*Luck is what happens when preparation meets opportunity.*'" It was all she could muster. Talk about luck. Breath seeped out slowly, along with all her anger at Rick. Dissipating in the puff of one irrational statement from Toddy Wilson.

"DO YOU THINK IT'S working?" Rick's voice was rough with anxiety. He paced the floor of Ash's office in front of the large plate glass windows. It was six o'clock and Genna had been missing over twelve hours. He'd contacted Ben Goodwin, the police chief, from Genna's driveway.

"This is a small town. Of course, it's working," Ash said.

Rick was ready to kill somebody.

"Don't worry. They've had all night," Lewis chimed in.

Rick had almost forgotten Lewis ensconced in the corner, rooted to the sofa in Ash's office, massive legs stretched out before him. His demeanor was so quiet and unassuming, Rick started at the sound of his voice. Lewis's bandages were gone, and the eastern sunlight bounced off his bald head.

Morning. A roaring sensation thundered in his ears. "Jesus, how do people get through this?" Rick hissed. He wanted to tear the streets up, but he had no idea where to start looking. She had to be okay. They had a life to live.

Once he'd realized she'd been snatched in front of her own house, he was besieged with shock, horror, fear, dread. That white hanky had been stained with a faint, sweet odor, and was now on its way to the forensics lab. Ben suspected chloroform.

She could be dead. The effects of chloroform weren't predictable. If not removed quickly enough, damage to the kidneys and lungs were imminent. Who knew what else? She was a small, delicate flower.

Ash had the brilliant idea of dropping hints to a few key people that Genna had been kidnapped. It spread like wildfire. At least *Ash* thought it was brilliant. It was their hope that the gossip mill would help them find her. She was a town favorite. Especially, since the fire. He scrubbed a hand over his face.

He was terrified. He needed a shower. He needed a shave.

"Excuse me, please."

He spun, eyes riveted to the door where a haggard, broken Plank stood erect. Rick froze, breath caught. It couldn't be.

Lewis brought himself to his full six feet, seven inches. The tension in Ash just as palpable.

Rick could not have uttered a word. His efforts were spent

trying to control the warning spasms. Fists clenched at his side.

"Plank." Ash stated, his reserve chilling. "Come in. Please."

"Your Genna," he started. His heavy accent sounded heavier, his dark and haunted gaze reaching for Rick.

"You have something to share?" Ash again. Rick met Ash's eyes, knowing this was it.

"*Ja*," he confirmed in his native tongue. His shoulders slumped forward, dejection emanating.

Plank's bleak eyes focused on Rick filled with regret...resignation. It raised the hackles on his neck.

"I may have information on your Genna."

"What kind of information?" Rick fairly growled. Hands clenched, he started forward, but Lewis stopped him, his large fingers digging into his shoulder.

His gaze turned fierce. "She was stealing my business."

There was more, Rick knew it. "What else?" he demanded.

Plank's expression grew grave as it moved from his to Ash, then back.

"You were damaging the property," Rick said. "You set fire to the place."

"*Nein!*" he said quickly.

"Then you know who, don't you?" Rick spoke softly. "Where is she, Plank? Is she hurt, or—" Rick wrenched himself free of Lewis's hold, but he didn't trust himself to move closer.

Plank stepped back, fear clouding his eyes. "I don't know where she is. But I think I-I might know who." He ended on a rushed of expelled air.

A deadly silence ensued and the urge to kill him mounted deep in Rick's gut. "Who—damn you—who?"

"The photographer. The boy." Plank's shoulders slumped.

"Boy?" Rick was confused. "You mean that *thirty-something-year-old-nerd*?" Suddenly, little things snapped into place. "Call the cops," Rick barked to Ash, but he already had the phone in hand.

"I-I paid him, t-to…"

"To fuck with the wiring? Loosen shingles on the roof? Saw through the rung on a ladder," he hissed the accusations. Plank visibly shrunk before him.

"No," he whispered. "I-she—"

"How did you do it?"

"H-he killed his father."

"That's preposterous," Rick bit out, but something triggered in the back of his mind. A few years ago, Theodore Wilson was found trapped in his darkroom. He'd suffered a painful death. It had rocked the community due to its unusual nature. Bloomington hadn't hosted a murder in recent memory.

"I fear he may have gotten carried away. I thought after the fire everything would end peacefully. But, now…" His voice faded. "There is something else I cannot understand." Rick drew back a fist to plant it in his face.

Tears filled the old man's eyes. "I feared the competition. It is wrong, I know. I am sorry. She is a sweet girl. I must go to hell. But still, I cannot place my finger. He is…I think he does some kind of drug. I cannot know what."

Lewis blocked his lash. Rick released a shaky breath, swung on his heel and ran.

"Toddy, you have to undo these ties. I can't possibly take care of business, trussed up like a roped calf." Genna decided the best way to handle Toddy was to treat him like a small child. It had worked the night before. He'd left her ankles unbound. But he'd securely confined her wrists again after her short bathroom and meal break. She hadn't realized geeks were so strong.

He hadn't even let her turn on a light. She had to make do with the moonlight streaming through a high window over the bathtub.

"Okay, but just for a minute," he conceded. "I need to see Lester today."

"Lester? Van Horn?" she asked him. "He's in real estate. What kind of business could you have with him?"

She'd caught him off guard, but he recovered. "I'm a photographer. I take pictures of potential house sales."

"Oh." Well, that *could* be true, she supposed. "Where's your mother?"

"At work, I guess. Why are you asking all these questions?"

"I'm just making conversation."

From what she gathered, they must be in the basement of his mother's house. Several windows, street high, were covered. A makeshift desk held a conglomerated computer with various green penlights, haloed due to the fact she didn't have her glasses. Her head was pounding because of the eye strain. There was a clock with an illuminated dial but she couldn't read it either.

Genna hadn't wanted to encourage his suspicions. He thought she was dumb, and that would work to her advantage. An overwhelming urge to giggle struck her, but she stifled it. No one *ever* thought she was dumb.

This morning would be different, she decided. He stepped closer to her to untangle the ties at her wrists. "I don't suppose you would let me wash my face?" she challenged, keeping her voice light. How many times had she heard Lorianne use the same cajoling tone that seemed to work wonders?

Toddy studied her. Genna was careful to maintain a blank expression, her nostrils twitched from his stench. "I-I suppose it would be okay," he relented, though it was cautious.

"Thank you," she gave him a brilliant smile. The ties dropped away. Painful pricks stung as she shook her hands to circulate the blood. She turned her head when he blushed. Wow, it worked.

"Don't latch the door all the way," he warned. She'd

expected that.

She pushed the door to, careful not to let it latch per his conditions. It was the only way to buy time. She could be cooperative when the need arose. After relieving herself, she turned on the faucet and did a quick search under the sink, finding nothing helpful. Then, because she couldn't stand it, she doused her face.

She left the water running, hoping it would serve as an adequate decoy and glanced up at the window. Being short had its drawbacks, but if she used the rim of the bathtub, it might be possible. This was certainly a time when being too skinny was not a hindrance.

"Where's the soap?" she called through the door.

"Try under the sink," he responded. She smiled. She opened the cabinet only to let it clap shut. For effect.

Genna moved quickly. She would only have one opportunity. She stood on the rim of the tub and tried the window. Oh, Lord! It was unlocked. With no regard to personal his property she punched through the screen. Using her arms, she maneuvered her body up through the opening. She was only halfway there when the bathroom door crashed back, a sign from God, and Toddy, that time was up. Gasping, she tried to haul herself the rest of the way up, but he grasped her ankle. She let out a scream and kicked her feet, with all the force she could muster.

Someone grabbed her beneath the arms and yanked. Her leg slipped free and she landed on top of a hard body with a thump, eyes squeezed tight.

"It's okay. You're safe." *Rick!*

A violent reaction trembled throughout her body. She grasped him about the neck. She would never let go.

"You did it, darling. You're safe."

She opened her eyes. The house was surrounded by police.

"T-thomas F-fuller said, '*I-if it were n-not for hopes, t-the heart would b-break...*'"

"Oh, my God." He buried his face in her neck. "I love you."

EPILOGUE

Genna contemplated her reflection in the bathroom mirror at Town Hall. Her dress was lovely—a soft blue, strapless bodice draped her waist. Wanda had outdone herself. Selma had insisted on makeup to enhance her pert features. And her hair. Well, that was a miracle in and of itself. Somehow she was going to have to make it down that walk in the same four inch heels she'd worn to the council meeting that night so many weeks ago.

The florist, Sarah Pendergrass, had created a beautiful bouquet with Pee gee hydrangeas, accented with pale blue tweedia and roses of soft pinks, whites, and peaches. Genna was so touched she'd been moved to tears, which prompted a stern lecture from Selma, who'd had to retouch her makeup. It happened at least two more times. Mrs. Finch helped too, flitting around patting her hand, as only Mrs. Finch could do.

But Genna's tears were not just from all the townspeople who'd stepped up for her wedding. The whole town had adopted her upon her parents' untimely death, as sweet as they all were. And, she'd appreciated it. No orphan had as loving a family.

No. Genna's tears threatened because she missed Lorianne. Desperately. It was only natural she would miss the best friend she'd ever had in her life. Especially on the most important day of her life?

Just last week she'd received a note from Lorianne, detailing her and Joanna's adventures through the London Theatre District, the Tower of London, the British Museum, shopping in Paris' Champs-Élysées, visiting the Eiffel Tower and Moulin Rouge. Lorianne deserved every speck of happiness that fell in her path. She *wanted* Lorianne to be happy.

Genna sniffed back more tears so Selma would not be forced into a third reparation.

Perhaps it would have been too much for Lorianne with Ashton so involved anyway, she excused. Heaving a deep breath she pushed away the melancholy thoughts with determined unselfish resolve.

This was the happiest day of her life. In less than an hour she and Rick would be married, lives intertwined for the rest of their days. She could explore the pulse in his neck, revel in his touch however long she desired. She'd already received *The Introvert and Extrovert In Love: When Opposites Attract*. It had arrived earlier that week in discreet brown paper wrapping.

Genna peeked through a window from inside the town hall. Rick stood near the Methodist Pastor, Reverend Jones, Ash next to him, not yet in their places.

"I waited too long to tell you I loved you," he said. He pulled her onto his lap.

"Were you really sitting outside my house every night?" She nibbled his earlobe.

"How did you know that?" His hand raked up and down her spine in an absent motion.

"Toddy saw you." She flicked her tongue along his jaw.

He scowled. "He has ceased to be a problem."

"He has?" She smiled against his neck. "He did end up with a couple of unexplained bruises."

"He did?" He countered with a smile of his own.

"On his face."

"Umm." He brushed her jaw with firm lips. "He was heavily into drugs."

"Oh." Her head fell back so he could nuzzle her neck. He bit lightly and she dug her fingers into his shoulders. She loved touching him. "I love you," she whispered. His response was a fierce hug and savage kiss leaving her no chance for escape. Like she'd ever want to escape.

He pulled his mouth from hers.

Her breath came out rapid and shallow. "Your mother seems very happy."

"Oh, yes. She's almost as happy as I am," he told her just before capturing her mouth again.

"Are you ready for your wedding, Genna, dear?" Ida Finch twittered, jolting her back to the present.

Wedding! She was getting married. Plans for updating and renovating her little house were already under way. She saw her future husband take his place, Ashton moving beside him. He glanced over his shoulder at the building. She could tell—he was ready.

Rick deserved the happiest bride in the world. All those lovely things he did to her with his mouth made her want to rush through all the pomp and circumstance. But the town, they deserved this too. She stepped back from the window and took a deep breath.

The small quartet cued up on the lawn, triggering a flutter of butterflies that tickled her belly. She snuck one last peek. The whole town suddenly overflowed the front lawn. The sun beat brightly against a lovely white arch erected at the end of the walk. Soon she would float down the steps between chairs arranged under the large trees facing the street. They swayed in the breeze like a graceful ballet.

Strange how her *glossophobia* remained at bay. She would have thought the idea of speaking her vows in front of the whole town would have her begging for elopement. But she found the sense of support comforting, fed into her notion that they were her family after all.

She turned to give Mrs. Finch a quick, fierce hug. "*'I would thank you from the bottom of my heart, but for you my heart has no bottom.'*"

"I had a feeling about this, you know," Mrs. Finch sniffed. "I told your Rick about it, too."

Genna gaped at her. "You did?"

"Yes."

"Of course you did," Genna smiled.

Genna reflected on Ash and brokering the deal with Mr. Plank to sell her his coffee shop. How sad his life had turned out, losing his family and livelihood as he had. Genna wanted to let bygones be bygones, but Rick and Ashton stood firm against the idea.

And to Mr. Plank's honor, he'd insisted on retribution. As a result, she'd sold her expansion space to Ashton for his parking venture after all. So she supposed it all worked out in the end.

The scary part had turned out to be Toddy's obsession for her. His glittering drug induced looks and unrealistic illusions were frightening.

His supplier had turned out to be the lecherous Lester Van Horn, Realtor, now residing behind bars. Genna shivered with the 'what ifs,' but pushed them away. She felt a bit sorry for Mrs. Wilson, but in the end Toddy should have been a more responsible adult.

She snuck another peek out the window. Ash wore a stern expression. His bleakness was not completely gone, but he'd rallied for the sake of their wedding and she was grateful. Whatever happened between Lorianne and Ash was destined for silence, but it was clear Ash was still a very unhappy man.

Genna steadied her breath, and primed herself before the doors of Town Hall. Destiny had prepared her to embrace her future. Well, destiny and *Getting Ready for a Lifetime of Love: 6 Steps to Prepare for a Great Marriage*. She hadn't even needed to read it. Not when she saw Rick, proud, tall and beautiful, standing there waiting. Waiting. For her.

But then her arm was snatched unceremoniously, jerking her back inside the echoing halls, startling her. She'd just survived a crazy man's abduction—she let out a short scream.

"Keep your voice down, you ninny," Lorianne chided her. "You'll have the whole town thinking you've been kidnapped again."

"You're here!" Genna's beautiful bouquet slipped to the floor, forgotten in her haste to squeeze Lorianne in an emotional and ferocious hug.

"That was all a bit dramatic, you know." Lorianne teased, reaching for her flowers.

Happiness overwhelmed her and she threw arms around her best friend. "Yes. Yes, it was, wasn't it?"

"Good God. Selma did your makeup, didn't she?" A tissue appeared in Lorianne's hand, dabbing at Genna's tears. "This eye stuff is too heavy!" she whispered in disgust.

THE PERFECT WEDDING WENT off without a hitch. Rick refused to relinquish Genna's hand throughout the ceremony. He didn't give a shit what Pastor Jones thought. Now that he had her, he wasn't about to let go. Even to Ash when he appeared asking for a dance at the reception. In his summarization, it was a small price for any of them to pay.

Admittedly, he'd found it slightly more difficult to deny Lewis, when he'd pulled himself up to his full six feet, seven inches. A linebacker could dish out pain. So he'd conceded, in that one instance.

Ash, he could beat the crap out of.

But now she was back, safely reattached to his hold once more. "Why the hell is Damon here? Are we stuck with him in this town forever?" Rick's breath touched her ear.

"I don't know, and maybe. Regardless, it looks as if he's decided on a new conquest," she answered.

"He's a bit short for Lorianne, don't you think?" Rick kept his voice low and steady. His thumb moved in a slow, rhythmic, steady motion across her wrist, back and forth. If they didn't get out of here soon, he would have a show for them they would not soon forget.

"Yes." Her husky tone sounded as ready as he was. He felt her tremble and smiled.

"Ash does not appear too happy about it either."

"No." Just a whisper. "All I can say is, '*Where love is, no disguise can hide it for long; where it is not, none can stimulate it.*'"

"Yes. I know, love. La Rochefoucauld," Rick finished for her.

He barely registered the round of applause when he touched his mouth to hers.

Dear Readers,

Thank you so much for reading *Quotable*. The idea actually came to me one day when I was standing in line to check out at Borders Books one year. I saw this huge book call *Quotationary*.

The very first quote I read turned out to be the opening sentence for this book. Please feel free to leave a review on any of the retailers: Amazon, Barnes & Noble, Kobo, and iTunes.

I would love hearing from you. Feel free to email me at kathy@klwheeler.com.

I can be found all over social media.
http://twitter.com/kathylwheeler
http://facebook.com/kathylwheeler
http://pinterest.com/kathylwheeler
Website / Blog: http://kathylwheeler.com

                                    Sincerely,
                                Kathy L Wheeler

Other Books
Kathy L Wheeler
Bloomington Series
Maybe It's You
Lies That Bind

Regency Rebel Lords of London
The Earl's Error

Martini Club 4 Series
Reckless – The 1920s
Pampered — The 1940s

Nose Job (Scrimshaw Doll Tale
The Mapmaker's Wife (Civil War novella)
Blood Stained Memories (A World of Gothic novella)

Kae Elle Wheeler
Cinderella Series
The Wronged Princess – book i
The Unlikely Heroine – book ii
The Surprising Enchantress – book iii
The Price of Scorn: Cinderella's Evil Stepmother
The English Lily (Scrimshaw Doll Tale)

ABOUT KATHY

KATHY L WHEELER (aka Kae Elle Wheeler) is an avid romance reader and writer. She was published through The Wild Rose Press, is an active member of Romance Writers of America, The Beau Monde and OKRWA where she has served several positions. She currently serves as editor of two newsletters: The Beau Monde's Regency Reader and the Novel Notes Newsletter. (facebook.com/novelnotesauthors).

Kathy has a BA in Management Information Systems with a vocal minor. She loves travel, musical theater, NFL, NBA, reading, writing, and karaoke. She and her musically talented husband recently moved to the Great Northwest. They have one grown daughter, who has two of the most adorable babies, a neurotic dog, and a bossy cat who acts as if she is the rescuer rather than the — *rescuee*!

http://kathylwheeler.com
facebook.com/kathylwheeler
twitter: @kathylwheeler
pinterest.com/kathylwheeler

48514208R00168

Made in the USA
Middletown, DE
16 June 2019